Also By Shelly Ellis

Chesterton Scandal series

Lust & Loyalty
Best Kept Secrets
Bed of Lies

Gibbons Gold Digger series

Can't Stand the Heat
The Player & the Game
Another Woman's Man
The Best She Ever Had

Published by Dafina Books

To
Love &
Betray

SHELLY
ELLIS

Dafina
BOOKS

KENSINGTON PUBLISHING CORP.
www.kensingtonbooks.com

DAFINA BOOKS are published by

Kensington Publishing Corp.
119 West 40th Street
New York, NY 10018

All Kensington titles, imprints, and distributed lines are available at special quantity discounts for bulk purchases for sales promotion, premiums, fund-raising, and educational or institutional use.

Special book excerpts or customized printings can also be created to fit specific needs. For details, write or phone the office of the Kensington Sales Manager: Kensington Publishing Corp., 119 West 40th Street, New York, NY 10018. Attn. Sales Department. Phone: 1-800-221-2647.

Dafina and the Dafina logo Reg. U.S. Pat. & TM Off.

ISBN-13: 978-1-4967-0881-6
ISBN-10: 1-4967-0881-4
First Kensington Trade Paperback Printing: December 2017

eISBN-13: 978-1-4967-0883-0
eISBN-10: 1-4967-0883-0
First Kensington Electronic Edition: December 2017

10 9 8 7 6 5 4 3 2 1

Printed in the United States of America

To Chloe,
Thanks for teaching me patience, humility, and how to
focus on the good moments and take my setbacks in
stride. It's an honor to be your mommy.

Acknowledgments

It's hard to believe this will be the eleventh full-length novel I've published, with eight of those novels written under the pen name Shelly Ellis. Sometimes, it feels like I've been writing books forever, and other times the memories of the nail-biting experience of submitting my first book for consideration by publishers is vividly fresh. The good part about simultaneously feeling a sense of accomplishment as an author while also still feeling new to the whole "writing thing" is that it makes you both eager and unafraid to take chances with your vocation. That is why I've felt brave enough to take my writing in yet another direction, launching yet another pen name, Shelly Stratton. As Shelly Stratton, I'll get to flex my writing muscles and write more serious fiction I've always been terrified to write but finally worked up the courage to try.

But back to Shelly Ellis. (Can't forget her! LOL.) She's no best-selling author, but I'm incredibly proud of the work I've done under that name and grateful to all the people who have assisted me in getting me where I am today. My support network, which includes my husband, Andrew, my parents, and even my daughter, Chloe, have made it much easier to do what I do. If it weren't for the coveted hours of unhindered time they give me to research and write, I would not have published eight full-length novels in four years.

I'd also like to thank my editors. From my first editor at Kensington, Mercedes Fernandez, to my current editor, Esi Sogah, these women have challenged me to become a better writer, have a greater understanding of the market, and to essentially try to give readers what they want. The education and guidance they have offered is invaluable.

I'd also like to thank my resident cheerleader (and agent), Barbara Poelle. If you've ever read her advice column in *Writer's Digest*, "Funny You Should Ask . . ." you know this woman knows A LOT about the publishing industry. She also has a great sense of humor. That knowledge and the ability to make me laugh have helped get me through some of the rougher times in publishing. Barbara is not only one of the first pairs of eyes that see my writing, but also the person I bounce story ideas off of. She counsels me through my writing career dilemmas. Having an agent as an author is great, but having an amazing agent is priceless. Barbara has taught me that.

And finally, thanks to all my many writer friends and readers out there. Without you guys, I probably would've thrown in the towel long ago. Thanks for making me and my work feel appreciated.

Chapter 1

Leila

Leila Hawkins walked toward the gold hotel elevator doors, listening as her high heels clicked on the marble-tiled floor. She trembled with each step she took.

A bellhop pushing a luggage cart loaded with suitcases nodded and smiled at her as she passed. "Good evening, ma'am," he said.

She turned away, not responding to bellhop's greeting, and dug into her purse, retrieving her cell phone. She tapped the glass screen and flipped through her text messages, finding the one that contained the hotel room number and the appointed time to meet.

9:30 p.m. sharp, floor 19, room 1926, the text read. *And don't even THINK about standing me up!*

Every time she saw those words, she gritted her teeth in frustration. Even now, she wanted to head back across the hotel lobby, out the revolving doors, and give up on this whole idea. But instead, she dropped her phone back into her purse and pressed the up elevator button. She waited patiently for the doors to open. When they did, she stepped inside the compartment and pulled out the room key that a courier had delivered to Murdoch Mansion earlier that day. She inserted the key into the wall slot and pressed number nineteen. She leaned her head back against the glass wall and watched the digital screen above her as the elevator ascended floors. The compartment felt stifling hot, and the urge to press the emergency button and bring the elevator to a screeching halt overwhelmed her.

Just then, Leila's phone began to ring, and she reached inside her purse again. She saw her mother's number on the screen and took a deep breath.

Not again, she thought in exasperation. Her mother had already called and texted her twice, and she had ignored the messages. She knew her mother wouldn't let up if she let this go to voice mail, too, so she pressed the green button to answer.

"Hi, Mama," she said.

"Lee, where are you?" her mother asked, the worry apparent in the older woman's voice. Leila could hear her whimpering infant daughter, Angelica, in the background. "You left here almost an hour ago. I thought you would be back by now!"

"I just . . . I just went out to run a . . . another errand."

"Another errand? At ten o'clock at night?"

"I know what time it is, Mama," Lee answered tersely. "I'll be back soon—probably in another hour, maybe an hour and a half." She looked up at the floor numbers again.

Eight . . . nine . . . ten . . . eleven . . .

"*What?* Lee, I don't . . . you can't just . . ." Her mother sputtered helplessly. "You should be *at home!* With all that's going on, honey, you need to be here with your children. You have to—"

"Please don't tell me what I need to do, Mama! I'm doing what I have to do."

"And what is that? You won't even tell me where you are!"

Fourteen . . . fifteen . . . sixteen . . .

"I have to go," Leila whispered before abruptly hanging up. She dropped the phone back into her purse and closed her eyes.

I'm doing what I have to do, she told herself again. And Evan would do the same for her if he were in the same situation.

Her fiancé had been in jail for almost a month now. Evan's lawyer had finally negotiated his release on a one-million-dollar bond after appealing to the circuit court after a lower court judge had refused to grant Evan bail because the prosecutors had claimed that he was a flight risk.

"Mr. Murdoch is a very wealthy man, your honor. He could hop on a jet and leave the country for Switzerland or Mozambique, for all we know!" the commonwealth's attorney had argued during Evan's bail hearing. "We might never find him!"

Luckily, Evan's lawyer had been able to convince the circuit court judge that the Murdochs' ties to the community—and Evan's responsibility to the business, not to mention his family—would keep him in town.

Evan would finally get out of prison in a matter of days, but Leila knew what awaited him when he exited the prison gates. He'd be greeted with lurid news stories detailing how he had tried to murder his half-brother, Dante Turner. He'd find that the stock prices of Murdoch Conglomerated had plummeted, and there were calls from shareholders and some board members to have Evan removed as CEO of the company his father, George, had built from the ground up. Evan would be shunned by the very people in Chesterton, Virginia, who had once clamored for his money and attention. And if Evan stood trial and was found guilty of attempted murder—a crime she knew in her heart he hadn't committed—his fate could be even worse: Evan could spend decades in prison.

Where did that leave her and the little family she and Evan had created? Leila and Evan weren't married; his divorce from his wife, Charisse, still hadn't been finalized. Would Charisse kick her out of the Murdoch estate? Where would they go?

Leila raised her hands to her chest, patting breasts that were still sore and full of milk. Her mother need not remind her that she was a mother, too, that her daughters, Angelica and Isabel, depended on her. She also had their lives to consider.

Accept it, a voice in her head insisted, sounding hollow. *You don't have a choice.*

Leila jolted as the elevator slowed to a stop. The doors opened, and she stepped into the carpeted corridor. She wasn't shaking anymore. Leila followed the gilded signs that pointed her in the direction of room 1926. When she reached the door, she hesitated only briefly before knocking. The door swung open a second later.

Dante stood in front of her wearing only a crisp white bathrobe with the hotel emblem on the breast. A glass of champagne was in his hand. He looked a little different than she remembered: his face had gotten fatter in the past year, and he looked wider through the middle. When Dante saw her, he leaned against the door frame and looked her up and down. She wanted to slap the smug smile off his face. She wanted to yank the glass out of his hand and pour his champagne over his head.

"I said nine thirty. You're late," he said.

She didn't respond. Instead, she strode past him into the hotel room. She looked around the suite as he shut the door behind her. The living room and adjoining kitchenette were in varying shades of cream, white, and gold, and decorated in an ornate, baroque style she viewed as gaudy, but she knew it suited a man like Dante perfectly, with his inflated ego and desperation to seem more important than he actually was.

"Make yourself comfortable. Have some champagne," Dante said, making it sound more like an order than an offer. She watched as he strode across the room and reached for a bottle that sat in an ice bucket on the kitchenette counter. "You look like you could use a drink."

"No, thank you," she mumbled, tugging off her coat and tossing it onto the sofa.

He poured a glass anyway and held it out to her, swirling the champagne around and around. "Come on! It'll do you good. It'll help your nerves. You look more wound up than a Swiss watch, baby."

"I'm not your baby, and I don't want a drink!" she snapped, making him pause and squint at her.

"You know," he began, lowering the champagne glass to the coffee table, "for a woman who needs a favor, you've got a lot of goddamn attitude." He pointed at her. "*You're* the one who reached out to me. It wasn't the other way around. If you're going to be a bitch, Lee, you can get the hell out now!"

That's right; she had reached out to him. As soon as Evan was arrested and she had found out the details of the charge against him, she had called Dante and asked him . . . no, *begged* him to recant what he had told the investigating detective. She had asked him to rise above his unjustifiable anger toward Evan and the other Murdoch siblings. Though they had never done anything to him, Dante'd had no problem cheating with Evan's wife, Charisse; attempting to blackmail Evan's sister, Paulette, into selling her company shares to him by threatening to reveal her affair with her ex-boyfriend; or representing a woman who had unsuccessfully sued Terrence, Evan's little brother, for millions of dollars.

But Dante could change, couldn't he? He could *finally* be a good man for once or at least be a decent human being.

"Please don't do this," she had pled over the phone. "Don't ruin his life like this, Dante. He could lose everything! You know he didn't shoot you!"

"I know no such thing," Dante had answered with mock innocence.

"*Enough!* Enough, all right? This isn't a fucking game!"

"Oh, but it *is* a game, sweetheart—and right now, I'm winning. I've got the queen in my sights and I'm about to yell, 'Checkmate!' unless . . . unless you can convince me differently."

"What the hell does that mean? What do you think I'm trying to do now?"

"You *know* what it means, Lee. You're a big girl. I wined and dined you and didn't get shit in the end. You lied to me! You told me you had nothing going on with Evan, that he was 'just your boss' and—"

"I didn't lie to you! While you and I were dating, Evan and I weren't together!"

"And you fucked him," he had continued, ignoring her, "and left me with a bad case of blue balls! You owe me, and if you want me to help get your man out of this mess, you know what you have to do."

Leila now stood in the hotel room, staring at Dante.

"So what will it be, Lee? Are you gonna play nice . . . or play the bitch?" he asked, tilting his head.

Out of the corner of her eye, through an open doorway, she could see the hotel bedroom. Only one lamp burned bright on one of the night tables. The rest of the room was mostly in darkness. Beside the lamp was a bottle of baby oil and a box of Trojan condoms with the lid already open. The satin comforter and sheets on the king-size bed were already turned down.

Leila wondered if Dante had left the door open purposely for her to see that. Maybe it was his way of gloating, of reminding her what she had to do tonight to get him to talk to the prosecutor and call off the case against Evan. She wondered if Evan's sister, Paulette, had felt the way Leila felt now when she had been blackmailed into having an affair with her ex-boyfriend more than a year ago. Did Paulette feel like an animal caught in the bear trap left with only two choices: gnaw off your own foot to escape or accept the inevitable?

Leila pursed her lips and forced herself to take yet another deep breath.

"I'm . . . I'm sorry. I'm just nervous. I don't want anything to drink because . . . well, because I can't have alcohol."

He furrowed his brows. "Why the hell not?"

"I'm breastfeeding," she whispered, lowering her gaze to the floor.

He chuckled. "Oh, yeah, I almost forgot you popped out a baby." He looked her up and down again. "You can barely tell." He reached out and wrapped an arm around her, catching her off guard. Dante pulled her close so that she was flush against his chest and torso. "You've still got that tiny little waist."

She fought the urge to smack his hand away and take a step back.

"It was a smart move to get knocked up by him. You won't get that alimony money, but a child support check from a rich guy like Ev isn't anything to sniff at, either. *And* you get it for eighteen years. You were—"

"I didn't 'pop out a baby' to get Evan's money," she argued, feeling her irritation perk up again. She met his eyes.

"I did it because I was in love with him. I *am* in love with him! That's why I'm here."

Dante laughed. "So you're fucking one guy to prove how much you love the other?"

"Exactly," she said coldly.

"Well, if that's the case . . ." He dropped his arm from around her, took a step back, and clapped his hands before rubbing them together eagerly. "Let's get to it, shall we?"

He then undid the knot in his robe belt and let both panels of the robe fall open. Leila glanced down and saw that he was naked. Her stomach dropped. Her pulse quickened. She teetered back slightly and he reached out for her again—more roughly than before. Dante wrapped one hand around the back of her neck and the other around her waist, drawing her close, bringing her mouth to his. It wasn't a kiss that could be mistaken for tender or loving. It was all mouth, all tongue, and she winced and tried her best not to pull away from him in disgust.

He reached for the zipper at the back of her dress and tugged it down with a yank that made her wonder if he had ripped the zipper off its track. He dropped his hand from her neck and groped her bottom, grabbing a handful.

"I'm gonna enjoy smacking that ass when I get you on all fours," he growled before kissing her again, then nipping at her neck and earlobe, lashing her with his wet tongue.

It's just one night, she told herself, as he tore one of her dress straps off her shoulders and panted in her ear.

It doesn't mean anything, she thought as he began to unhook her bra. He reached underneath one of the cups and grabbed her swollen breast. This time, she did wince.

Leila was doing this for Evan, for her children. She had no other choice.

Tears began to prick her eyes, but she fought to hold them back.

"I was going to do this in the bedroom, but I don't

know about you, Lee—I can't wait for that shit," Dante said, wrenching his mouth away from hers. "We can do it right here."

He pushed her back against the sofa so that she landed on one of the padded arms and almost fell to the carpeted floor. He hiked the hem of her dress up to her waist.

"Condom. Condom!" she muttered against his lips.

"Yeah, yeah, yeah," he said with a grin, before climbing between her legs. "Don't worry. I'm not putting it in yet," he insisted, though his erection pressed between her thighs then the crotch of her panties. He kissed her again, grabbed her wrist, and dragged down her hand. "But you're gonna have to help me out, baby."

She fought the urge to recoil from him. Instead, she wrapped her hand around his manhood.

"That's right, baby," he whispered against her lips. "You're doing a good job," he urged as she began to slowly stroke him, hating every second of it.

"Just wait 'til Ev hears about this," Dante groaned as he closed his eyes and threw back his head.

At his words, she froze. Her body went stiff as if she were zapped with a Taser.

You son of a bitch, she thought, tightening her hold around him into a crushing, viselike grip. She yanked—hard—and Dante's face contorted with pain. He let out a girlish scream. He dropped to his knees and grabbed his crotch as soon she released him seconds later.

"You . . . you fucking *bitch!*" he said, still on all fours, gulping for air. He raised his gaze and glowered at Leila with outrage, looking like he wanted to strangle her. "Are you fucking crazy? Were you trying to rip my dick off? What the fuck was that?" he shouted, gradually standing upright, grimacing as he did it.

"No, what the fuck did you mean by 'wait 'til Ev hears about this'?" She hopped off the sofa arm, lowering her dress hem. "This was supposed to be a secret. I told you I would only do this if this stayed between you and me! That's what I said!"

She watched as Dante closed his robe and retied the terry-cloth belt. He limped toward the kitchenette, not answering her.

"Oh, my God." She slowly shook her head. "You *were* actually going to tell Ev about this, weren't you? You were going to shove it in his face?"

Despite being in pain, Dante laughed. He leaned down, opened the refrigerator, and removed a soda can.

"Were you going to tell him while he was still in jail, or wait until he got out . . . give it to him like a 'welcome home' present?"

Dante placed the cold can on his crotch. "What's the point of a win if you can't do an end zone dance, huh?"

Leila balled her fists at her sides. She should have known Dante would do this. He was a man with no ethics, no heart, and no soul. She was a fool to make any agreements with him. It was the equivalent of making a deal with the devil.

She grabbed her purse from where it had fallen to the hotel floor along with her coat and made her way across the living room.

"I'd think twice about this if I were you, Lee!" he called out to her, stopping her in her tracks. "From what I've heard, the prosecutor has a pretty good case against your boy. They have my testimony and the testimony of a few other people who saw him threatening me at a restaurant in D.C. less than two months before the shooting. They said he grabbed me and he pushed me. Even a cabbie saw him threaten my life." He set his soda can on the coffee table and shoved his hands into his robe pockets. "Ev could go away for a *long* time. Are you sure you want to be responsible for that?"

She turned around to face him. "I'm not responsible for it—*you* are, you petty asshole! And even if I did have sex with you, I know now there are no guarantees with someone like you. You're a snake," she snarled. "Your word means *nothing*."

"Sticks and stones may break my bones, but words will never hurt me," he sang.

"You are a piece of shit, Dante . . . and if someone finally does manage to kill your ass one day, it's well deserved."

He raised his brows. "Better hope I didn't get that on tape, sweetheart."

She was tired of sparring with him, with arguing with him. She felt like a fool and just wanted to go home and wash the sensation of his tongue and kisses off her skin. She wanted to scrub her hand with soap and scalding hot water one thousand times. She strode to the door.

"See you in court, Lee!" he called as she swung the hotel door open. "I'll be the black man who *isn't* wearing an orange jumpsuit."

He laughed as she slammed the door shut behind her.

Chapter 2

C. J.

At six thirty a.m., like clockwork, C. J. Aston opened her eyes to her darkened bedroom. She felt the soft bedsheets against her face and saw slivers of light coming through the drawn bedroom blinds. She hadn't been roused by an alarm clock. She had something better to wake her up.

"Good morning," she murmured dreamily as she felt her fiancé nuzzle the back of her neck.

Terrence Murdoch didn't return her greeting but instead shifted the hand that had been resting on her hip for most of the night to her breasts. He massaged her through the cotton of her T-shirt at first but quickly raised the hem and let his fingers graze over her bare skin, running his thumb over her nipple, making her tingle all over, making her skin prickle with goose bumps.

She turned to face him and, in the dark, could faintly make out the outline of his handsome face. She ran her hand along his cheek only inches away from the eye that had been mangled in a car crash almost a year ago. He usually hid his eye from the rest of the world, but he didn't hide it from her. She raised her head to kiss him, opening her mouth, letting her tongue intermingle with his.

This is how they had woken up every morning for the past month or so, since she had moved back to Chesterton permanently and moved in with Terrence. She would wake up to find him kissing her bare shoulder or she'd be moaning in her sleep only to open her eyes to find his head between her thighs. They'd make love, share a shower afterward, eat breakfast, and she'd head to the newsroom where she was reporter for the *Chesterton Times* while he'd head to the gym. C. J. had noticed lately, though, that after they had made love, Terrence would linger in the bed a lot longer. He would stare at the ceiling with his brow furrowed and his face grim. She knew he was thinking about his brother, Evan. She knew thoughts about his family and the future weighed heavy on Terrence's mind.

But right now, he seemed to be solely focused on her.

Terrence tugged her T-shirt up from her waist and over her head. She was naked underneath and felt the cool air in their bedroom on her skin. She tried to tug her arms out of the sleeves and toss her shirt aside, but he stopped her movements, holding her bound arms over her head on the bed.

"Don't move," he ordered in a harsh whisper.

She instantly went still.

He withdrew his hands from her shirt before grazing them over her breasts. He lowered his mouth to each of the nipples, in turn flicking his tongue over them and suckling them, making her moan. He shifted his mouth to her stomach, leaving a wet trail of licks and nips, and he descended lower and lower.

She longed to touch him but didn't dare move her arms from above her head.

This was all part of the fun, as Terrence would say.

Besides, he was the one who had taught her about the

joys of sex, the one she had given her virginity to. She trusted Terrence totally.

When he spread her legs open, she was almost squirming in anticipation. He lowered his mouth between her thighs and gently blew on her clit, startling her, making her cry out. He then began to lick and suck, and her cries grew even louder. She was squirming so much, he had to hold her hips in place to keep her from falling off the bed.

After a few minutes of delicious agony, he drew his mouth away. Every part of her—one part in particular—was throbbing. By then, she was practically panting to have him inside of her. Ever so slowly, Terrence climbed on top of her. Even in the dark, he could see her eagerness. He started to chuckle.

"You ready for me, baby?" he asked.

"You know I am, Terry. Just *do* it!"

He kissed her cheek, her chin, her forehead.

"Come on," she whimpered.

He laughed again.

"Fine," she grumbled, lowering her arms from over her head and shoving him off her and onto his back, catching him by surprise. "If you won't do it, then *I* will!"

She then straddled him and lowered herself on top of him. He slid smoothly inside her, and she groaned at the familiar sensation. She braced her hands on his broad shoulders and began to rock her hips.

Within seconds, the cocky smile disappeared from Terrence's face. He closed his eyes and bit down hard on his bottom lip, guiding her hips as he increased the tempo of their lovemaking, grinding against her. She got lost in the sensations of the moment, gazing down at him in the dark, feeling herself drawing close to orgasm, only to have everything flipped—literally. This time Terrence flipped her back onto the mattress and again onto her stomach.

Before she had the chance to ask him what he was

doing, he raised her hips so that she was in the kneeling position and he crouched behind her. She only had a few seconds to brace herself before he entered her again.

She cried out his name and fisted the bedsheets in her hands. As he pounded into her, C. J. could hear the headboard thumping against the bedroom wall and the mattress squeak beneath them. She spurred him on, shouting for him to keep going, not to stop. She could feel herself drawing close again.

When she did come, she screamed. She had long ago stopped being embarrassed by the noises she made while in the throes of passion. Terrence's release came soon after. He squeezed her hips and let out a long, tortured groan as he swelled inside her. He collapsed on top of her seconds later, sending hot blasts of air against her ear and neck. She fought to regain her breath, too. They lay that way for quite a while—in a crumpled, sweaty heap on top of the sheets. She glanced at the alarm clock on his night table. When she saw the time, she let out a panicked squeak. It was 7:16! Had that much time really passed? She was going to be late.

"Terry . . . Terry!" she said, reaching behind her and nudging his shoulder.

"Huh?" he answered drowsily.

"I'm sorry, baby, but I've got to start getting ready. I have to be out of here by eight if I'm going to make it."

"Shit, that's right . . . you've got that job interview today."

She nodded . . . well, she *attempted* to nod. It was hard to do with him still sprawled on top of her.

He sighed and reluctantly rolled onto his back. "Sorry. Didn't mean to slow you down."

"Oh, believe me," she said with a smile, kissing him again before she hurriedly rose from their bed, "you don't *ever* have to apologize for what you just did! I enjoyed it immensely. Unfortunately, if I try to enjoy more of it, I'm never going to make it down the Dulles Toll Road and to my interview on time."

He nodded absently, reached for his eye patch, and put it on, making her frown. She turned on a nearby table lamp, filling their bedroom with bright light. She grabbed a scrunchie for her hair.

"You're going to get out today, too?" she asked, pulling her hair into a ponytail, preparing to head to their bathroom. "Got some stuff lined up? Meeting one of your boys?"

Terrence shrugged. "I don't know . . . maybe."

She squinted. C. J. didn't like the equivocal tone of Terrence's voice or the unfocused look in his eye.

Terrence had a history of depression and had battled lows in the past: one after a car accident that almost killed him, and another when they had briefly broken up. She worried the dark mood would sweep over him again. Though C. J. knew she was already running late, she sat back on the bed and gazed at him.

"You have to get out of the house, honey. You have to *do* things. Live your life. That's what your therapist said, right?"

He rolled his eye. "I don't need a pep talk, C. J. I'm *fine*."

"No, you aren't fine. I know you aren't!" She reached out and cupped his face. "I know you're worried about Evan, but—"

"How can I *not* be? My brother's locked in jail with murderers and rapists, and there's not a damn thing I can do about it! He's always had my back, C. J. . . . *always!*"

She nodded. "I know, baby."

"He's never raised a hand to anyone! He pays his taxes on time. He's never been charged with anything before. He's the fucking last person who should be locked up!"

"Evan is going to be okay. It's *all* going to be okay!"

"You don't know that," he argued, making her drop her hand from his cheek.

"You're right. I don't . . . but I have to believe it. You do, too! And if we're proven wrong and the worst case scenario happens,"—she leaned forward and kissed him again—"your family will handle it. You'll work through it. I'll help you. We're family now, too, right?"

Finally, ever so slowly, a smile broke across his face. "I was smart to ask you to marry me."

"Yes, you were! And I was smart to say yes."

He chuckled and tossed back the bedsheets. She watched as he slowly rose to his feet, letting her eyes travel over his naked body—the smooth, coppery skin, the sinewy muscle, six-pack abs, and sculpted backside. She would *never* get tired of staring at this fine-ass man!

"Take your shower and get ready for your interview," Terrence muttered. "I'll make breakfast."

C. J. rushed into the kitchen thirty-five minutes later, shoving her feet into a pair of high heels. As she drew near the granite kitchen island, Terrence extended a cup of espresso toward her. He retrieved a pan from the burner and used a spatula to scrape a pile of scrambled eggs onto a plate already covered with toast and bacon. He set the plate on the kitchen island next to a fork and knife.

"Dig in, babe."

C. J. did as he ordered. She grabbed one of the slices of bacon and popped it into her mouth. She then adjusted the lapels of her new business suit jacket and gestured down to herself. "How do I look? Do I look okay?" she asked between chews.

He glanced at her and nodded. "You look fine. Why?"

"*Why?*" she repeated with widened eyes, making him chuckle. "Are you kidding?"

"I just mean you look good!" He shrugged. "Why wouldn't you? Don't you always?"

"You're sweet—but a liar! Sometimes I look like a hot mess! Unlike you, Mr. Former *Supermodel*." She gestured toward him and sighed. Terrence had put on his prosthetic eye and was now wearing a T-shirt and sweats. "You haven't even showered or shaved, and you look like you just stepped out of an issue of *GQ*!" she lamented before drinking more of her espresso.

He laughed again, leaned down, and kissed her cheek. "You look great. You're just nervous. That's all."

"Well, I should be! I have an interview with one of the biggest newspapers in the country!" she said, digging into her breakfast. "I'm going to talk to one of the editors I've admired for years! I wrote a paper in college on his Iraq War coverage, you know."

"Yeah, I know." Terrence nodded as he dumped the rest of the eggs onto another plate. "You've told me—*several* times."

"I just don't wanna mess this up. It's a great opportunity, Terry. It's my chance to finally break out of small town news."

"And you won't mess it up," he said before shoving a forkful of eggs into his mouth. "You'll do fine. I know you will."

C. J. wished she had as much confidence in herself as he did. She puffed air through her cheeks and glanced at the digital clock on the microwave behind Terrence. Her eyes nearly bulged out of her head. "Damn! I better get going or I'm going to be late."

"You're not going to finish breakfast first?"

"No time!" She grabbed a slice of toast and another slice of bacon and folded them together. "I'll have to eat this in the car."

"Good luck!" he called after her as she grabbed her

leather satchel from one of the kitchen bar stools and ran toward the front door.

"Thanks!" C. J. said before blowing a kiss to him over her shoulder. She unlocked the door and swung it open. When she saw what was in the condominium's hallway, she slammed the door shut.

"Shit!" she spat. "Goddamnit!"

"*What?* What's wrong?" Terrence said, walking out of the kitchen into the living room.

C. J. waved toward the door. "There's a news crew waiting out there with a camera and everything."

"*What?* How the hell did they get in the building?"

"I don't know. I guess someone let them in the front door. But none of that matters now. They're here, and I bet they're waiting to talk to you."

Since word had spread about Evan's attempted murder charge, several of the local stations had tried to gain interviews with Terrence and his sister, Paulette, to discuss the case and the volatile sibling rivalry between Evan and Dante. So far, both had staunchly refused to talk. Even though C. J.'s editor had begged her to try to convince Terrence to give an exclusive interview to the *Chesterton Times*, she had also refused. But the Murdoch family's silence only seemed to make the local news outlets more persistent. They called the condo constantly, and one news crew had even shown up at Terrence's gym.

C. J. knew how this went; she was a reporter, too. But for once, she was on the receiving end of a media frenzy, and it wasn't fun.

"They want to talk to me, not you, though. Can't you just walk past them?"

"Maybe. But it's more likely that as soon as I come through that door, they're gonna pounce. Some of the reporters know I'm your fiancée. They might want a comment from me, too. I guess I can try to wait them out then leave." She glanced down at her wristwatch. If she left in thirty minutes and broke a few speed limits, she might be able to still make it to her job interview fashionably late, but it would all depend on morning traffic. "Or maybe I should just reschedule."

Terrence rubbed his neck and closed his eyes. "Open the door."

She looked up from her watch and blinked. "Huh?"

"Open the door! I'll talk to them."

"Terry, honey, the *last* thing your family needs is a shot of you cussing out a TV crew on the morning news!"

He shook his head. "I'm not going to cuss at them. I'll talk to them. Maybe if I finally answer their goddamn questions, they'll leave me and Paulette the hell alone!"

She inclined her head. "*Are you sure* you really wanna do this?"

"No, I'm not sure, but it doesn't seem like I have much choice. You've gotta get to your interview, right?"

She opened her mouth to argue with him, but he didn't give her a chance. He stepped forward and swung the door open. When he did, C. J. hopped back and hid, taking cover behind one of the entryway walls. Terrence was immediately met by a cameraman and a bottle blonde with big hair, wearing about twenty pounds of makeup. She held a mike and stuck it straight at Terrence's face while frantically waving the cameraman behind her to step forward. A spotlight suddenly shone down on Terrence, making him squint.

"Mr. Murdoch! Mr. Murdoch, hi! I'm Susan Schuler at Channel 6 News! How are you this morning?" the reporter drawled while brandishing her bleached-white grin.

"I'm dandy," he said dryly. "Just ask your questions and make it quick. If you could keep it under five minutes, I'd appreciate it."

The reporter's smile faded a little. She cleared her throat.

"Well, uh . . . We were wondering if we could talk to you about the charges your brother Evan Murdoch is facing."

"What do you want to talk about?" Terrence asked, leaning against the door frame.

Though C. J. knew he was furious at the woman's question and the presumption it had taken just to show up at his door at eight o'clock in the morning, he didn't show it. Even from this vantage point, peeking from behind a wall, she could see that he had the veneer of total calm, almost as if he were having a conversation at a dinner party.

"Are you surprised that your brother was charged with attempted murder? Had you witnessed any violent behavior from him in the past?" the reporter asked.

C. J. watched as Terrence waited a beat, as his jaw tightened as if he was torn between spewing a series of expletives or slamming the door in the woman's face. Instead, he exhaled, pushed back his shoulders, and stood upright.

" 'Surprised' isn't the right word. It angers me that the police managed to trump such a *bogus* charge against my brother and that a prosecutor would move forward with that charge. But no . . . I'm not surprised."

The reporter narrowed her blue eyes at him and drew even closer. "I'm sorry. What do you mean by that, Mr. Murdoch? Then why aren't you surprised?"

"I mean my brother is a black man in America. It wouldn't be the first time one of us was railroaded by the legal system—and I'm sure it won't be the last."

"Are you making allegations of racism in this case? You think the police are racist?"

"I'm not alleging anything. I'm just pointing out the obvious. It seems a bit far-fetched that a man who hadn't even gotten a speeding ticket before or owned a gun permit suddenly decided to track someone down and shoot him in cold blood in a parking garage. Not to mention the fact that my brother had an alibi for that night . . . an alibi that was validated by *several* people! But hey, I'm not an investigator. I guess I'm not as smart as they are," he muttered sarcastically.

"But Mr. Turner claims your brother is the one who shot him," the reporter charged.

"Mr. Turner claims a lot of things. Anyone who's known him personally knows to take whatever he says with a grain of salt."

"So you're saying Mr. Turner is lying?"

"That's *exactly* what I'm saying. And if the jury decides to listen to the truth—the *whole* truth and nothing but the truth—they'll realize that."

The reporter turned to the camera. "Well, there you have it! The whole truth and nothing but the truth. Well said!" She faced Terrence again. "Thank you for speaking with us today, Mr. Murdoch!"

Terrence nodded and forced a smile. "No, thank you."

"All right. We've got it," the cameraman boomed as he turned off the overhead light and lowered the camera from his shoulder to his side.

"Wonderful! Just wonderful!" the reporter said.

She stared openly at Terrence and coyly batted her false eyelashes. She then gnawed her glossy lower lip. If C. J. was reading this woman right, it looked like she was flirting.

You've gotta be kidding me, C. J. thought with exasperation, fighting the urge to laugh. She didn't want to give away her hiding spot.

"Really . . . thank you *so* much for talking to us, Mr. Murdoch," the reporter said. Her voice sounded breathy now. "We'll get out of your hair."

He nodded again.

"I mean I can only imagine how difficult this is for you. You must—"

Terrence didn't give her the chance to finish. "Have a good day," he said, before slamming the door shut.

When he did, C. J. eased from behind the wall and did a slow clap.

"*Bravo,* baby! That was amazing!"

He blew a puff of air through his cheeks and walked back into the living room. "Thanks," he mumbled.

"No, seriously, you were smooth ... articulate ... charming. I've never seen you like that before in front of a camera. I'm a reporter. I've seen people freeze up when they talk to the press, but you didn't. I would've thought you were trained to do it!"

He shrugged. "I guess I learned it from modeling and after years of schmoozing at boring-ass galas. Never thought I'd have to do it to defend my brother from an attempted murder charge, though."

"All the same," she said, linking her arms around his neck and giving him a kiss, "you did good. If Evan could've seen it, I'm sure he would have been proud of you."

"Maybe." He slapped her rear end. "Better head out, babe. It's ten minutes after."

"Ah, crap!" She removed her arms from his neck and ran toward the door. "I'm out!" she shouted over her shoulder before grabbing her coat from the hallway closet, swinging open his door, and excusing her way past the news crew. She then fled down the corridor to the elevators.

C. J. fidgeted anxiously in the office chair, flipping through the leather file folder that contained her résumé and clips of articles she had written. The *Washington Daily* already had both. She had sent them two weeks ago when the human resources department had told her they wanted her to come in for the first round of interviews. This was her second round—this time with *the* Ralph Haynes, managing editor of the news desk and Pulitzer Prize–winning war correspondent. She told herself to take several deep breaths. She told herself to not freak out.

Be more like Terry, she thought.

Terrence had faced down a news crew with no prior warning after rolling out of bed, and he had handled himself masterfully. She could certainly handle this.

"No big deal," she whispered. "I've got this."

"You've got what?" Haynes's booming baritone rumbled behind her, making her jump in her chair. He shut his office door and walked toward his desk.

"Uh, nothing! Nothing," she mumbled, sitting upright and forcing a smile. She pointed at a series of photographs on display on the wall behind his desk. "I was just wondering if those were pictures of you in Iraq? From the war?"

He glanced over his shoulder at the wall, adjusted the wire frames of his glasses, and sat down. He nodded. "Yeah, not too long after Operation Phantom Fury."

"That's amazing," she gushed, "that you were there, I mean. That you saw all that stuff and got to report on it. That would be my . . . my absolute dream! I would—"

"It was hot, bloody, and I saw a lot of good men die," he replied blandly, leaning back in his office chair. He interlocked his fingers behind his head, revealing damp circles at the armpits of his dress shirt. "Believe me, you wouldn't have been as eager to be in the thick of that as you'd think."

She grimaced. "Maybe. But your writing was awe-inspiring, Mr. Haynes! So vivid and honest. I've admired it for years!"

He nodded again, looking indifferent. "So tell me a little about yourself, C. J."

"Well, I've . . . I've been working at the *Chesterton Times* for almost three years now. My beat covers the local government and businesses. Sometimes I—"

"Don't," he said, waving his hand. "Don't do that."

"I'm sorry . . . Don't . . . don't do what?"

"Don't rattle off your résumé to me! I've already read it. Remember? Tell me what I *can't* find in your résumé or LinkedIn profile. Tell me about what makes you . . . *you.* Out of all the candidates who applied for this job, why should I add you to my news desk? What makes you so special?"

She squinted, thrown off by the pointedness of his question and his hostile tone. She clasped her hands in her lap and began to squeeze them. She could feel herself growing hot under her cotton-blend blouse.

"Well, uh . . . well, I'm a tenacious reporter who—"

"For example," he began, as if he hadn't heard her, "why did you change your name from Courtney to C. J.? What's the story behind that?"

C. J.'s stomach dropped. How did he know her name was really Courtney? She continued to stare at him blankly.

"You didn't think I'd let that slip by me, did you?" He reached for a pencil on his desk and began to twirl it around and around. "Come on, C. J.! This is a newspaper. You looked like a strong candidate, so I did a little more checking into your background. Call it . . . I know . . . a reporter's curiosity."

Of course, she thought. A few quick searches on Google could have brought up that information, especially since she had appeared at several events with her family to help support her father's congressional campaign. She hadn't spoken to her family in months, but that didn't mean that those old news stories would disappear.

"That's . . . that's f-fine," she stuttered. "I-I understand."

"So why did you change it to C. J.?" he persisted. "And why did you move here from North Carolina? I'm sure with your father's connections, he could have easily gotten you a position at one of the newspapers down there—with him being Reverend Pete Aston and all."

At that, her forced smile disappeared. Her back went rigid. "I don't *need* my father's connections, Mr. Haynes. I can stand on my own two feet."

"Whoa! Sounds like I pricked a nerve there! I guess your relationship with your daddy isn't amicable?"

"My relationship with my father is not relevant to this conversation. So I suggest we steer the conversation back to the subject of how I'm qualified to work at your news desk."

He chuckled. "Do you now?"

"Yes, I do. And if we aren't going to do that, then I think I'll leave right now!"

"You're just going to leave? Just like that?"

"Yes, *just like that!*" She rose from her chair.

"Do you know how many reporters would sell their left kidneys for an opportunity to work on my news desk? And you're just going to walk out on an interview?"

"Look, I want this job," she said, as she grabbed her leather satchel from the floor, "but I don't want it enough to be talked to like this. I'm a good reporter and a hard worker. If you can't see that, then it's your goddamn loss!"

At that, Haynes smiled. "Well, I'll be damned."

"Excuse me?" she asked, her frown deepening.

"I've had plenty of candidates come in here with great résumés and clips, kissing my ass and telling me how great I am and how great the paper is. They laughed at all my jokes. Hell, they'd probably stand on their heads if I asked them to! But what I'm looking for is a reporter who isn't easily intimidated, who doesn't cave under pressure. I need someone who can steer the conversation and not take shit. That's a real reporter!" He eyed her. "I can't say for sure if you're it, C. J. Only time will tell. But . . . I'm willing to give it a try. I'll give you a chance."

C. J. blinked in amazement. "Wh-what?"

"I'll let HR know my decision. You should get the formal offer letter in a few days." He suddenly stood up and extended a hand to her. "Welcome aboard."

She was struck speechless again. It took her a few seconds to recover and finally shake his hand. "Th-thank you! Thank you so much for this opportunity, sir!"

"You're welcome." He eyed her again. "And don't make me regret it!"

Chapter 3

Paulette

"Baby, you've gotta see this," Antonio said.

"Huh? See what?" Paulette Murdoch asked over her shoulder while standing at the kitchen counter, where she was currently stirring a puréed mix of apples and carrots in a plastic bowl. Behind her sat her husband, Antonio, at the kitchen table with their infant son, Nate. The baby was perched in his high chair, banging his plastic spoon on his serving tray, eagerly awaiting his breakfast. He was also making babbling noises that to her motherly ears sounded a lot like, "Speed it up, woman! I'm starving!"

"Your brother's on TV," Antonio said, motioning to their small flat-screen television, which was mounted under one of their kitchen cabinets.

"If it's yet another news story about Ev, I'll pass." Paulette scraped last of the purée into the bowl. "I've seen enough of them already. I don't need to hear any more of that trash."

"It's not Ev. It's Terry."

At that, she whipped around from the counter and faced him, sending a splatter of apple and carrots flying.

She almost dropped the entire bowl to the tiled floor, but caught it before she did. She quickly placed it on Nate's tray.

"*What?* Why is Terry on the television?" she asked as she raced across the kitchen and grabbed the TV remote from the table, turning up the volume.

"I'm not alleging anything. I'm just pointing out the obvious," she heard her brother say before she pulled out one of the kitchen chairs and fell back into it. Paulette watched the entire interview, stunned. Terrence answered all the reporter's questions and even thanked her for doing the interview.

When the newscast segued to the next story, Paulette dazedly shook her head. She dropped the remote back to the table with a clatter. "Why the hell did he do that? We said we weren't going to talk to the press!"

Antonio scooped baby food into Nate's mouth, wiping a smear from the little boy's chubby chin with the edge of his bib. "Terry did a good job, though, baby."

"It doesn't matter! We said we weren't going to talk to them. We weren't going to grant interviews! That's what we agreed to!"

The cordless on their granite counter began to ring, drawing their attention and making her grumble loudly.

"See that!" she shouted, pointing at the phone. "See there! It's probably a reporter calling right now, trying to get me to talk . . . to share some dirt about Ev, *but am I talking?* No!"

"But Terry didn't share any dirt," Antonio said over the sound of the ringing. He lowered the baby spoon, making his son whimper. He then quickly raised it to Nate's mouth again. "Terry stood up for Ev. He—"

"I bet this has something to do with his girlfriend . . . his *fiancée*," she muttered with a sneer. "I bet she talked him into it."

"Why do you think she did it?"

"Well, she's a reporter, isn't she? I'm shocked she hasn't plastered all this stuff in her little newspaper already! I guess it's only a matter of time." She crossed her arms over her chest and shook her head. "I can't believe Terry is getting married to her . . . to *her!* This is the same woman who snuck into a hospital, lied, and tried to get an interview with him after his car crash. I mean . . . come on now!"

"I thought we were talking about how you guys agreed not to talk to the press. How did we get on this stuff about Terry getting married?"

"It's all connected!" She hopped out of her chair and stomped back to the kitchen counter. "She could be *using* him, Tony. She could break his heart!"

"Baby—"

"He and Evan trust her, but *I* don't," she continued, tapping her chest and tossing peels of red-delicious apple skin into their farm sink. "I'm done with trusting people who only take advantage of us!"

"Baby—"

"We trusted Dante, too—and look where that got us! Look where it got Evan! Now he's behind bars and that son of a bitch is still walking the streets!" She turned on the garbage disposal switch, filling the kitchen with a grinding sound, then turned it off. "Evan is coming out on bail at the end of the week, but what if a jury finds him guilty, Tony? Evan could spend decades in prison! He won't be able to see his little girl grow up, and you know how much he's always wanted to be a dad! He could be—"

Paulette stopped mid-tirade when she felt her husband place his hands on her shoulders. When he gave her a light squeeze, she lowered her head and choked back a sob.

"It's okay," he whispered into her ear. "Let it out."

She whipped around to face him and pressed her face into his chest, letting the smell of his cologne and the laundry detergent in his sweater fill her nose. She wept softly while he held her in his strong arms and their son continued to babble from his perch at the kitchen table.

Less than a year ago, they wouldn't have been able to do this—stay locked in an embrace. Antonio had wanted nothing to do with her after she had cheated on him with her ex-boyfriend, Marques Whitney. She had wanted to beg him for his forgiveness, but she ultimately ended up forgiving him when he finally confessed to her that he had murdered Marques the night he found out about her affair.

Paulette opened her reddened eyes and gazed up at her husband. She remembered the moment on Christmas Day when the cops had burst into Murdoch Mansion with handcuffs in hand. She'd thought they were going to take Antonio away from her, that their life together would be the final domino that tumbled in the series of dominos she had set into motion with her bad decisions. When the cops instead placed her brother in handcuffs, Paulette had felt a mix of horror—and relief. It was an overwhelming relief that left her feeling guilty to this day. And she would be burdened with that guilt until her brother was released, until the charges were dropped against him or he was found not guilty.

Meanwhile, she and Antonio would continue to attempt to put the past behind them, each trying desperately not to remember and replay what the other had done. Antonio was a kind, loving husband and father—not a cold-blooded murderer, she told herself. Paulette was a warm, giving wife and mother—not a cheater who may have given birth to her murdered lover's baby; she was sure that was the mental reminder Antonio had to give himself on a daily basis. They would pretend to be whole again until, eventually, their pretense became reality.

The doorbell rang, and Antonio loosened his grip around her. "That's probably Mama," he whispered.

Paulette nodded and reluctantly pulled away from him. She wiped her eyes with the back of her hands and sniffed. "Oh, no," she said, wiping at his chest, "your sweater's a mess now!"

"It's fine." He kissed her cheek. "It's just tears, honey. They'll dry."

"Maybe you can change before you head out to work," she called to him as he walked out of the kitchen and into their foyer. She watched his receding back.

"No time, baby. I told you . . . it's fine."

Paulette heard him unlock and open their front door soon after. She then heard Antonio's mother say, "Where's my little baby?"

At the sound of Reina's squawky voice, Paulette leaned against the kitchen counter and cringed.

Reina was supposed to watch Little Nate while Paulette ran a few errands today. The older woman was always whining that she never got to babysit him. Though Paulette could just as easily have put on her Baby Björn and taken Nate to the grocery store and the dry cleaners with her, she had decided to ask Reina to watch the baby for a few hours—more to appease her husband than anything else. Paulette felt she owed Antonio more than she could ever give him. She would do almost anything to make him happy, and what made Antonio most happy was to have the two most important women in his life getting along. Unfortunately, Reina didn't make that easy to accomplish. Since Paulette and Antonio began dating, the older woman seemed to make it her mission to belittle and be hostile to Paulette. Her vengefulness had only picked up ferocity over the years.

"Where's my grandbaby? Where's my Little Tony Tony Tony?" Reina crooned as she walked into the kitchen.

"His name is Nathan," Paulette muttered under her breath.

She watched as Reina tossed her crocodile handbag onto the kitchen island and spread her arms wide, looking a lot like the Stay Puft Marshmallow Man in her all-white turtleneck and slacks. She sauntered toward Nate, whose entire face was now smeared with his breakfast. Antonio trailed in after her.

Paulette pushed herself up from the counter and painted on a smile. "Good morning, Reina. How are you today?"

Reina gave her a withering glance. "Fine. I didn't know you were here."

"Well, I *live* here," Paulette said, drumming her nails on the cool granite, feeling her anger perk up again.

"*Really?* Couldn't tell that from the way the house looks," Reina muttered as she surveyed the kitchen, wrinkling her nose at the disarray. "When's the last time you cleaned this place up?"

Paulette inclined her head, keeping her smile firmly in place. "Probably the last time you minded your own business."

Antonio loudly cleared his throat and gave Paulette a warning look. She threw up her hands in a *"She started it!"* gesture.

Reina ignored her comment, leaned down, and undid the harness holding Little Nate in his high chair. She scooped him into her arms and held him against her oversize bosom. "Such a handsome . . . Oh, look at this mess all over your face!" she cried as she reached for one of the paper towels and began to wipe Little Nate's mouth. "I swear your mama don't know how to feed you!"

Paulette's eyes narrowed into thin slits. She opened her mouth to respond just as Antonio suddenly interjected, "Actually, Mama, I'm the one that was feeding Nate. I was doing it while uh . . . while Paulette was straightening up the kitchen."

"Uh-huh," Reina grunted, still giving Paulette the side-eye. "Well, it was nice of you to help out, baby. You're the good man that I raised you to be."

Paulette noticed that Reina had made no mention of her being a good woman, but she decided not to take the bait.

"Well, I should be heading out," he said, walking across the kitchen. He kissed his son on the forehead and his mother on the cheek. "See you later. Have a good time."

"You be careful driving to work! I heard there was an accident on I-66," Reina said, bouncing Nate up and down as she sat in one of the kitchen chairs.

Antonio nodded and turned to face his wife. "Behave yourself. *Be nice,*" he mouthed, making her sigh.

"I'll try," she mouthed back just before he kissed her good-bye.

The kiss was warm and tender and lingered on a lot longer than she had expected, getting more and more heat with each passing second. When she parted her lips and darted his tongue inside her mouth, she pulled away, giggling. She playfully slapped his shoulder, and Antonio gave her a wink. He smacked his lips and smiled.

"We'll finish this when I get back home," he whispered before turning and walking toward the kitchen entrance. He then grabbed his briefcase from one of the kitchen chairs, waved, and disappeared behind one of the Ionic-style columns leading to the foyer.

We'll finish this when I get back home . . .

Just the promise behind those words made her touch her kiss-swollen nips. It made her nipples harden into pebbles.

Along with trust, intimacy had disappeared from their marriage because of her affair and the aftermath. It was only a few months ago that they had shared the marital bed again, and it was as lovely and steamy as she remembered it. Her cheeks warmed just imagining what they would do in that bed tonight after they put Little Nate to sleep.

Paulette turned from the kitchen entrance with a winsome smile. That smile quickly disappeared when she met Reina's condescending glare.

"Like I said, my son's a good man . . . a good *husband,* too," Reina said, reaching for the diaper bag that Paulette had finished packing only an hour ago.

"I know he is."

"Yeah, well, make sure you remember that!" Reina tossed the diaper bag strap onto her shoulder. "Tony may not be so forgiving—next time!"

Paulette did a double take. *Next time?*

Had Antonio told his mother that she had cheated on him? He was close with his mother, but he hadn't divulged such an embarrassing secret to Reina, *of all people?*

"What did you say?" Paulette asked just as the older woman strode out the room.

"Come on, baby," Reina said to Little Nate, pointedly ignoring her daughter-in-law. "Come with Grandma."

Paulette stared after Reina with a mix of bewilderment and fury.

Chapter 4

Dante

Dante turned the corner then pulled up to the curb in front of the rundown D.C. row house where he had spent the first eighteen years of his life. He parked his Jag, reached inside his pocket, removed a medicine bottle, then twisted open the lid and shook two OxyContin pills into his hand. He considered the pills then shook out two more before tossing all of them into his mouth. After he swallowed, he glared at his reflection in the rearview mirror, taking in the bags under his eyes, the five o'clock shadow along his chin, and frown lines around his mouth that he was sure hadn't been there a year ago.

He was in a bad state today, and he blamed Leila Hawkins for it.

Dante knew he wouldn't have drunk as much champagne, then eventually hard liquor last night, or called that poor excuse for an escort, if Leila hadn't rejected him—*again*. Just who the hell did she think she was anyway, getting him all excited, only to blindside him?

"Dick tease," he murmured.

But that was all right. She would regret her choice when she saw her baby daddy, Evan, carted away in handcuffs after a judge sentenced him to twenty years to life for his attempted murder charge. She'd be begging Dante to ride his dick after that, but this time *he* would be the one turning *her* down.

With that resolved, he turned away from the rearview mirror and threw on a pair of Ray-Bans as he climbed out of his Jaguar and slammed the door shut. He cringed at the sound.

Dante hoped his hangover would get better soon, because he had something important to do today—specifically, checking on his childhood home and his daughter, Kiki, who had moved in a few weeks ago. He had left the smart-mouthed teenager a series of text messages and made phone calls to the house over the past two weeks to check on her and make sure the row house was still standing. But all his messages and calls had gone unanswered. It made him wonder just what the hell Kiki was doing in his mother's old home. He'd figured that it was about time he found out.

The chain-link gate squeaked loudly as he wrenched it open, and he slowly made his way up the sidewalk and the porch steps. He unlocked the front door and shoved it open. The instant he did, an overwhelming smell smacked him in the face and made his weary eyes widen.

"What . . . the . . . *fuck?*" he shouted over the hip-hop music blaring on the stereo. He ripped off his sunglasses and stared in outrage at his living room.

His mother's old scuffed mahogany coffee table was now littered with plastic baggies and mounds of weed. A digital scale sat at the center, where a young man with cornrows was carefully weighing one weed bundle, squinting as he did it. Kiki sat in Dante's recliner, inserting several hand-rolled cigarettes into zip-lock bags. When Dante entered the room, the two stopped mid-motion and looked up at him, startled.

"What the fuck are you doing?" he yelled at his daughter, marching across the room and pressing the button to turn off the stereo music. "Why is all this shit in my house? Are you trying to get this place raided?"

Kiki lowered the recliner's lever and slowly sat forward in her chair, flipping her purple braids over her shoulder as she did it. She set the plastic baggie on the table next to several others. "We ain't gonna get raided. Don't make it a big thing when it ain't!"

"*Don't make it a big thing?*" he cried. "Do you realize you're running a fucking drug den out of my front parlor!"

"Yell it a little louder, why don't you?" Kiki said drolly. "Besides, it's Grandma's front parlor—not yours!"

"Yo, Kiki," the young man murmured, jabbing his thumb in Dante's direction, "who the fuck is this dude?"

"I'll tell you who the fuck I am!" Dante charged across the room toward the sofa where the boy was perched. "Despite what my daughter says, *I'm* the owner of this house. And *you're* gonna have to get the hell up out of here and take all this shit with you!"

"Man, I ain't goin' nowhere!" Kiki's friend shot to his feet, glaring up at Dante, curling his thick lips in challenge.

The young man was about a foot shorter than him, had a rail-thin build, and a voice that was so high Dante wondered if he'd gone through puberty yet. He didn't find him remotely intimidating.

"Boy, don't make me have to toss your ass out on the sidewalk!" Dante spat.

The young man's sneer turned into a menacing smile as he raised the side of his white T-shirt, revealing the black handgrip of a Glock tucked into the waistband of his saggy jeans and boxers. "I'd like to see you try, nigga'!"

"Stop!" Kiki shouted, hopping to her feet and standing between the two. "Just stop! Why are you faking, Tee? You ain't gonna' shoot my daddy! He's been shot enough already anyway." She shoved the young man back onto the couch and then turned to face Dante. "Let me talk to you right quick."

"There's nothing to talk about," he said through clenched teeth. "Get this shit out of my house!"

"Daddy, don't be like that!" she pleaded, tugging up her hip-huggers and leaning her head toward his kitchen. "I just wanna talk to you . . . in *private*. It ain't gonna take long!"

He stood silently for several seconds then threw up his hands. "Fine. Say whatever you have to say—but I'm warning you, I'm not budging on this."

They both strolled into the kitchen, which he also noted was covered in drug paraphernalia, making him slowly shake his head in exasperation.

Dante had only met Kiki a few months ago after she had revealed she was his daughter, and he was already regretting letting her move into the home he had inherited from his late mother. He was also starting to regret letting her wedge her way into his life. Kiki was becoming the thing that Dante despised the most: a liability. He had hoped he could teach her how to hustle properly and use her wits and ruthless cunning to move ahead in the world. Kiki had already shown potential with the way she'd helped him take care of Renee Upton. Renee was a woman he had briefly dated who had, after he rejected her, tried more than once to kill him. Kiki had been the person to find the crew to kill Renee instead.

Dante had been grateful. He had given Kiki a place to live, let her drive his car, and had taken her under his wing. And *this* was how she repaid him?

"What were you thinking, Kiki?" he exclaimed. "I can't

believe you would bring this shit into my house!" He gestured to a bag that showed more bundles of weed sitting on the linoleum counter.

"You told me I couldn't keep living here for free! You said I had to get a job and start paying you some rent—so I got a job!"

"I meant a job as a receptionist or a . . . a sales girl at the Gap, for Christ's sake! Hell, I didn't even care if you got a job at McDonald's or Burger King. But I didn't ask you to become a fucking drug dealer! I certainly didn't expect you to set up shop in my house."

She sucked her teeth. "Like you're one to talk."

"What the hell is that supposed to mean?"

"It means I saw all those bottles you used to keep in your medicine cabinet!" she snarled, making him fall silent, making his stomach drop. "I saw all those pain pills you were eating like candy. You thought I was stupid and I didn't know how you got those pills?" She shook her head. "Well, I wasn't. I know you got a dealer, too! So you really trying to preach to me about making some money off of bud when you do what you do?"

He didn't have a response to that. He hadn't known that she had found out about the addiction to painkillers he had developed soon after Renee had shot him. It was now to the point that he took twenty to thirty pills a day, making it a rather expensive habit. He was spending about six to eight grand a month to keep himself stocked with pills. And the high seemed to get harder and harder to chase. Each week he was gobbling more and more pills. He had tried a few times to go cold turkey, but the withdrawal symptoms were just too painful: the chills, the body aches, the severe stomach cramping, and the seemingly endless vomiting that would have him sitting on his bathroom floor with his head propped on the toilet seat. He'd feel like he was dying and he would only get relief after opening the medicine cabinet and shaking pills into his hands. It was a monkey he worried he would never get off his back.

Kiki inclined her head and smiled. "Now instead of getting mad, you could see this as a way for you to make some money, too. If you let us keep working out of here, we could cut you like . . . I don't know . . . a monthly fee or some shit. Even you could use some extra cash!"

"I don't want anything to do with your little drug operation. If the cops find out what's happening in here, they could shut this whole place down. My name would be associated with it. Did you forget that I'm a lawyer? I can't afford to get disbarred!"

She took another step toward him and dropped her voice down to a whisper. "Nobody would know you were part of it. It would just be me and Tee. That's all."

"*You and Tee?* Oh, that makes me feel *so* much better!" he shouted sarcastically. "Until today, I'd never met that kid before in my life! I've known him all of five minutes, and he's already threatened me with a gun!"

"She," Kiki corrected, making Dante squint.

"Huh?"

"It's *she*, Daddy. Tee's a girl—*my* girl," she said proudly, licking her lips and placing a hand on her hip.

"You mean you're a couple?"

She snorted. *"Couple,"* she repeated in a baritone voice, making fun of him.

"When the hell did you turn into a lesbian?"

She shrugged and leaned back against the countertop. "I didn't *turn* into anything. I've always liked both, and I just got tired of dudes being assholes and trying to get you pregnant then leave you. I don't have time for that shit! Tee and I understand each other. Plus,"—she grinned— "she knows how to eat that pussy."

He held up his hand and cringed. There were some

things he didn't want to know about his own daughter. "Spare me the details."

She chuckled and pushed herself away from the counter. "Come on. I'll introduce y'all since we'll all be working together now. *Right?* Let's see what we can work out."

He pursed his lips, contemplating Kiki's offer.

In no way did Dante want to get involved in his daughter's little weed empire, but she was right about a few things. One was that he couldn't exactly take the moral high ground about her becoming a dealer when he had a heavy drug habit himself. Another was that he could definitely use the extra money Kiki and Tee would pay him. Dante's savings were being depleted at an alarming rate thanks to his drug habit. Since he had been fired from the law firm of Nutter, McElroy & Ailey, he'd been trying to get a position at a new firm and get clients where he could. But it wasn't easy. As a parting shot, Dante had admitted to law firm partner Edgar McElroy that he had been secretly screwing Edgar's wife. Furious, the old man seemed to have made it his mission to kill Dante's legal career—and he was doing a splendid job of it.

Finally, Dante slowly exhaled. "Okay, I'll talk to her, Kiki, but you two better give me a decent cut of this whole enterprise, because if you don't, then—"

"Then you'll toss us out on the street." Kiki nodded. "I heard you the first time. Don't worry, Daddy! I got you."

Chapter 5

Evan

"Inmate number 14587889!" the guard behind the counter barked as he looked down at a chart in front of him. "Evan Murdoch!"

Evan slowly raised his head and stepped out of line toward the laminated counter. "I'm Evan Murdoch," he said.

The guard glanced up from the sheet at Evan, peering at him through the steel grate. He looked down again.

"Got any dress-outs?"

"Uh, yes," Evan said with a nod. "Yes, I do."

"Yes . . . *what?*" the guard asked tersely, looking up from the chart.

Evan's jaw tightened at the guard's challenging tone, but he forced his blank facial expression to stay in place.

He had learned to train his reactions. Any show of emotion could land him with a guard yelling and sending spittle into his face, or it could earn him a hard shove or a lightning-quick punch from another inmate who wanted to bully him into a fight. He had the bruises to show for his past mistakes, the moments when he hadn't used caution and had let his emotions get the better of him. He wouldn't make those mistakes again.

"Yes, sir," Evan said evenly, watching as the guard snickered.

"You haven't gotten out the door yet, Inmate. Mind your P's and Q's." The guard then turned slightly to riffle through the stack of bags adjacent to him on the counter. He paused at one bag, scanned the label, then compared it to the sheet in front of him. He picked up the bag and tossed it at Evan. It was filled with clothes that Leila had sent for him wear on the day he would exit the jail and had to turn in his inmate uniform. Those inmates who didn't have relatives or friends to send them clothes had to choose from the thrift store finds the jail had in reserve.

"Sign this," the guard said, turning the chart toward Evan.

Evan reached for the ballpoint pen the guard handed him and signed on the line the guard had pointed to.

He then picked up the bag.

"Nice duds," the guard commented, glancing at the Armani label on Evan's shirt that showed prominently through the clear plastic.

Evan didn't respond.

He emerged from a steel door into the receiving area a few hours later, rubbing his wrists, relieved to finally be rid of the steel cuffs that had left an indentation in his skin. The dingy room was filled with people sitting in the beat-up plastic chairs and standing along the walls. A few children ran in circles, tossing candy bar wrappers at one another while a woman yelled at them in rapid-fire Spanish. An elderly woman sat in one of the chairs, engrossed in her knitting.

"Ev!" a voice called out to him. "Evan!"

He turned slightly and saw Leila rising from one of the chairs. She strode across the room toward him. He could see that she was shaking and gulping for air as she did it. Tears were in her big brown eyes. When she reached him, she flung her arms around his neck and began to weep.

"Oh, baby! Baby, I missed you! I missed you so much."

He wrapped his arms around her, too, and held her close, breathing in the smell of her hair and the intoxicating scent of her perfume, sinking into her warmth and suppleness. He had longed to embrace her like this, counting the days and then the minutes until he would see her again. He had even dreamed about her during those lonely, harrowing nights in his jail cell.

Evan continued to hold her close as she wept on his shoulder. But her cries eventually tapered off. Reluctantly, he released her.

"Let's go home. I wanna see our baby," he whispered.

That had been the other thing he had dreamed about while in jail. He longed to cradle Angelica in his arms, to have her little hand cling to his finger. He had been gone for a little more than a month and could only imagine how big she had gotten in his absence. He knew babies developed quickly their first year. Each week that passed was filled with milestones he had missed.

Leila grinned and nodded. "Of course," she said, wiping her eyes with the backs of her hands. "Angelica wants to see her daddy, too. So does Isabel. We all missed you, Ev."

They exited the prison doors and walked into the parking lot. Evan closed his eyes and breathed in the fresh air.

It was overcast that day. The cement and asphalt were wet and filled with puddles thanks to the melting snow all around them. Icicles still clung to the sparse trees along the parking lot. The prison's exterior and the neighboring buildings seemed to all be of the same drab gray color as the clouds above. But the skies might as well have been clear blue and the sun might as well have been shining for how good Evan felt to finally be free again.

No guards barking at him to wake up or turn off his lights. No prisoners yelling taunts of "What the fuck you lookin' at?" or "I'ma get in that ass, rich boy!" as he passed.

But Evan knew this freedom, however glorious, might not last. A year from now if a jury found him guilty he could very well find himself back here, walking through those doors again in handcuffs. Or maybe he could be sent to a worse place—a maximum-security federal prison on the other side of the country.

How the hell am I going to survive that?

His hold on Leila's hand tightened at the prospect of having to let her go all over again.

Feeling his crushing grip and seeing the desperation in his eyes, she frowned. "Everything okay, baby?"

He nodded. "I'm . . . I'm fine," he lied.

They walked the short distance to his Lincoln Town Car, where his driver, Bill, stood smiling as he held the door open for them.

"Good to have you back, Mr. Murdoch," Bill said.

Evan gave a halfhearted smile and thumped Bill on the shoulder. "Good to be back."

Though he had no idea how long he would be back. He couldn't count on the world suddenly righting itself. He had to prepare for the worst and plan accordingly.

He and Leila climbed inside the car's backseat, and Bill slammed the door shut behind him. They were still holding hands.

"I'll admit that I'm selfish. The whole family wanted to wait for you in the parking lot, and I told them to meet us at the house instead." She cupped his face and gazed lovingly into his eyes. "I get to have you all to myself, for a little while at least." She kissed him again.

He vaguely nodded and stared over her shoulder at the passing scenery outside the passenger window, taking it all in: the buildings, the trees, and the cars. What was once so mundane now took on much more importance. He had seriously started to question when and if he would ever see these things again.

"I cleared out my schedule for the next few weeks." She raised his hand to her lips and kissed his knuckles. She drew closer to him on the leather seat. "I'm not doing any work for any of my clients. I just want to spend time home alone with you and the kids, and we can—"

"I can't, baby," he said, shaking his head, pulling her hand from his face. "I have to get back to the office. We get news in prison, too, you know. I saw that Murdoch Conglomerated is falling apart. I can't lounge around at home while that happens—even if I wanted to."

"Of . . . of course," she said, lowering her eyes, looking embarrassed and crestfallen. "I understand."

He placed a finger under her chin to raise her face so that she was looking at him again.

"And I'm going to check in with my lawyer to see about my divorce from Charisse. We went through all that bullshit to get her to finally sign the paperwork, and she did it more than two months ago. It should've gone through by now. If it hasn't, I'm going to tell my lawyer to light a fire under the judge's ass and speed it up. I want us to get married ASAP."

"Oh, Ev, baby, I . . . I want to marry you, too, but we can do all of that in time! Let's just focus on—"

"We don't have time, Lee! You know that and I know that. I don't know how long I'll be out of jail or if all this shit is behind me . . . behind us."

"I know that, honey, but—"

"No 'buts.' We *need* to do this. I have to make sure

you're taken care of. The only way I can do that for sure is if you become my wife."

She slowly nodded. "O-okay, whatever you think is best. Whatever you want."

"This is what I want," he said before turning around to look out the tinted window again.

They carried out the rest of the ride to Murdoch Mansion in mutual silence with only the soft murmur from the heating vent and business radio filling the car compartment. When the Town Car slowly pulled into the circular driveway and he stared at the soaring portico and snow-covered hedges, he sighed.

"We're home," Leila whispered, leaning toward him.

"We're home," he repeated.

A minute later, he and Leila stepped through the mansion's French doors, and Evan was greeted by the sight of his family standing in his foyer.

If he'd thought he'd been emotional when he walked out of the prison, he wasn't prepared for the emotions that overcame him when he saw his infant daughter nestled in her grandmother's arms or when he saw his brother and sister turn to look at him.

They had all been talking and laughing with one another but instantly fell quiet when Evan entered the room, like someone had flicked a switch, turning off all sound. He stared at them, also at a loss for words.

Isabel, Leila's daughter, was the first to break the silence. She ran across the foyer and leaped at Evan, almost making him stumble back through the open door. She threw her arms around his waist and held him tight.

"I thought you weren't coming back," she sobbed into his dress shirt. "I thought they took you away like Daddy and you were going to jail forever! I thought we'd never see you again, Evan!"

Watching the little girl cry as she clung to him made Evan's heart break.

His relationship with Isabel had been far from perfect this past year. He had tried to win her over, to show her that he loved her mother and, if given the chance, could care for her, too. But she had gone to great lengths to show Evan over and over again that he wasn't her father. That title belonged only to Bradley Hawkins, in Isabel's eyes—even if the man was a son of a bitch who had cheated on Leila for most of their marriage and had manipulated Isabel into doing things that no eight-year-old should ever be coerced into doing. Isabel's coldness toward Evan had forced him to back off, to give up any hope of developing a relationship with her. Fortunately, a thaw had started to settle between them before he had gone to jail. But he'd had no idea that Isabel had warmed to him this much, that she had cared this much about him.

"It's okay, Izzy," he whispered, hugging her back. "It's okay. I'm home now."

After Isabel's sobs subsided, Evan released her and hugged his sister, Paulette, who was also crying. He then embraced his brother, Terrence, who kept a brave face, but Evan could tell Terrence was equally emotional.

"Damn, Ev! I missed you, bruh!" Terrence croaked through sniffs as they thumped each other on the back.

Evan chuckled, released him, and took a step back. "Missed you, too, Terry. You been behaving yourself while I was gone?"

Terrence shrugged. "As much as can be expected."

The welcome-home party continued in the great room where the servants had set out a buffet lunch for the half dozen or so attendees. But Evan didn't have much of an appetite. Instead, he spent most of his time cradling Angelica, staring down at her with the same reverence as he had the day she was born. He also spent the next two hours holding Leila close, even as he spoke with others.

As the sun began to set behind the floor-to-ceiling windows, Evan removed his arm from around Leila's waist. He did it with great reluctance. He longed to maintain the physical connection that had eluded him for more than a month, but he had something very important he had to do instead.

"I'll be back, all right?" he whispered to her, then leaned down to kiss slumbering Angelica's crown, gently brushing her dark, curly hair as he did it.

"*Back?*" Leila frowned up at him quizzically. "Where are you going?"

"Not far. I just need to talk to Terry for a sec."

"Oh," she uttered as he kissed her cheek and walked away. Despite his explanation, she still seemed disconcerted. Her worried expression didn't disappear. "O-okay. But don't run off for too long!" she called weakly after him as he strode across the room to his brother, who was talking to C. J. He tapped Terrence on his shoulder.

"Can I talk to you?"

Terrence nodded.

"In private," Evan whispered, glancing around the room. "It won't take long."

"Lead the way."

As the two men walked toward the great room's door, Evan could feel several eyes upon them—particularly Leila's.

Yes, it might seem odd and maybe even rude to walk out of his own party, but frankly Evan didn't care. What he wanted to say to Terrence he had to say without an audience.

Evan walked down the hall with his brother trailing behind him. He then pushed open the door of his study.

"Oh, man! I don't think I will *ever* get used to this

room no matter how many times I come in here," Terrence whispered in awe as he strolled into the study, staring at the wood paneling, the twelve-foot-tall bookshelves along the walls, and the high ceilings. He shoved his hands into his jean pockets. "I know it's your home office now, but I'll always associate it with Dad. I remember coming in here back when he was alive. You knew when Dad called you into the study, you had fucked up."

Evan chuckled as he walked toward the large oak desk and turned on the old Tiffany lamp. Despite it still being somewhat light outside, the cavernous study was always dark thanks to its heavy velvet curtains. "That is definitely true."

"He made me sit in that chair," Terrence said, gesturing to one of the leather wingback chairs, "after getting suspended from school when I was sixteen for that big prank I pulled. You remember?"

"Yeah, I remember," Evan said as he pulled out the swivel chair and fell back into it. When he did, he released a sigh of contentment. He'd never imagined that he would miss the little things like the feel of a comfy chair. A twenty-seven-day stint in prison had taught him different. "Dad looked like his head was about to explode," Evan continued, looking up at his brother. "When you walked in here and he shut the door behind you, I wasn't sure if you'd make it back out alive."

"I wasn't sure, either," Terrence said, thumping his hand on the back of the chair. "He didn't beat the hell out of me, but he cut me down pretty good with his words—the way only Dad could. I wish he would've smacked me. It would've been less painful!"

Evan shook his head. "Dad wasn't one for proportionality, was he? Did he tell you he was disowning you?"

"Pretty much. He told me I was a total waste of time and space, and if I ever embarrassed him and the family like that again, he would kick me out of the house. 'Don't think being my son means I won't turn my back on you like any other sorry son of a bitch out here, because I can and I will. Then what will you have? Nothing. No one.'"

"Jesus," Evan exhaled as he lowered his eyes to the desk their father had once owned. He slowly ran his hand along the ornate gold trim. "'Don't bring shame to the family name.' That's what he used to say."

"All the damn time," Terrence muttered.

"I wonder what he would say about me now . . . about everything that's happened. He'd probably give me the same threat as he gave you that day—maybe worse."

"No, he wouldn't! He'd know you didn't do this, Ev. It's that bitter, psychotic asshole Dante who's—"

Evan raised his hand to silence his brother. "I don't wanna talk about him, Terry. Don't even say that mother-fucka's name to me again. Okay?"

Just the thought of Dante could send him into a bubbling rage as hot as magma.

When Evan hadn't been fantasizing about Leila or Angelica during those cold, lonely nights in prison, he would think about Dante. He'd wish that he *had* been the one to pull the trigger in that parking garage—or had killed his half-brother by some other means: strangulation, stabbing, or possibly kicking and beating him to death. If he ever came face-to-face with Dante again, he didn't know what he would do. If found guilty of attempted murder, Evan decided he might try killing Dante after all.

If I'm going to go to prison for twenty years, I might as well go for a good reason, he now thought, clenching his fists.

He exhaled and loosened his hands, resting them on top of the desk again.

"Talking about . . . him," Evan said, "isn't why I brought

you in here, Terry. I don't want to waste any more time on that."

"So why *did* you bring me in here?"

"Look, I don't . . . I don't know what the future holds anymore. I never did, but I know that for certain now. I don't know if this bogus attempted murder charge will get dropped—or if I could face some serious jail time if a jury finds me guilty. Either way, I figured I should be prepared. I . . . I have to set my house in order."

He raised his eyes to look at his little brother. As expected, Terry's facial expression was grim.

"I'll try my best to pull Murdoch Conglomerated out of the quagmire it's in now, but . . . but I'll also encourage the board to start looking for a new CEO to lead the company if I—"

"No! Hell no, Ev! That's *our* company." Terry pointed at his chest. "Dad wanted you to lead it. He said so on his deathbed! You can't just—"

"We have to have a contingency plan, Terry," Evan said firmly. "I have to prepare for the worst."

Terrence fell silent.

"I also want you to become trustee of the estate in my absence. I know money management isn't your thing, but I have people lined up who can help you. I would feel more comfortable with you overseeing it. I know I can trust you."

"Ev . . ." Terrence slowly shook his head. "Come on, man! Stop talking like this."

"I also want you . . ." Evan lowered his eyes again. His throat tightened. "I want you to look out for Lee for me. Look out for the kids."

"You're not going back to jail. You're going to beat this! We—"

"Terry, just promise me you'll take care of them," Evan said, talking over his brother. "I know you and C. J. will probably want to start a family of your own one day, but . . .

but I don't want Lee to have to fend for herself. I'll make sure she's set financially, but just . . . just watch out for her. Watch out for my little girl, all right?"

Terrence closed his eyes and then opened them. Gradually, he nodded. "Of course. Of course, I will, Ev! You know I'll take care of Angelica and Isabel like they were my own. But I won't have to do that because you're going to be here to help raise them. There's no way we're going to let that son of a bitch win and take you away from Lee and the girls . . . take you away from us."

Evan stared up at his brother. He wished he could be as confident as Terrence, but he couldn't.

Chapter 6

Leila

"Roly-poly, roly-poly, roly-poly," the women chanted over and over again, filling the workout room with their voices.

Leila leaned over her infant daughter, who lay on the yoga mat in front of her. She cooed to Angelica as she wiggled the baby's arms and legs in a circular motion. She gazed into Angelica's eyes—soulful, dark eyes, much like her father's—and smiled, enjoying the feel of her daughter's soft rolls under her fingertips and her comforting baby smell. Angelica gazed back at her with her lips parted, entranced by her mother's soothing voice.

"I still don't understand why *we* have do it," Paulette whispered sharply, snapping Leila out of her tranquil reverie. "She doesn't have any friends who can help her out?"

Leila glanced at her sister-in-law, who leaned over Little Nate, who was splayed on a yoga mat in front of his mother, though he seemed more interested in eating his toes than in today's exercise.

Both women were attending a baby and mommy yoga class at the Chesterton Rec Center to bond with their babies and catch some girl time together, but so far it seemed that Paulette hadn't gotten the memo that this was supposed to a fun, *calming* outing. She seemed far from calm; she was downright irritable.

"We don't have to do it," Leila whispered back. "I just thought it would be a nice gesture if we did. You know . . . to help her out. Terry said—"

"I have better things to do with my life than help some chick I barely know pick out a wedding dress, Lee. You never should've told Terry we'd do it, especially without consulting me first."

Leila sat back on her shins, releasing a deep breath in exasperation.

Perhaps Paulette was right. Maybe Leila should not have volunteered herself and Paulette to help C. J. select a wedding gown for her and Terrence's ceremony in a few months, but she really hadn't thought it would be that big of a deal. Terrence had been kind to her and the girls while Evan had been in prison, stopping by the mansion at least twice a week to check on them and see if they needed anything. Was it that hard to return the favor?

Terrence had also mentioned in passing at Evan's welcome-home party a few weeks ago that C. J. had no one to help her choose a wedding dress. The poor girl had basically been tossed out of her family and had no close girlfriends to rely on. Leila remembered selecting her own gown for her first wedding. It had been a touching moment, having her mother standing behind her in the mirror at the bridal shop. The two women had been in tears as Leila donned her veil and gazed at her reflection. It broke Leila's heart that C. J. wouldn't have a similar heartfelt experience with her own mother before she tied the knot.

"Besides," Paulette muttered, rolling Nate's little arms, "I don't know why they're making a big deal about it anyway! She probably doesn't care what dress she gets—just as long as it's the most expensive one in the store!"

"Oh, stop," Leila huffed. "You don't know that."

"She probably wants some crazy elaborate reception, too," Paulette continued, ignoring Leila, "when they should just keep it simple since he'll probably be footing the bill anyway. I doubt she'll pay one dime!"

At that, Leila gave Paulette the side-eye. She remembered Paulette's own wedding day, and it hadn't been understated. Between the Vera Wang dress, bushels and bushels of flowers, the huge wedding party, and extravagant reception, Paulette's wedding had to have cost well into the six figures. And Paulette hadn't paid for anything out of her own pocket; Evan had footed the entire bill.

"You and Ev kept it simple," Paulette said, turning to Leila. "You didn't make a big deal about it! Why should they?"

Leila sighed and gazed down at Angelica again. The infant had grabbed onto her mother's finger—her ring finger, which now sported a wedding band.

Yes, she and Evan had finally tied the knot last week in a simple ceremony presided over by the justice of the peace with only Paulette, Terrence, and Diane in attendance. It had lasted all of ten minutes with simple "I do's," ending with a peck done so quickly that Leila wondered later if she and Evan had really kissed. He had left soon after to return to his office at Murdoch Conglomerated for a scheduled meeting. And Leila had been left with the feeling that they hadn't gotten married, but that Evan had simply checked off a line item on his to-do list. Their marriage was one of many things he had wanted to accomplish just in case he did go to jail for a long time.

Evan wanted her and the girls to be legally protected. Leila respected that. That's why she didn't have the heart to tell Evan or anyone else that she would have wanted a bigger wedding. She'd wanted the pomp and circumstance of a church ceremony and an intimate but beautiful reception to celebrate them *finally* becoming a married couple. Instead, she had gotten an anticlimactic end to the drama that had been her and Evan's relationship for the past two years—hell, the past *twenty years!*

Leila was no longer Evan's mistress; she was officially Mrs. Evan Murdoch now. But she felt no triumph or even relief. She wore his ring, but she didn't feel any closer to him. When he wasn't at the office, he was barricaded in his study on the phone with his lawyers, reviewing his case and going over what could happen to his assets and the Murdoch estate during imprisonment. What little precious free time Evan had, he spent cradling and rocking Angelica or reassuring Isabel, who was terrified of losing yet another father figure to prison. He rarely talked to let alone held Leila anymore. He hadn't kissed her in days and hadn't made love to her in weeks, not since that first night after he had returned home from jail.

But she felt shallow and petty pointing out those things to him. His future and livelihood were in jeopardy. Who cared that she needed a hug or that she longed for reassurance that he still loved and wanted her? She needed to be here for him, to give him all of her support. *That's* what mattered.

"All right, ladies," the instructor in the front of the class called out, yanking Leila's attention back. "That brings an end to today's yoga class. I hope you all enjoyed your special time with the little ones and come back to us next week! Namaste!"

Wow, it's the end of the class already, Leila thought bemusedly as she watched all the women rise to their feet, taking their babies with them. She must have been pretty lost in thought not to even notice.

Leila scooped Angelica into her arms before lowering

her into the car seat she had set along the workout room wall. As she buckled the carrier's straps into place, Paulette wrangled Little Nate into a Baby Björn on her chest. Both women put on their coats and slowly made their way to the doors.

"Look," Leila said, hefting the baby carrier at her side, "if you really don't want to go to the wedding dress shop with us, you don't have to. It's not like you're contractually obligated to do it."

"No, I'm not contractually obligated, but you said I would do it, Lee! Now it'll look messed up if I don't go. It'll seem like I don't like the girl!"

Leila barked out a laugh as they stepped in the rec center's hallway. Their voices bounced off the high ceilings and steel lockers surrounding them. "But you *don't* like her, Paulette! You've made that pretty clear."

"I did *not* say I didn't like her." Leila watched as her sister-in-law tossed her long hair over her shoulder and out of reach of Little Nate's fingers and mouth. "I don't know enough about her to feel one way or the other—and frankly, neither does Terry! I just don't understand why he's jumping into this so fast. They've been a couple for less than a year and have already broken up at least once! And didn't she dump him only to start dating her ex-fiancé again? I mean—"

"Paulette," Leila began softly, placing her hand on the younger woman's shoulder, "Terry is a big boy . . . a *grown* man! He knows what he's doing, and he's allowed to follow his heart. He's been supportive of you and your brother in all the decisions you guys have made, right?"

Paulette paused. Her face went somber.

"So cut him a break," Leila said. "Support *him* this time!"

Paulette stared down at the crown of Little Nate's head. "But she could really hurt him! You remember what he was like right after his accident—when his depression was at its worst."

"I do." Leila nodded. "I also remember that it was his relationship with C. J. that helped him get better."

Paulette sucked her teeth. "I'd credit his therapist for that."

"Either way, he's asking for our help this time around . . . and he's not asking for a lot. It's just a bridal appointment. A couple of hours at most. You can do that, right?"

After some time, Paulette raised her eyes and loudly grumbled. "Fine. I'll do it."

"Good," Leila said, beaming. "Now let's move on to more important matters, like lunch. Miss Tracey said she was making something special today. I'm eager to see what it is."

Miss Tracey had been the cook at the Murdoch Mansion for the past thirty years. She had been recruited by the late Angela Murdoch during the early days of her marriage.

"Gah, I miss Miss Tracey's food so much!" Paulette exclaimed as they pushed through the heavy steel doors to the parking lot. "It's one of the perks of living at the mansion that I miss the most!" She smirked. "Maybe I'll steal her and get her to cook at my house instead."

"Are you sure you want to get into a bidding war with Ev?"

Paulette quickly shook her head. "Oh, no! Nope! No thank you!"

Less than a half hour later, Leila pulled Evan's Range Rover into the mansion's circular driveway. When she did, she whipped off her sunglasses and peered at the spectacle in front of her. Her mouth hung open, agape.

Leila watched as three men clad in dark suits unloaded suitcases and shopping bags from three Lincoln Town

Cars parked in front of the stone steps. They all carried the suitcases to the open French doors. Several more suitcases sat on the ground behind each sedan's bumper.

"What in the . . ." Leila murmured.

Evan hadn't mentioned that any guests would be arriving at the mansion today—but it looked like they were getting a visit from someone. Whoever it was had brought enough luggage to clothe a small army.

A minute later, Leila was cradling a slumbering Angelica against her chest. She shut the driver's side door, still transfixed by all the luggage streaming out of the open trunks.

"What in the world is going on?" Paulette asked behind her, making Leila jump, startled. She hadn't realized that her sister-in-law had been standing there.

"I have no idea." She lifted her diaper bag and tossed the strap over her shoulder. "Guess we better find out."

They mounted the stone steps and walked through the open doorway. When they did, Leila saw an elderly woman standing near the staircase, pointing to one of the portraits on the entryway walls. A handsome young man in his mid to late twenties stood at her side with a fur coat thrown over his arm, smiling in the direction she was pointing.

The woman had creamy, wrinkled skin in sharp contrast to the jet-black, curly afro that was closely cropped to her head. She wore a tight-fitting, V-necked red dress that was cut so low in the front it barely contained her bountiful bosom. A bright pink Birkin bag dangled at her elbow. A sizable diamond bracelet hung from her wrist. When Leila and Paulette walked into the foyer, she turned and tore off her Chanel sunglasses. She grinned.

"Here they come now!" she said, tapping the younger man's shoulder. "I told you someone would come home eventually, Michael. You were worried for no reason, honey! I told you we wouldn't have to fend for ourselves!"

"Aunt . . . *Aunt Ida?*" Paulette said, squinting at the woman.

"In the flesh, girl!" Aunt Ida exclaimed, throwing out her wingy arms with a flourish.

Leila stared in shock. *Aunt Ida? This was* the *Aunt Ida?*

Leila knew Paulette, Evan, and Terrence had an aunt—their father, George's, only surviving sibling—who lived on the other side of world. Since her twenties, Aunt Ida had spent her days using the Murdoch money to fund her jet-setting lifestyle, hopping from homes in St. Croix to Paris, marrying four husbands along the way. Aunt Ida held from a generation in their family before they were called the Marvelous Murdochs in Chesterton, just the "high-yella Murdochs."

In the twenty-plus years Leila had known their family, she had never met Aunt Ida in person, but it looked like she was finally meeting the mysterious woman today.

Aunt Ida chuckled as she sauntered toward them. "I'd give you a hug, Paulette, if you didn't have the little rug rat strapped to you. I don't want to crush him, and frankly, I'm allergic to babies. It's the reason why I never pushed one out. So you're just gonna have to settle for a kiss on the cheek instead."

She leaned forward and did exactly that, catching Paulette off guard.

"Well, look at you, all grown up!" she cried, rubbing Paulette's arms. "I see you have your mama's genetics . . . the pretty face and that lovely, thick hair!" She looked Paulette up and down. Her smile disappeared. "And those hips . . . You know, Angela couldn't lose the baby weight, either, no matter how hard she tried! I hope your husband likes 'em thick, honey, or he might turn you in for a slimmer model!"

Leila's mouth fell open again—this time in outrage at

the older woman's rudeness. Who the hell did she think she was?

"Aunt... Aunt Ida... what are you doing here?" Paulette sputtered.

"Well," the older woman began as she strolled around the foyer, gazing up at the high ceilings, "I decided it was about time I pay the homestead a visit to see what the hell was going on, considering that my Murdoch Conglomerated stock is now worth only half of what it was six months ago. It seems that boy, Evan, is running the company into the ground, and I wanted to find out what he plans to do to make it right again before we all end up in the poorhouse! Since he doesn't seem to—"

"Ev's doing everything in his power to save Murdoch Conglomerated," Leila said, stepping forward, drawing Aunt Ida's attention. "And he didn't run the company into the ground. He's the one who made it better. If you want to blame anyone for ruining the company, blame Dante Turner. It was his false charges that landed Evan in this mess in the first place!"

The older woman inclined her head and squinted up at Leila. "And who might you be?"

"I'm Leila Murdoch," she said, pushing back her shoulders. "I'm Evan's wife."

"*Really?*" Aunt Ida cried. "I was under the impression that Evan's wife was a blond white woman."

"That was his first wife—Charisse. I'm his second."

"His second. *Already?*" The older woman threw back her head and laughed. "Well, it seems Evan's personal life is going along just as splendidly as his business sense!"

"Excuse me?" Leila said, dropping a hand to her hip. She was about to give Aunt Ida a piece of her mind just as the older woman waved forward the young man who had been silently standing near the staircase newel posts.

"Come over here, Michael, honey! Say hi to Paulette and Leila here. Meet my niece and my new niece-in-law!"

He did as the older woman ordered, strolling toward them with a brilliant smile. He stood a little over six feet with light eyes, tan skin, and a face that looked like he could star in his own Ralph Lauren ad.

"Paulette and Leila, meet Michael . . . my fiancé," she gushed, linking arms with him.

"Your fiancé?" Paulette choked.

Good God, Leila thought with disgust. *She's old enough to be his damn grandmother!*

"Pleased to meet you," Michael said, offering his hand to Paulette first.

Paulette seemed to hesitate before giving his hand a quick shake.

"And you, too, Leila," he said, turning to Leila with his hand extended. "It's a pleasure."

Though Leila wasn't in the mood for introductions, she knew it wasn't *his* fault that Aunt Ida had decided to just barge in here and force herself upon her relatives. The poor guy was probably being dragged along for the ride.

"Pleasure to meet you too, Michael," Leila said, adjusting Angelica in her arms and shaking his hand. She then attempted to pull her hand back, but he held on a few seconds longer, much longer than necessary—making her frown.

"I can't wait to meet your husband, Mrs. Murdoch," he said, finally letting her go. "Especially since we'll be living under the same roof for the next few weeks. Ida has told me so much about Evan, I feel like I know him already."

"*Weeks?*" Leila repeated, choking on the word. "Did you . . . did you say you're going to be staying here for *weeks?*"

"Aunt Ida," Paulette rushed out, hoping to intervene,

"you don't really want to stay here, do you? Wouldn't you be much, *much* happier in a place all to yourself?" Paulette raised her brows. "Maybe a five-star hotel in D. C. with room service or even a . . . a personal concierge? I'm sure we could recommend a place that would be just . . . just fabulous!"

"No, I think I'd be perfectly happy staying here," Aunt Ida said. She linked her arm through Michael's and stared up at him, fluttering her false lashes. She trailed her index finger along the front buttons of his shirt. "I told Michael here that we'd get to test out one of the four-poster beds in one of the rooms upstairs. I don't think we can wait to make it to the city."

Paulette's eyes widened. Leila cringed.

"And besides, I haven't been back home in ages. I was getting nostalgic."

"Look, I hate to ruin the nostalgia," Leila began, "but this is Evan's house now, not yours."

She paused when Paulette gave her a warning glance to tell her to keep quiet. She slowly shook her head, but Leila ignored her. Leila believed in respecting her elders, but this was ridiculous.

"He's not here right now, but he should know what's going on at the very least. Before you move in your things, shouldn't you speak with him first?" Leila asked.

"No, I will not speak with my nephew first," Aunt Ida said, lowering her eyes from Michael and turning to fix Leila with an icy glare. "Because even though Evan Murdoch's name is listed as owner of this property, this house was built by Henry and Lucille Murdoch . . . *my* father and mother." Aunt Ida then gestured to the staid portrait showing the original mansion owners. "So as far as I'm concerned, I have just as much claim to this house as every other person in this family. Maybe more! I may stay for a few weeks—or a few months. I haven't decided yet." Aunt Ida smiled up at the young man again. "Come on, baby. Let's go pick out our room."

Leila and Paulette then watched helplessly as the couple strolled up the stairs leading to the east and west wings.

Chapter 7

C. J.

C. J. clicked computer keys then paused to flip through her reporter's notebook.

"Hey, can I borrow your highlighter?" her cubicle mate and fellow metro desk reporter, Allison, called out to her.

Allison sauntered toward her desk in the crowded newsroom. The skinny blonde then flopped back into her chair and leaned forward to boot up her laptop.

"Sure," C. J. said absently, reaching into a coffee cup full of pens, pencils, and markers. She pulled out a yellow highlighter then held it out to Allison. The other woman grabbed it and popped off the lid before tugging a thick, binder-clipped document out of her tote bag.

They were the youngest on the metro desk—the newest recruits at the *Washington Daily*. She and Allison had bonded immediately and often grabbed coffee and biscotti together at the little shop downstairs, sharing stories about sources and marveling at the fast pace of news reporting in the big city.

"Ugh, the trains were *super* slow today! It took me forever to make it back here. Doesn't WMATA realize I'm on deadline?" Allison asked, adjusting her glasses and squinting at her laptop screen. "Still finishing up that Advisory Committee meeting piece?"

"Yeah, three hundred more words to go before I'm done, I think. I should have *just* enough time to file it before I have to leave."

C. J. glanced at the digital clock on the bottom right-hand side of her screen. "Two thirty," she whispered before returning her attention to her notes. It'd be a tight deadline, but she'd have to do it to make it back to Chesterton by four o'clock.

"Where are you running off to after this?" Allison asked. "Another assignment?"

"No, I'm . . ." C. J. paused from typing. She wrinkled her button nose. "I'm trying on wedding gowns."

"Wow! *Really?* I'm jealous!"

"Don't be," C. J. muttered under her breath, returning her attention to her news story.

Though she was excited to marry Terrence, she wasn't excited about today's outing to the bridal shop. She hadn't found out until after the fact that Terrence had asked Leila to help her pick a wedding dress. To make matters worse, his sister, Paulette, was going to tag along.

"*Why* would you do that, Terry?" she had shouted yesterday while they lay in bed together. She had stared at him in shock, like he had sprouted a second head.

"I'd thought you might need some help, babe! To get a second opinion," he'd said, bewildered at her reaction. "It'd give you a chance to bond with them, too. You know getting all girly and everything."

Yes, because that's exactly what I want to do—bond with the rest of the Murdochs, she'd thought mockingly.

Well, actually not *all* the Murdochs were bad. Leila Murdoch was always very sweet to C. J. and tried to make her feel welcome. Evan, Leila's husband, was okay, too, even though C. J.'s relationship with Evan had started on a bad footing. Her stories about Murdoch Bank and Murdoch Conglomerated hadn't enamored her to Evan—and when Evan had accused her of dating Terrence solely to gather information for the hit piece he claimed she planned to write about their family, he didn't become her favorite person, either. But C. J. and Evan seemed to have put that ugly part of their shared past behind them.

In contrast, Paulette Murdoch hadn't made any effort to get to know C. J. or to be nice to her. Terrence's younger sister could be downright aloof sometimes, making C. J. suspect she didn't like her, though C. J. couldn't fathom why.

I've never done anything to the girl, C. J. now thought as she typed.

C. J. wondered if Paulette believed she wasn't good enough for Terrence, that the preacher's daughter wasn't worthy of being a Murdoch.

C. J. had grown up far from poor; her father, Reverend Pete Aston, was rich by most standards. But growing up in the church had taught C. J. not to flaunt her wealth. Her brother, Victor, might be comfortable with his Prada shoes and Movado watches, but C. J. had always liked to keep things simple. She drove a Honda Civic, not a Mercedes. She did her own hair and nails. She considered buying a two-hundred-dollar dress at Macy's a splurge.

But the Murdochs had Victor beat in their displays of affluence. A person only had to see the Murdoch Mansion and its surrounding ten-acre estate, the fancy cars, the boats, and the servants to know these people had money— lots and *lots* of money.

C. J. wasn't from that world, nor did she want to be.

"So what's your fiancé like, anyway?" Allison chirped, breaking into her thoughts. "You hardly ever talk about him for a guy you're supposed to be marrying in five and a half months!"

"Oh, he's just an . . . an average guy. I met him not too long after I moved to Chesterton. We started dating. We still live there. You know. *Yada, yada, yada!*" She shrugged, forcing herself to seem casual. She started typing again. "There isn't too much to tell."

"There's a lot more to tell! In all our conversations, you haven't even told me his name."

"It's . . . It's Terry."

"Terry? That's it? *Just Terry?* Does Terry have a last name?"

C. J. loudly grumbled. "Ally, please . . . I'm trying to get some work done here!"

"Fine, I'll let you get back to your work." Allison cocked an eyebrow. "But if I were a paranoid girl, I'd swear you were hiding him or something. What is he, a CIA agent?"

"No, he's not a CIA agent, and I'm *not* hiding him!" C. J. cried in exasperation.

But she was being vague about Terrence for a reason. When people in Chesterton figured out that she was engaged to a Murdoch they always acted strange, like she was suddenly a different person, like she had morphed into a celebrity they had to fawn over. The Murdochs weren't as infamous outside of Chesterton, but they were still well known enough locally that she was wary of throwing the name around.

"Well, if you aren't trying to hide him, then you won't mind sharing a few more details about him, like, for instance, what does he do for a living?" Allison persisted. "What does he look like? Is he tall? Is he short? Does he—"

"C. J!" someone called out to her, breaking into her and Allison's conversation.

Saved by the bell, C. J. thought as she saw their editor, Ralph Haynes, striding toward them. She instantly sat upright in her desk chair.

She had been working under Ralph for a few weeks

now, but she was still a little awestruck and intimated by him. He was an exacting editor, often asking her to rewrite entire stories or call more sources. He was definitely keeping her on her toes.

"Hi, Ralph. What's up?" she asked, forcing a smile.

Though she had been a chatterbox only seconds ago, Allison went mum as Ralph approached. She reached for her water bottle and turned around in her chair to face her wall calendar, pretending to write something on one of the day slots, trying her best to avoid drawing Ralph's attention.

If C. J. was intimidated by Ralph, Allison seemed outright frightened by him.

"Did you see my notes on the story you filed this morning?" he asked C. J., frowning down at her.

"Uh . . . no. No, I didn't!" She frantically clicked laptop keys so that she could call up the file in question. "I didn't know you—"

"Well, there's a shitload you've got to do to beef it up. You're not in small town news anymore. I didn't put you on my news desk to do half-assed stories!"

She flinched. "I didn't . . . I didn't think it was half-assed, Ralph. I really tried to—"

"I don't want to hear excuses. I want you to pick up the phone," he said, pointing to her desktop phone, "and call the commissioner and a few council members to get them to weigh in. And I want more background about the housing development. Clean up the story, then send it to me for review."

C. J. swallowed. That sounded like a lot of time-consuming work, which would make her late for her bridal appointment. She didn't have Leila's or Paulette's cell numbers to update them that she might be a little late.

"Is there a problem?" Ralph asked with raised brows, noticing her hesitation.

"No, there isn't a problem! I'll . . . I'll make those changes and additions and get it back to you right away."

"Good. I look forward to seeing those edits." He gave a curt nod before moving onto the next cubicle to eviscerate another reporter.

Allison slowly turned away from the cubicle wall once Ralph was out of earshot. "Are you going to make your gown thingie?" she whispered.

"I'll be a few minutes late." C. J. winced once she saw all the red in the edited document and all Ralph's notes in the margins. "Okay, maybe more than just a few."

Allison snickered as she resumed highlighting her document. "My hat's off to you, C. J.! I don't know how you manage to keep this job and a personal life at the same time. I can barely make it home to feed my cat!"

C. J. rushed into the bridal shop at a near run—fifty-five minutes late. When she entered the carpeted dressing room, she was immediately met by melodic choral music playing on background speakers, walls awash in pale pink and white, and three women sitting on the white satin banquette in the center of the shop with facial expressions that varied between annoyed and bored. They simultaneously looked up at her when she entered. Leila smiled at her, and Paulette rolled her eyes and sucked her teeth. A petite older woman wearing a fox fur–trimmed beret lowered the champagne glass from her ruby red lips to the glass coffee table in front of them and laughed.

"See! She didn't keep us waiting a whole hour! She made it here by the skin of her teeth, but she still made it. You owe me twenty dollars, honey!" the older woman said, pointing to Paulette.

Paulette rolled her eyes again and crossed her arms over her chest.

"I'm so . . . *so* sorry," C. J. said, gulping for air. She was out of breath from racing from her car, which was illegally parked four blocks away and would likely be towed by the time she got back. She tugged the strap of her satchel over her head and forced a smile. She blew a tendril of curly hair that had fallen into her face out of her eyes. "I really didn't mean to keep you guys waiting. I got a last-minute assignment that I had to do and . . . well, never mind. Anyway . . . thanks so much for staying!"

"No problem!" Leila said. "We're glad you made it!"

"Oh, yeah, no problem! It's not like we have anything better to do than sit around waiting for you," Paulette mumbled dryly.

C. J.'s cheeks reddened.

Yeah, I was right, she thought. Paulette Murdoch didn't like her, and she suspected that, because she had made them wait so long, Paulette probably liked her even less now—if that were possible.

"Uh," Leila said, after loudly clearing her throat, "C. J., have you met Aunt Ida?"

C. J. turned away from Paulette, shook her head, then waved. "No! No, I haven't. But Terry's told me so much about you. It's a pleasure to finally meet you!"

That was a lie. Terrence had given only a few vague details about his aunt.

"She's rich. She's blunt and way too horny for one man's appetite," Terrence had confided a few days ago after he had gone to Murdoch Mansion with the rest of the family to welcome his aunt back to Chesterton. C. J. hadn't been able to attend because of a news assignment. "Basically, Aunt Ida is the female version of what my dad would be if he was still alive today," he'd confided.

"Aunt Ida wanted to . . . uh . . . tag along for the wedding dress shopping," Leila now explained. "Isn't that right, Aunt Ida?"

"Absolutely! I also wanted to meet the girl that our

Terry plans to marry," the older woman said, pushing herself up from the banquette. She strolled toward C. J., looking her up and down. "So you're the one who won Terry's heart?"

C. J. bashfully nodded. "Yeah, that's . . . that's me!"

Aunt Ida inclined her head. "I have to admit you aren't quite what I expected. I thought you'd be more . . ." She fluttered her fingers in the air then ran her hands up and down her torso. "I don't know . . . *va-va-voom*, maybe?"

C. J.'s forced smile disappeared, and Aunt Ida quickly patted her on the shoulder. "Oh, don't get me wrong, honey! You're fine for any regular fella, but for a tall glass of water like Terry, I was just expecting more glamour, more sex appeal." She laughed again before reaching down to retrieve her glass of champagne and taking another sip. "Believe me, if it wasn't for the fact that he was my nephew, I'd take a slow, *long* drink from that glass any day!"

"Well," Leila exclaimed, clapping her hands, "C. J., you probably want to . . . uh . . . start trying on dresses now. Right?"

C. J. nodded, still staring at Aunt Ida. Terrence had warned her that the woman was blunt—but she wasn't quite prepared for just how candid Aunt Ida would be. "Yeah, sure. Might as well!"

A salesgirl introduced herself and showed C. J. toward the back of the shop to one of the dressing rooms. C. J. tried her best to concentrate on choosing a gown but couldn't. Dress shopping had never been her forte, to even her mother's great disappointment. The last wedding gown C. J. had worn had been for her last "almost wedding" (she had run out on the groom fifteen minutes before the ceremony) and her mother had chosen the dress. C. J. had only offered her halfhearted input, not particularly excited about the dress *or* the groom. Even now as the salesgirl fired questions at her, C. J. felt like the young woman was talking to the wrong person. C. J. felt like she was taking a test she hadn't studied for.

"Were you thinking A-line, ball gown, or mermaid?" the bouncy salesgirl asked, staring at C. J. eagerly as they sat on the plush velvet benches in the dressing room.

"Umm, well . . . I hadn't really thought about that."

"Okay," the woman said, nodding her dark head. Her eager grin stayed in place. "That's fine. I can pull different silhouettes so you can see how they look and start narrowing down from there. Any particular fabric you had in mind? Were you thinking lace or organza . . . maybe satin?"

"Uh, sure! That . . . that sounds good."

The salesgirl squinted. "So which one: lace, organza, or satin?"

"Umm . . . *all of them?*"

The salesgirl lowered her head and laughed. "I'll pull a few dress in your size and be right back."

Ten minutes later the salesgirl and her assistant returned with so many gowns that they filled up the walls of the dressing room. C. J. stood in her bra and panties, shell-shocked. She watched as the young women began to open the dress bags and hold up different gowns for her to consider.

There were so many choices. How could she possibly pick just one, let alone the *right* one?

That's why Leila, Paulette, and Aunt Ida are here, a little voice reminded her.

Yeah, she thought sardonically as she stepped into one of the dresses and the salesgirl raised the zipper and began to fasten hooks. *And I bet they're gonna be so helpful!*

Leila seemed to be making an effort to be kind and accommodating, but she could only imagine what Paulette or Aunt Ida would say once they saw her walk into the main room and stand on the podium. The proverbial knives would be out. Those two could slice her into pieces.

Feeling like a soldier heading before the firing squad, C. J. walked back into the room wearing a simple white satin mermaid wedding gown. She thought the ruching complemented her curves and the heart-shaped neckline showed the right amount of cleavage. It also hugged her round booty.

Something Terry will definitely like, she noted.

When she stepped on the podium, the salesgirl adjusted the train. C. J. stared down at the faces of the three women.

"*So?* What do you think?" she asked.

Leila tilted her head. "It's . . . nice," she said politely, in the same tone that one would use to describe the weather.

Paulette glanced up from her cell phone, shrugged, then looked at her cell phone screen again.

"It's boring!" Aunt Ida exclaimed before sipping from her champagne glass. "It looks like something I would wear to a dinner party!"

C. J. frowned down at the dress.

Who the hell would wear a white satin mermaid gown to a dinner party?

Aunt Ida waved off the dress like she was waving off a fruit fly. "Not acceptable! We can do better! Try on another one, sweetheart."

Grudgingly, C. J. raised the hem of the dress and walked off the platform.

She returned a few minutes later wearing a cream-colored ball gown with a little embellishment along the bodice. She turned to the three women expectantly.

"*Better?*" she asked.

"I really like you in that color," Leila said, nodding.

Aunt Ida sighed. "I guess it's better, but where's all the Swarovski crystals and pearls, honey? Where's all the *bling?*" she drawled. "Believe me . . . girls like us can't go simple with what we wear. We need as much help as we can get!"

"Aunt Ida," Leila said tightly, eying the older woman.

"I'm just saying she's no beauty queen! She knows that. But, darlings, neither am I! That's why I always make sure I'm covered in flash," she said, motioning to her diamond bracelet and necklace. "It draws the attention instead!"

"We . . . uh . . . we have a similar dress with much more adornment along the bodice and train!" the salesgirl piped, stepping forward.

"You do?" Aunt Ida asked hopefully.

Meanwhile, C. J. stood mutely on the platform. She was still recovering from the insult: *"She's no beauty queen."*

No, C. J. would never describe herself as beautiful, but she had never considered herself unattractive, either. From the way Aunt Ida was describing her, though, you'd think she'd be better off not choosing a wedding gown but walking around with a paper bag on her head her entire wedding day to hide her ugly face!

"Yes, we do! There's this gorgeous Lazaro that just came in last week," the salesgirl said to Aunt Ida, still eager to make a sale and oblivious to the devastated bride-to-be standing beside her. She paused and finally glanced back at C. J. "Of course, it's at a much higher price point. It's—"

"This dress is fine," Paulette said, finally speaking up. "No need to bankrupt my brother over a dress she's only going to wear once."

C. J. gritted her teeth. She was ten seconds away from cursing out Paulette and Aunt Ida but decided, for Terrence's sake, to just grin and bear it, to just get through this ordeal.

She and the salesgirl returned to the dressing room, try-ing on more gowns that C. J. quickly eliminated. She finally settled on a Chantilly lace and charmeuse empire-waist dress with caplet sleeves and a ribbon at the waist that was held together with a small diamond broach. She thought the dress was romantic. She felt like a character in a Jane Austen novel wearing this dress.

C. J. proudly marched onto the platform, daring her entourage to say anything bad about the gown.

Aunt Ida lowered her champagne glass and squinted. "Did they steal someone's tablecloth to make that?"

Paulette burst into laughter as C. J.'s shoulders fell.

"It does *not* look like a tablecloth," Leila snapped.

"I swear that my grandmother used to have something similar on the mahogany table she kept in her foyer! An old doily, I believe it was. It's the very same pattern."

At that moment, C. J. felt like a trash can that both Aunt Ida and Paulette had been lobbing garbage into for the past hour. She felt almost full to the brim with their putdowns. Instead of making her feel worthless—which is what she was sure the duo had intended—it made her angry.

C. J. shook her head. "To hell with this," she mumbled before marching off the platform, no longer in the mood to try on wedding gowns.

She wasn't going to be abused any more by these women. She started to head back to the dressing room but stopped, thinking better of it. She whipped around to face them again, balling her fists at her sides.

"You know what? For all your damn money and *supposed* class, you are some petty, malicious, tacky bitches!" she spat, making Paulette's snorts and giggles abruptly taper off and Aunt Ida's mouth drop open. "Thanks for welcoming me to the damn family!"

She then strode across the shop back to the dressing room.

"Well, if you can say anything about her, she's got backbone," Aunt Ida muttered just as C. J. slammed the dressing room door shut behind her.

She yanked off the dress, ripping off one of the pearl buttons as she did it. She hurled the dress to the floor in frustration and paced back and forth, furious at Aunt Ida and Paulette—and furious at herself for losing her cool. She was still fuming when she heard a soft knock at the dressing room door twenty minutes later.

"What?" she snarled.

"It's me . . . uh, Lee," Leila answered. "Can I come in?"

C. J. didn't answer her. She closed her eyes and chewed her lower lip instead.

"They're gone. You don't have to worry about dealing with them anymore. I swear it's just me out here. And I . . . I come in peace," she called out weakly.

C. J. threw on the complimentary robe that the shop had given her, knotting the belt. With great hesitancy, she undid the lock and slowly swung the door open.

Leila stood in the doorway, giving a smile that looked more like a pained grimace. "Hi," she whispered, stepping into the dressing room.

"Look, I'm sorry I flipped out like that." C. J. dropped her eyes to the carpeted floor. "I just didn't expect to—"

"Oh, don't apologize!" Leila insisted with a chuckle, shutting the door behind her. "They deserved it—and I told them so. They *were* being petty, malicious, tacky bitches. But I've gotta tell you . . . Paulette isn't usually like this. I'm sorry you're seeing this version of her." Leila sat down on one of the padded benches and sighed. "She's soft-spoken and sweet most of the time. She's been that way as long as I've known her . . . since she was a little girl. But she's . . . well, she's scared for her brother . . . for Terry. So she's lashing out at you."

C. J. furrowed her brows in confusion. "*Scared?* Scared of what?"

"She knows he's fallen hard for you—and that's never happened before. Terry's had plenty of girlfriends but none that anyone would take seriously. You're the first one that he's been this intense about, that he'd even considered moving in with, let alone marrying! But you guys haven't known each other for long . . . well, not as long as Paulette *thinks* you should've. She's worried that you'll break his heart and send him spiraling into depression again."

"Oh."

And just like that, C. J.'s anger dissipated. She'd had no idea Paulette felt that way. She'd thought that Paulette believed she wasn't good enough for Terrence: not beautiful, rich, or classy enough—not on his level. She'd had no idea Paulette was being such a bitch because of her protective feelings for her older brother.

"And Aunt Ida was behaving that way because . . . well, I'm not even going to try to defend her," Leila said, throwing up her hands. "I barely know her, but I'm pretty sure she's uniformly rude to everyone. That woman just can't be helped."

"Look, Leila, I don't want to hurt Terry," C. J. whispered. "I love him. That's why I want to marry him."

"I know that. And I think you guys will make each other very happy. Terry has a strong personality. Everyone expected him to hook up with one of the airheads he always used to date, but I knew better. He needs a woman who can challenge him . . . match him toe-to-toe. From what I've seen so far, C. J., you fit the bill!"

C. J. laughed. "Thank you for saying that."

Leila nodded then rose to her feet. She walked back toward the dressing room door, grabbed the handle, then paused to turn back around to look at C. J.

"Even if some of us are giving you a hard time, you *are* welcomed to the family, C. J."

"Thanks."

Leila nodded again before opening the door and closing it behind her.

Chapter 8

Paulette

"That's two hours of my life I'll never get back," Paulette muttered as she pulled into her driveway. "What a waste!"

Not only had she gone to the bridal shop against her better judgment, and been made to wait for almost an hour for Terrence's fiancée to finally show up, the ungrateful woman also had the nerve to insult her!

"This will be the first *and* last time I ever do a favor for that bitch," she snapped as she threw her Mercedes into park, removed her car keys from the ignition, and shoved open her car door. Less than a minute later, Paulette stomped up her walkway, still fuming. Her high heels clomped on the brick path.

She just wanted to kick off her shoes, relax, and spend some time with her son, whom she had left in the care of her mother-in-law, Reina. But Paulette stilled near the front door when she heard Little Nate's muffled, shrill screams. Being his mother, she had heard his cries before, but he had never sounded like this. He sounded like he was being strangled to death, like he was being tortured.

"What the hell is she doing to my child?" Paulette questioned aloud.

All thoughts of C. J. Aston and the disastrous bridal shop visit were shoved out her head. Her hands shook as she shoved her key into the door and unlocked it. When she opened her front door, she saw Reina and Little Nate framed by the archway leading to the living room. Reina was holding a milk bottle to Little Nate's mouth, even as the infant wailed and tried to turn his head away.

"What on earth . . ." Paulette murmured as she tossed her purse aside. It landed with a thud on the hardwood floor. She slammed the door behind her and ran across the foyer toward Reina, who was sitting on their sofa, holding the wriggling baby in her arms. In her haste, Paulette almost tripped over one of Nate's discarded toys. She caught herself before she did.

"What's wrong with him?" Paulette cried, tugging him out of his grandmother's grasp. She held Little Nate close, kissing his forehead and cheeks, tasting his salty tears on her lips. "It's okay, honey. Mommy's here! It's okay!" she cooed.

Reina flapped her hands in the air in capitulation. "Oh, just go ahead and take him! He's been crying his head off for the past hour. I've got no idea what's wrong with that boy! I laid him down for a nap and he woke up yellin'."

"Why didn't you call me to tell me?" Paulette asked, patting his back and bouncing him gently even as he continued to scream bloody murder. "I could've come home if he was *this* bad off!"

"I've raised a child to a full-grown man, thank you very much," Reina said, raising her dimpled double chin defiantly. "I know how to take care of babies—even *yours*."

"Well, you weren't doing a very good job of it, if Nate's

like this!" Paulette shouted angrily, gesturing to her son. "Did you do anything different today? Did you—"

"No, I didn't do a damn thing different! I changed him. I fed him," Reina said, counting off the tasks on her fingers. "I took him for a walk in the park! Before his second nap, I gave him a big bowl of my egg and potato salad and then I—"

"*What?* You gave him . . . *potato salad?*" Paulette squinted in disbelief.

"Yeah, it was homemade! Not that cheap store-bought stuff you try to pass off as yours."

When Paulette continued to stare at her aghast, Reina raised her brows.

"That boy is way too skinny for his age with you giving him all that mashed up, puréed nonsense!" She flicked her wrist. "He needed something to put some meat on his bones."

Ignoring her mother-in-law, Paulette felt the baby's stomach beneath his rubber duckie and umbrella cotton onesie instead. It was as hard as a rock—as expected. His stomach was so swollen that she bet if she stripped him down to his diapers, he'd look like one of those poor African refugees in the Save the Children ads on television. She knew now why he was screaming so much; he was constipated and filled with gas. He was probably in horrific pain.

As Reina continued to talk about fattening up Nate and giving him "decent, real food" and Nate continued to wail, Paulette seethed. She felt like flames were about to sprout out of her ears.

"I told you," she began through clenched teeth, "not to feed him that . . . that shit!" she yelled, making Reina fall silent. "Every day I label the jars for what he should eat— and you ignore them! Now I come home to this?"

Reina blinked rapidly, as if she couldn't see straight.

She shoved herself to her feet, though it took a few tries to do it successfully. "How . . . how *dare* you talk to me like that!" she sputtered. "There isn't a damn thing wrong with what I feed that boy! If you would just—"

"There *is* something wrong with what you feed him! Every time you give him your recipes to 'fatten up him,' he can't poop! You think that's normal?"

Reina pushed back her shoulders and stood at her full height. She glared at the younger woman, and Paulette glared right back at her. They looked like two prizefighters in the boxing ring, each preparing to land the first punch.

"I gave that food to Antonio every day since he was four months old!" Reina charged, pointing her finger into Paulette's face. "He never had any problem doing number two! He was regular as—"

"I don't care what you fed Tony when he was a baby! Tony was your son, but this one is *mine!*" She shoved Reina's finger away, making the older woman bluster all over again. "I let you babysit Nate because Tony begged me to, *not* because I wanted to let you do it. Frankly, I wouldn't trust you with a pet goldfish, but I did it to please my husband. But if you want to keep babysitting Nate, you better damn well do what I tell you to do! *Understand?* Stop feeding him that crap!"

"Well, he probably would've been able to take what I gave him if he had Tony's genes," Reina sneered. "But maybe that boy doesn't. Maybe he isn't Tony's baby!"

Paulette stilled again, feeling the blood drain from her head. "What . . . what did you say?"

"You heard me! I said maybe that baby of yours," Reina said, gesturing to Little Nate, "isn't my son's child. The older he gets, the less he looks like him."

Paulette stood mutely, too stunned and too furious to form words.

"Didn't think I knew the truth, huh? But I do! I know

how you were when you two first got married. Uh-huh, couldn't keep your legs closed, could you? You had no problem jumping from one bed to the next! That's right . . . I'd get a DNA test if I was my son! No point in him raising some other man's baby!"

If it wasn't for the fact that she was holding Little Nate, Paulette swore she would've punched her mother-in-law in the face at that moment. This was despite her refined up-bringing and her mother Angela's constant admonish-ments to carry herself like a lady. Years of judgment and condescension by Reina had finally pushed Paulette to her breaking point, and she was ready to beat the hell out of this fat old woman. But instead, she turned on her heel, marched out of the living room and across her foyer. She then swung open her front door and pointed to the view of her lawn, brick walkway, and driveway.

"Get the hell out of my house! Get out and don't you ever *think* of coming back!"

Reina's entire body went rigid.

"You heard me! Get out!" Paulette screamed.

She prepared herself for another yelling match, for an-other onslaught of insults and allegations. Instead Reina reached down and yanked her tote bag from the couch. She slowly walked toward Paulette, taking her sweet time as she made her way toward the front door. When she stood next to Paulette in the doorway, she paused to stare at her. Bold challenge was in her eyes.

"Tony's gonna hear about this. He's gonna hear about how you treated his mama, and you're gonna have to suf-fer the consequences."

"Tell him whatever the hell you want. I don't care if Tony sends you a golden engraved invitation to come back to this house, you better not ever darken my doorstep again!"

Reina chuckled, infuriating Paulette even more. "We'll see about that, Miss High and Mighty. Tony would *never* choose you over me! Be ready to eat some crow, heffa," she spat before strutting out the front door.

"Bitch," Paulette muttered as she slammed the door behind Reina. Its thud was drowned out by Little Nate's wails.

Hours later, Antonio arrived home from work. Paulette had finally gotten Little Nate asleep after plying him with milk infused with prune juice and literally unplugging him with Vaseline and a baby thermometer, testing her fortitude as a new mother *and* her queasiness. She had just closed the door to the nursery, leaving the infant slumbering to the sound of the nursery rhyme music that played on his mobile, when Antonio opened the front door. Paulette winced as she walked stiffly down the staircase, sore and exhausted from the tension and activity of the day. Antonio lowered his briefcase to the tiled floor. Paulette knew from the look on his face that he had already spoken with his mother and he was about to unleash a lecture that she was in no mood to hear.

"Before you start," she said, holding up her hands as she descended the last riser to their foyer's Afghan rug, "you first need to hear what she said to me."

Antonio released a loud grumble and tugged at the knot in his tie. He leveled her with tired eyes and a withering gaze. "You told my mama never to touch our child again and that she had to leave your house and never come back." He began to remove his suit jacket. "What the hell could she possibly say to—"

"She said Nate probably wasn't your baby because I couldn't keep my legs closed when we got married." Paulette raised her brows. "Is that a good enough reason to kick her out?"

He paused mid-motion with one arm still in his suit sleeve. He gaped. "She didn't . . . she didn't really say that, did she?"

"Yes, she did, Tony!" Paulette crossed her arms over her chest. "Which made me wonder just what exactly have you told her about our marriage? Did you tell your mother that I cheated on you?"

He sighed and closed his eyes.

"Well, did you?"

"I didn't . . . I didn't tell her outright what happened, but she kind of . . . well, she figured it out, I guess," he said, opening his eyes again.

"*You guess?*"

"I told her we were having problems, okay? I may have let it slip that I was sleeping in the guest room. Then you just . . . just popped up with Little Nate. Mom asked me why I didn't tell her you were pregnant. I tried to make up an excuse, but I guess I . . . that I wasn't very convincing." He shrugged. "I tried, baby. Really, I did."

Paulette didn't believe that for one second. If Antonio wanted to hide a secret, he was more than capable of doing it.

He's done it before, she thought with an inward shudder, remembering how he had lied about what had happened the night of Marques Whitney's murder. He'd made up an elaborate story about staying up late at night in his old childhood bed at his mother's house while agonizing over the state of their marriage, when he was really secretly tracking down Marques all night. He had waited for a chance to sneak into Marques's apartment, then beat and strangle him to death. And Antonio had not only lied to her about that night—but also to the investigating detective. He'd done it so convincingly that she'd been appalled that she had ever doubted Antonio's innocence. The only reason Paulette had discovered the truth about the murder was that Antonio had slipped and revealed himself to her brother Evan. If it hadn't been for that, she'd still believe that her husband was incapable of committing murder—let alone covering up the horrendous act. But of course now she knew better.

"Your mother was totally disrespectful, Tony."

"I know that, baby, but—"

"Instead of apologizing for what she did, she basically accused me of being a whore! Who does that? Who does that to their own daughter-in-law? She said I don't even know if Nate is your son!"

"But you don't know!" he blurted out with irritation, making her flinch and take a step back from him.

She watched as he gritted his teeth and took another deep breath. He ran his hand over his head. "Baby, I didn't . . . I didn't mean that."

"Yes, you did," she whispered, now hurt. "You meant every word."

Antonio said he'd accepted Little Nate as his son regardless of whether that was true, but she worried if some part of him would always wonder if it *was* true. Would the question eat him up inside? Would it add yet another wound to a marriage they were fighting so hard to heal?

"Look, baby," he said, reaching out for her, but she took another step back, out of his reach. He dropped his hands to his sides. "Look, I love Nate. You know that! And I love you, too."

"So show me, Tony."

"What do you mean 'show you'? I do it every damn day! I provide for my family. I take care of—"

"I mean show me that we come first! I refuse to come second place to Reina Williams. I'm not doing it anymore!"

The foyer fell silent. Antonio shook his head again. "I hate being put in the middle like this. Can't you just . . . just hear her out?"

Paulette firmly shook her head. "No."

"Be the bigger person and try again! She's my mother, for Christ's sake!"

"No. I'm *done* with her, Tony!"

"So what are we going to do when we need a babysitter? We can't leave Nate with just anybody!"

"I'd trust Nate with a dog walker before I let your mother take care of him again," she snapped, before walking toward the kitchen.

"Oh, come on, Paulette! *Really?*"

"I'm going to heat up some leftover fettuccine because I'm hungry and too exhausted to cook," she called over her shoulder, not looking back. "You can either join me or go eat dinner with your mama. It's up to you," she said, leaving her husband to stew alone in their foyer.

Chapter 9

Dante

"It's not the end of the world, Trevor," Dante said, casually leaning back in his chair and adjusting his tie. He spread out his hands and smiled. "We still have the option to—"

"Don't you dare patronize me, Turner!" his client, Trevor, ordered icily. "They wanted to settle! They made the offer, and you didn't think to let me know about it!"

Dante reached for his buttered croissant, tore a piece off, popped it into his mouth, and chewed. He resisted the urge to roll his eyes, though he was growing bored with Trevor Malcolm's drama-queen antics.

The retiree was suing his doctor and a medical group for misdiagnosing his acute ulcer as irritable bowel syndrome. The case had been dragging on for months. The medical group had finally offered to settle out of the court for a hundred thousand dollars.

"Trevor, listen to me! We can get more out of them," Dante said, gazing at the perturbed man sitting across from him at the coffee shop table.

The coffee shop was not far from his condominium and had become his new office of sorts, now that he no longer had his spacious office at his old law firm in Tyson's Corner.

"I'm sure they'll offer a higher sum! This is just their first offer. If you'd accepted it, it would've been like leaving money on the table. Just let me—"

"But you didn't even tell me about it!" Trevor argued, pounding his fist on the bistro table and drawing the uneasy stare of the barista behind the lacquered counter. "You let the deadline for a response pass without even mentioning it to me! The only reason why I found out about it is because the doctor reached out to me personally and asked why I rejected it. I could've used the money!"

"I didn't mention it to you because it was a bad offer," Dante said tightly, trying his best to control his temper. "As I told you before, I—"

"Bullshit, Turner! Bullshit!" Blue veins erupted along Trevor's forehead, and the cords stood out along his reddened neck. "You work for me! You don't get to make decisions on what offer is too low or just right. I make that call because I'm paying *you*—not the other way around!"

Dante jaw tightened even more. He certainly needed Trevor Malcolm's two-hundred-dollars-an-hour fee. He still hadn't succeeded in finding a position at another law firm and was now forced to take on clients independently, putting up his own shingle, as it were.

Dante kept silently reminding himself that he had rent and bills to pay as well as an expensive drug habit he had to fund. The money his father, George, had given him he had spent on a hefty down payment for his luxury condo, and his savings were low.

You need this money. You need this money, he kept silently reminding himself, repeating it like a Tibetan chant.

But bowing his head and biting his tongue had never been Dante's strong points. The more Trevor yelled and blustered, the more Dante wanted to tell him to take each dollar bill of the hundred thousand dollars the medical group had offered and individually shove them up his pale, hairy ass.

"*I'm* the client and *I* damn well call the shots!" Trevor insisted, pounding on the table again.

"Whatever you say, Trevor," Dante muttered before taking another bite of his croissant.

"Unless you want me to get another lawyer. Is that what you want me to do?"

"Like I said . . ." Dante finished chewing and wiped his hands with a paper napkin, growing more uninterested in this argument every passing second. "Whatever you say," he answered with a bland, painted-on smile.

"*Whatever you say . . . whatever you say . . .*" Trevor repeated snippily before shaking his gray head. "I never should've went with you," he spat, making Dante stop smiling. "I should've stayed with Nutter, McElroy and Ailey— like Edgar told me to. 'You're a fool if you give your money to that washed-up bastard,' he said. But I didn't listen. I said you were fully capable. I *thought* you could handle it. I guess I was wrong!"

Dante tensed at the man's words. Under the table, his hands curled into fists.

"Did you really think the doctors lowballed their offer, or did you just drop the ball, Dante, like you've dropped the ball before? Missed phone calls . . . botched contracts . . . hearings that you weren't prepared for . . ." He raised his chin triumphantly as Dante's brows knitted together. "That's right! I spoke to a few of your other clients. They all gave me the same story. They told me that you've been messing up, that you've lost your touch. They're all thinking of firing you and getting representation elsewhere. But you know, what I can't understand is how you got to be this way. It wasn't just the shooting. A bullet didn't bring you to this pitiful a state! It's something else, isn't it?" He scanned Dante as if he were a book filled with endless pages. "Something changed in you. Is it alcohol? Had one brandy too many? Or maybe drugs?"

Dante's face must have changed again, because Trevor began to nod knowingly. He pointed at Dante, sneering at him like he was a smashed fly on a windshield. "It *is* drugs, isn't it? Of course it is! All you lawyers are fond of having a bit of cocaine every now and then."

He pantomimed doing cocaine by holding a finger up to his nose and sniffing for exaggeration. He snickered.

"But you've obviously let it get out of hand! We can all tell. You better be careful, or you'll end up like all those other junkies on the side of the road, begging for—"

Trevor didn't get a chance to finish. Dante leaped across the table and grabbed the other man by his necktie, yanking him forward so hard that his chin collided with the metal tabletop. Trevor screamed as the jolt made him bite down hard on his tongue. The barista behind the counter shrieked and dropped the iced mocha with whipped cream she was holding. All of the coffee shop patrons turned and stared at Dante and Trevor in alarm.

Worries about billable hours lost and about destroying what little professional reputation he had left all disappeared. Dante was all fury and retribution right now. He didn't care what the aftermath would be.

"Don't you ever . . . *ever* try to give me advice or tell me who the fuck I am! You don't know me, motherfucka!"

"You're crazy," Trevor gurgled as the blood from his bitten tongue pooled in his mouth. It started dribbling over his bottom lip. "You're fucking crazy!"

"Maybe I am," Dante said as he let go of Trevor's tie. He stood and grabbed his coat from the back of his chair. "But you won't make the mistake again of disrespecting me, now will you?"

"You're fired!" Trevor yelled as Dante strode to the coffee shop door. Out of the corner of his eye, Dante could see Trevor frantically grabbing paper napkins from the dispenser and wiping at the smear of blood along his chin. "You're fired and I'm hiring another lawyer to . . . to sue you! I'll . . . I'll sue you for assault! I'll tell all your other clients what you did! I'll tell them that you've lost it . . . that you—"

Trevor's words were cut off as Dante let the shop's glass door fall close behind him. He shrugged into his wool coat and walked down the sidewalk back to his Jaguar, his body still tense with impotent rage. Puffs of steam burst into the cold air with each angry breath he took.

How dare Trevor tell him that he had lost his touch! How dare he call him a junkie! Dante longed to do a lot more to Trevor than what he had already, but he fought the urge to turn back around and go storming into the coffee shop again. He wanted to beat Trevor senseless, but he knew if he went back now, he stood a good chance of getting arrested.

No, he thought, shaking his head, *that's not an option.*

But someone had to feel his wrath. He had to find someone who would suffer the brunt of his anger.

Suddenly, a thought dawned in Dante's head. He halted a few feet away from where he had parked his car.

Evan's arraignment was scheduled for today. The prosecutors had told Dante that it wasn't necessary for him to attend the hearing since Evan would only be entering in a plea of not guilty. No evidence would be presented. But Evan would definitely have to be there in person to enter a plea.

Could he goad Evan into a fight after the hearing was over? He had heard that his half-brother had been released on bail, but if Evan assaulted Dante, he could very well end up in jail again—this time permanently.

A smile crept to Dante's lips.

Oh, that would be perfect, he thought. It would make a lovely end to the bad day he was having. He hadn't gotten to see it the first time Evan was arrested—to his great regret. Maybe he would get to see it this time around.

With that, he removed his keys from his pants pocket and pressed the button to open his car door. He then glanced at his wristwatch. He had less than thirty minutes to make it to the courthouse. He would have to drive fast if he wanted to make it there on time.

Dante sat on the wooden bench, waiting ten feet in front of the white metal doors leading to the courtroom, eagerly anticipating the moment when they would open.

Though he was a lawyer, he had never been enamored with courthouses. Conference rooms were where he usually preferred to be—not here. Real courthouses weren't like the ones in the movies, which made them seem like glamorous places filled with polished wood, glistening marble, and lawyers in sleek suits. In film, every jury room had an air of tension as the forces of good and evil battled to tilt the scales of justice in their favor. In contrast, *real* courthouses were boring places with bleached linoleum tiles, crowded jury waiting rooms, overworked prosecutors and public defenders in bargain-basement attire, and glum-looking clerks who stood behind counters all day. Standing in line at the MVA was more exciting than sitting around a courthouse, in Dante's humble opinion. Thankfully, he wouldn't have to sit around here much longer.

The double doors finally opened, and he watched as a steady stream of people exited: a woman wearing a nondescript dress, an old man in a baggy suit, a couple who whispered to each other, and a police officer who was scanning his cell phone. The doors swung shut then opened again. This time, Leila walked into the hall. She whispered something through the cracked door, not looking in Dante's direction.

He marveled at the transformation Leila had made in the two years since they had first met. She'd gone from the secretary wearing polyester-blend blouses and skirts you could get off the sale rack at JCPenney's to the wife of a millionaire who oozed wealth and prestige from the triple string of pearls at her throat to the tortoiseshell Louboutin pumps on her feet.

She had revealed to him during one of their dates long ago that even though she had been friends with the Murdochs for decades, she had grown up poor like Dante.

Well, you ain't poor no more, are you, baby, he thought flippantly. *So much for not caring about money, huh, Lee?*

His eyes traveled over the simple gray dress she wore that hugged her curves in all the right places. A less than demure split was on the side of the dress, revealing one of her long legs—legs that Dante wistfully remembered he had been standing in between naked more than a month ago.

I came this close, he thought with a mix of frustration and longing. *This close and I could have had her!*

But he hadn't had her and probably never would—a fact that still pissed him off.

Seconds later, Evan exited the courtroom. Leila reached for his hand and held it, but Evan barely seemed to notice, still lost in a daze.

Lucky son of a bitch, Dante thought. *He doesn't even realize what he has.*

Evan embodied everything Dante secretly envied and outright hated about the Murdochs. Evan had been educated at the best schools, had been given the best opportunities, and their father had set aside the cushy position of CEO at Murdoch Conglomerated for him. Now he had a woman like Leila on his arm.

What infuriated Dante the most about his brother wasn't

the money, education, or pedigree but that the world had been handed to Evan—and Evan seemed completely unaware of it. He didn't appreciate it at all. Instead, Evan seemed to almost resent the burden of wealth and power, whereas Dante would have *relished* it. If he had been raised and nurtured by George Murdoch, Dante would have taken the family company to even greater heights! Under Dante, the Murdochs could have had the same stature as the Walton family who owned Walmart. But like his hookup with Leila, it was a lost cause. It would never happen.

That didn't mean that he should let Evan go about leading his tranquil life, though. He would make sure this man suffered—heartily.

"So I heard congratulations are in order!" Dante called out just as Evan and Leila began to walk down the corridor to the elevator doors.

At the sound of his voice, Leila's back stiffened. Evan whipped around to face him. It was as if someone had struck a match and tossed it into bowl filled with lighter fluid: Evan's face flared with rage. He looked so furious that Dante almost burst into laughter. Instead he slowly rose from the wooden bench and walked toward them.

"I heard you two tied the knot. I didn't get an invitation to the wedding, but frankly . . . I wasn't expecting one." Dante smiled. "So it's official now, huh?"

As he drew closer, he could nearly see the gusts of hot air coming out of Evan's flared nostrils. He could almost smell the sweat pouring out of Evan as he fought to keep himself under control.

But he's gonna lose it today. I'll make sure of that.

"You guys didn't get the chance to go on your honeymoon? Oh," Dante snapped his fingers and inclined his head, "I'm sorry. I forgot! You're facing an attempted murder charge and can't leave the state, can you? That kind of puts a damper on travel plans."

"Let's get out of here, baby," Leila whispered to Evan, shooting daggers at Dante with her dark eyes. She looped her arm through Evan's and tried to walk away, but Evan didn't budge. He just continued glaring at Dante.

"Why are you in such a rush to get away, Lee?" Dante asked, coming to a stop a few feet away from the couple.

"I have *nothing* to say to you," she snarled, pulling at Evan's arm again, but he stayed firmly in place.

"You have nothing to say to me? *Really?* But you had plenty to say a few weeks ago in that hotel room in Reston when you were begging me to show your man a little mercy."

Leila gave a barely noticeable flinch, making Dante want to burst into laughter all over again.

"But we did a lot more than talk, didn't we, baby?" he asked, giving her a wink.

She made a panicked glance at Evan to see his reaction. For the first time, Evan's face went blank; he wasn't sure how to respond to the news that his new wife had cheated on him. His eyes turned away from Dante and shifted to Leila.

"Don't worry, Ev! It didn't get too down and dirty. I only let her—"

"You son of a bitch!" Evan yelled as he lunged forward with his arm extended, like he was reaching out to grab Dante or he was about to throw a punch. "I'm going to beat the shit out of you!"

But Leila stopped him. She held onto his arm with all her might, fighting to hold him back. She threw her body between the two men.

"Don't . . . *don't*, baby!" she said, staring up at Evan. "You know what he's doing!"

When Evan tried to pull away from her and walk around her, she placed her hands on both sides of his face. "Listen to me! Listen to me, Ev! Don't fall for it. He's not worth it! *He's* not important—we are."

At that, Evan's shoulders relaxed. The flames dimmed in his eyes a little, and Dante nearly groaned in exasperation.

You've got to be fucking kidding me!

"I need you. Your family needs you, honey!" she pleaded. "Don't let that bastard send you back to jail!"

Dante chuckled. "Oh, this is touching . . . so touching. Too bad she—"

"Shut up! Just shut the hell up!" Leila spat, whipping around on him like a coiled cobra poised and ready to strike. "Don't say anything else, you piece of shit!"

"What are you, his guard dog now?" Dante spat.

She didn't answer him but instead continued to stare at him with the same contempt and imperious air as Evan had. It felt almost like a betrayal.

"Do you really think you're one of them because he put that big-ass rock on your finger? Well, you're not! You're not a Marvelous Murdoch, Lee—and you never will be! You're just like me—a poor relation. And one day you won't even be that. You'll be his cast-off when he finally decides to move on to wife number *three!*"

Leila ignored him. She turned and began to walk again, holding Evan's hand. Evan followed her—reluctantly. Dante watched them until they reached the end of the hall, boarded the elevators, and the doors closed behind them.

Chapter 10

Evan

Evan gazed out of his office's floor-to-ceiling windows, staring at the choppy water of the Potomac River and the gray clouds gathering over Reagan National Airport. The scene was apropos; it reflected his dark mood.

He had been staring out the window for more than an hour, lost in thought, replaying his confrontation with Dante earlier that week. Each time he thought back to the argument at the courthouse, his mind created a different ending. Instead of Leila quietly tugging him away and ushering him down the hall to the elevators, he would march straight up to Dante and start punching him in the face. Or he would wrench out of her grasp, charge back down the hall, wrap his hands around Dante's neck, and start strangling him. He would only stop once the bailiffs and police officers pulled him off.

Only his half-brother could suck him into these black holes of fury. Evan usually considered himself a level-headed, pragmatic man, but Dante Turner knew how to make him feel like the Incredible Hulk. He'd want to just start smashing cars and knocking down walls from all his bottled-up rage. But Evan knew Dante's end game: it was to destroy him and taint everything he held sacred. He had even managed to make Evan doubt Leila's fidelity—something he never thought he would do.

"He's not worth it, baby," Leila had whispered soothingly to him as they sat in the backseat of his Lincoln Town Car on the way back to the mansion from the courthouse. She'd held his hand as she said it. "He's not worth the dirt on your shoes."

"I know that," Evan had spat, yanking his hand out of her grasp. "But that son of a bitch always knows what buttons to press. He knows what shit to say to push me over the edge—even when it's not true. Because I *know* it's not true. It can't be."

"What can't be true, honey?"

"Those things he said about you. What he said you . . . you two did. You never met him at a hotel. You could never fuck someone like that or even consider it!"

She fell quiet.

"It's all bullshit . . . *Right?*"

Leila didn't immediately respond. Instead, she broke his gaze, and for a split second, Evan had panicked. He had wondered if what Dante had said was true, after all.

Leila met that son of a bitch in a hotel room in Reston, he'd thought, horrified. *She fucked him. Dear God! She did it!*

His grip on her hand had tightened. His pulse had quickened. Finally, ever so slowly, she'd shaken her head.

"Of course not, baby," she'd whispered, rubbing his shoulder, calming him instantly. "How could you even ask me that? This is the same man who claimed you shot him in a parking garage one night. You can't believe a damn word he says!"

Leila was right. It was ridiculous to even consider believing Dante. And no matter what Dante said or did, Evan couldn't let him get to him like that again. There was too much at stake now.

"Have you seen the email?" Joe Cannon asked as he burst through Evan's open door and strode into his office. "I can't believe the bastard did it!"

Evan slowly turned away from the floor-to-ceiling windows, mentally snapping back to the present. He blinked.

"The bastard did what?" he asked distractedly as Joe, the chief operating officer of Murdoch Conglomerated, stalked toward his desk. *"What bastard?"*

They couldn't be possibly talking about Dante, were they?

No, Evan thought. His half-brother didn't lurk in dark corners in everyone's lives—just his and his family's.

Joe looked angry enough that his head was about to explode, which was rare for the genial older man. He was trailed by Ed Morgan, the company's vice president of marketing and communications, whose face was almost green, like he was physically ill.

"Payton!" Joe snarled. "That son of a bitch submitted his resignation. The coward did it by email!"

Evan stared at them both. "Payton . . . wait, Payton as in *Payton Thurston?* Our director of public affairs?"

Both Joe and Ed nodded in unison, making Evan slump back in his leather office chair and close his eyes.

Payton had been with the company for almost seven years. He was the person who spoke to the press and appeared at summits and conventions. In lieu of Evan, Payton was the public face of Murdoch Conglomerated. Now that Evan was facing attempted murder charges, Payton had been pushed even more to the forefront, being a less controversial figure than the company's CEO. Payton's resignation couldn't have come at a worse time.

"Jesus," Evan whispered, scrubbing his hand over his face. He opened his eyes again. "Did he say *why* he's leaving? What happened?" he asked, frantically clicking his computer mouse and tapping on laptop keys, searching for Payton's resignation email.

"Issues with his family . . . unable to dedicate his full attention to his duties . . . yada, yada, yada," Ed said, waving his hand dismissively.

"He couldn't hack it!" Joe charged. "The jackals started circling, and he ran for cover!"

Ed shook his bald head and sighed. "Payton is fine at announcing new products and doing photo ops and ribbon cuttings, but crisis management just isn't his strong point."

"The boy has no balls!" Joe shouted. "Let's just call it what it is, Ed! He didn't even have the balls to tell his boss to his face that he was quitting. Instead he snuck out the back door like a—"

"Stop," Evan said tiredly, holding up his hands. "Just stop, all right? I get that you're angry. Hell, I am, too! But none of this is helpful. We're short a company spokesperson when Murdoch Conglomerated's image is already shattered. The board will go ballistic when they find out Payton jumped ship, not to mention what the damn press will say! I don't need griping. I need an action plan." His gaze shifted between both men. "Now what are we going to do? You think Payton's assistant can take over?"

"*That nitwit, Kyle?*" Joe exclaimed, raising his bushy white eyebrows. "The only reason why he's even on the payroll is because he is Payton's wife's nephew! He wouldn't know how to write a press release, let alone how to preside over a news conference with bloodthirsty reporters! Something like that is completely beyond him!"

"Fine," Evan said, drumming his fingers impatiently on

his glass desktop. He zeroed in on Ed again, who still looked like he had just received a stage-four cancer diagnosis. "Is there anyone in your department who can step forward and fill the position for now?"

Ed shook his head. "None have press experience, and I don't know if we could train them quickly enough to be ready for what's going to come at them." Ed shrugged his bowed shoulders. "I guess I can do it myself if—"

"No," Evan said, "you have enough duties as it is, and we have that big launch later this month. I want you to focus on that." He grumbled to himself then sucked his teeth. "I guess we'll have to recruit someone from outside of the company . . . though I have no idea who. We should call up that firm that—"

"I have someone in mind who might work," Joe piped, stopping Evan mid-sentence.

Evan and Ed stared at him in amazement.

"*You do?*" Evan asked.

Joe nodded.

"Who?" Ed inquired eagerly.

"Before I say who it is, just . . . just hear out my reasoning. Okay?" Joe began.

He seemed to hesitate. He nervously adjusted his tie, making Evan wary of where this was going.

"Now he doesn't have a lot of communications or media experience, but he's *strongly* connected to our brand and has an emotional investment in the company. He's handsome . . . articulate . . . charming, but doesn't come off as disingenuous. I never would have thought of him before but . . . but when I saw a broadcast not too long ago and saw how he held his own with a reporter, I thought, 'That boy has potential! He's got talent!' I wondered why none of us had considered it sooner."

"*Who* are you talking about, Joe?" Evan asked.

"For the love of God, just spit it out!" Ed shouted.

Joe waited another beat. He opened his mouth, closed it, then opened it again. "Terrence," he said.

"Terrence?" Evan asked, squinting in confusion.

"Terrence Murdoch."

"My brother?"

Joe nodded.

Evan didn't know how to respond at first because he was so taken aback. A laugh tickled his throat. It finally burst forth into full-on, stomach-cramping laughter.

"You think Terry should be our company spokesperson? You're joking, right?"

He swiveled in his chair to look up at Ed, expecting him to be laughing, too, or at least to look incredulous, but instead the other man's eyes had narrowed with concentration. He didn't look sick anymore. He was actually nodding in agreement now.

"You two can't be serious! *Have you lost your minds?* Look, I love Terry to death but . . . but he can't be our director of public affairs! He's never worked a nine-to-five! His last job was modeling—and he hasn't modeled in years! He doesn't know a damn thing about public relations or—"

"But you didn't see the interview, Evan," Joe insisted. "Your brother handled it like a pro, and that reporter was asking him some pretty serious questions about your case and the allegations. Payton *never* could have done an interview like that. With a little training and finessing, Terrence could get even better! The seeds are there. I can see it. Trust me!"

"And it might be good to have another Murdoch step forward to represent the company, Evan—at least temporarily," Ed argued, shoving his hands in his suit pockets. "It would show the board that the Murdoch name—the brand is still good. If this works out, it could silence the naysayers."

"Or it could make *even more* of them call for my head on a silver platter!"

Joe leaned against his desk. The expression on his pale, wrinkled face was dire. "Look, Evan, we have to accept the facts. Murdoch Conglomerated is at a crisis point. I worked for your father for twenty-two years. He wasn't a perfect man, but he fought for this company. He did whatever he had to do to help it survive and thrive. I know how much blood and sweat he put into Murdoch Conglomerated to make it what it is today. And I know *you* know it, too."

At the mention of his father, Evan's gaze involuntarily flickered to the portrait of George Murdoch hanging on the wall near the door. It was the only holdover from when his father had been CEO of Murdoch Conglomerated and had occupied this very office. Even his father's image seemed to be judging Evan at that moment—and finding him lacking.

Are you really going to let this destroy us? his father's image seemed to silently ask. *Are you going to let those sons of bitches kill everything I built?*

Evan lowered his eyes and stared down at his glass tabletop.

"If we want the company to survive, we have to take some risks, Evan. This is one of them," Joe said.

Evan finally raised his gaze. He exhaled. "Fine. I'll talk to Terry. I'll ask him. But I think I know what his answer will be."

"No! Hell no! Are you crazy, Ev?" Terrence exclaimed a day later, lowering his bottle of Stella Artois from his lips and slamming it to the restaurant table.

Evan slouched back into the padded booth and sighed. "I knew that's what you would say," he murmured as the waiter placed their ceviche appetizers in front of them.

He had decided to broach the topic of Terrence becoming Murdoch Conglomerated's new director of public affairs over dinner, hoping to butter up his little brother with a good meal and liquor. But it hadn't worked. Terrence had still reacted as expected.

"Why the hell—" Terrence bellowed then caught himself. He glanced around the high-end tapas restaurant, his eyes landing on the nearby table of elderly women who were currently enjoying bowls of gazpacho. He leaned over the table toward Evan.

"Why the hell," he began again, this time in a whisper, "would you want me to work at Murdoch Conglomerated . . . let alone be the spokesperson *for the whole damn company?*" He ruefully shook his head. "Whatever you're smokin' must be some good shit! Share some with me!"

"I didn't smoke anything, and it's not just me who thinks you'd be a good fit. A few other executives made the suggestion. I'll admit that I was . . . doubtful, at first," he explained diplomatically. He took a sip of red wine. "But then I went online and saw that interview you did with Channel six news. It made me *proud,* Terry. I didn't know you had that in you. They were right. You held your own that day!"

"But it was *that day,* Ev! I don't know if I could do that again, let alone do it over and over and over. I swear like a sailor! You know that! What if I drop a few f-bombs on Fox Business News?"

"You know how to code switch. I've seen you do it at dinner parties and galas. You know how to carry yourself and how to schmooze when the time calls for it. You won't drop any f-bombs on live TV. I know you won't," Evan assured. "And if you're really that worried, ask C. J. to coach you! She's a reporter. She can help. I'm sure she'd be happy to do it!"

Terrence rolled his eyes. "Look, Ev, even if . . . *even if* by some chance I manage to talk to reporters and do interviews with no problems, I know there has to be more to it than that! I didn't finish college, but I'm not stupid! What about coordinating publicity campaigns and social media? What about—"

"Terry, we would bring in someone who can handle the day-to-day strategic stuff like that. We just need you to be the face and the voice. That's all!"

Terrence gritted his teeth. "I can't do it. I just can't!"

"You can't or you *won't?*"

"I can't! I'm not a 'suit and tie' guy! I never have been. I hate that corporate shit!"

"You hate that corporate shit, but you're happy to live off of its proceeds, though, right? What do you think made your trust fund, Terry? What do you think pays for your condo and your Porsche and your personal trainer?" Evan barked, drawing the attention of the diners at the tables nearby. "Dad busted his ass wearing a suit and tie, working long hours, and building the company for you to have a good life . . . for *all of us* to have everything we've ever wanted! And now you're saying you're too good to work? You're too good to do the same?"

Terrence winced, making Evan immediately regret his words and his anger. He took a deep breath and counted to ten.

"Look, I'm . . . I'm sorry. That didn't come out right."

"No, it came out like you meant it. I've been freeloading off of Dad's legacy. You don't think I know that?" Terrence paused. "C. J. keeps hinting that I should get a job. That I should do more than go to the gym and hang out with my boys all day. Maybe she's right. But what you're asking me to do is a big damn leap, Ev! What if I fuck it up?"

"Believe me, I know what I'm asking you to do isn't easy. I know it may seem intimidating. Maybe even . . .

scary," Evan began, pushing his wineglass aside. He gazed into the tea lights at the center of the table, mesmerized by the flickering flames. "But I'm going to be honest with you, Terry . . . I'm scared, too. I've never been in this situation before. Our shares still aren't doing well. We're getting all this negative press. I never thought there was a chance I could be let go as CEO of our *own* family company. The fire is getting so big, and I have no idea if I can put it out. But I have to *try*. I have to do something!"

Terrence's hard visage softened.

"No, I didn't say that right," Evan whispered, tearing his gaze away from the flames. He was actually finding it harder to do this part, to humble himself. "*We* have to do something, because I realize I . . . I can't do this all on my own anymore. I . . . I need your help, Terry. I need you to do this for the company . . . for our family."

At that, Terrence pushed back his shoulders. He looked his brother in the eyes.

"Okay. I'll do it, Ev."

"You will?"

Terrence nodded and reached for his Stella Artois again and raised it for a toast. "I'm probably gonna fall flat on my face, but . . . what the hell, right? Let's do this!"

Evan smirked before raising his wineglass and tapping it against his brother's beer. "Let's do this."

Chapter 11

Leila

Leila slowly made her way down the west wing corridor, tightening her silk robe's belt as she walked. She glanced down at the baby monitor in her hand, where there was a black-and-white image of little Angelica slumbering in her bassinet beside Leila and Evan's king-size bed. The bed was now empty, which was why Leila was doing her midnight stroll.

It was the same nightly ritual of her walking to his study on the first floor and wishing him good night. He'd mumble good night in reply and return to his work. She'd fall asleep alone and wake up alone because Evan often got up early to head to his office at Murdoch Conglomerated. Despite him being out of prison, this was the only real chance she got to see him nowadays.

Suddenly, Dante's words echoed in her head, making her slow her pace.

"You're not a Marvelous Murdoch, Lee—and you never will be! You're just like me—a poor relation. And one day you won't even be that. You'll be his cast-off when he finally decides to move on to wife number three!"

But she wasn't a "cast-off," and there wouldn't be another Mrs. Murdoch after her. She and Evan were meant for each other, and they would make this marriage work. It was just a trying time for them now, but these bad days wouldn't last forever.

"Things will get better," she quietly reassured herself.

As Leila neared the center of the corridor, she paused and frowned. She thought she had heard someone screaming. Leila took another few steps then halted again on the marble tile. She listened more closely.

There it was—a high-pitched scream. It sounded like a woman in distress. She started walking again. She picked up her pace until she was almost running. She stumbled in her slippers and nearly dropped the baby monitor, trying to find the source of the screams. Was it her mother, Diane? Dear God, was it Isabel? As she neared Aunt Ida's bedroom door, the screams got even louder. Now frantic, Leila pounded on the closed door with her fist.

"Aunt Ida! Aunt Ida, are you okay?" Leila shouted. She tried the brass doorknob. It was locked. She pounded again on the wooden slab. "Do you need help? Can you—"

The door suddenly swung open and Leila jumped back in surprise. Aunt Ida stood in the doorway with a bedsheet wrapped around her petite frame, revealing bare feet. Her face and shoulders were doused with a fine sheen of perspiration. Her curly afro was matted and soaked with sweat. An irritated expression was on the elderly woman's face. In the distance, Aunt Ida's fiancé, Michael, lay on the four-poster bed across the room, naked, with a pillow over his crotch and a sardonic smile on his handsome face.

Leila's eyes widened when she realized what she had really stumbled upon. She loudly swallowed.

"I'm . . . I'm sorry! You were . . . were screaming. I thought something was . . . I thought something was wrong."

Aunt Ida leaned against the doorframe. "The only thing

that's wrong, honey, is that I was this close to comin' when you interrupted me," she sneered.

Leila grimaced.

"Do you know how hard it is to get a decent orgasm this far past menopause? Huh? *Do you?*"

Leila stared at her mutely, at a loss for words. Her cheeks warmed with embarrassment.

"I guess the next time I'll leave a 'Do Not Disturb' sign on the damn door," Aunt Ida quipped before muttering to herself, stepping back into the room, and slamming the bedroom door shut in Leila's face.

Leila turned back toward the hall, releasing a loud breath. "Jesus," she whispered, torn between wanting to hide her face and burst into laughter.

"Do you know how hard it is to get a decent orgasm this far past menopause?"

Just the memory of the perturbed look on Aunt Ida's face as she said those words sent Leila into a fit of giggles.

Serves her right if she couldn't get off, she thought, then had to clap her hand over her mouth to keep from laughing even harder. Aunt Ida had barged into their home, and now Leila had barged into the old woman's one chance to reach orgasm. There seemed to be some cosmic fairness to the situation.

Leila continued down the corridor and finally drew near the center staircase.

"Hey, Leila!" she heard someone shout behind her.

She turned to find Michael jogging down the corridor toward her. He was no longer naked, thankfully; he was now wearing a robe.

"Leila, wait up!"

She anxiously glanced around her, wondering why he was out here right now.

Shouldn't he be getting back down to business?

She hadn't had much interaction with the young man

since the first day he and Ida had arrived. In fact, for the most part he seemed happy to sit silently beside Aunt Ida while the older woman did all the talking.

"Hi, Michael," she said, forcing a smile, "look, I'm sorry that I interrupted . . . uh, you guys."

He chuckled. "It's fine. Ida decided take a shower, and I needed a break anyway. She's not lying about how hard it is to get her going. We'd been at for the past couple of hours."

"Oh," she said, not knowing how else to respond out loud to that revelation.

TMI, she thought, glancing again at the stairs, desperate to get away from the awkward moment.

"I just wanted to apologize if she came off as rude. That's all."

"Really, you don't have to apologize! Again, I didn't mean to interrupt you. I understand that you guys were . . . well . . . busy."

"Just as long as there's no hard feelings."

She shook her head. "No! None at all! Don't worry abo—"

Her words faded when he abruptly stepped forward and dragged her into a hug, crushing her against his bare chest. Leila stood frozen as he wrapped his arms around her. He rubbed her back through the silk of her robe.

"I know we just showed up on your doorstep, but you've been so nice to us," he whispered into her ear, sending a warm blast of air against her cheek. Alarm bells started to go off in her head. They were similar to the alarm bells she had heard faintly when he shook her hand more than a month ago. "I can't thank you enough, Leila."

She shoved back from Michael. "I told you, it's . . . it's no big deal."

"I hope I can reciprocate the kindness. If you ever need anything . . . anything at all. I'm here for you."

A polite smile was still on his tan face, but she would know that predatory, smoldering gaze anywhere.

He had just finished having sex with one woman, only to make moves on another? She wondered if Aunt Ida knew this about Michael. Did she know the wolf in sheep's clothing she let sleep in her bed every night? Leila wondered if she should tell Aunt Ida what he had just done.

It probably wouldn't matter anyway, she thought, eyeing him. *And Ida probably wouldn't believe me.*

But Leila resolved that she would have to keep her distance from this young man. She turned away from him and headed down the stairs.

"Good night, Leila," Michael called after her, leaning over the railing.

She didn't respond.

A minute later, Leila knocked on the cracked door to Evan's study, then pushed the door open. She found him sitting at his father's immense mahogany desk, as expected. Several stacks of paper were around him. His laptop was at the center of the desk, and the glow of its screen lit up his face.

Leila painted on a pleasant smile. "I haven't seen you all evening. I just wanted to check in and see what you're doing and . . . and say good night," she said softly as she stood in the doorway.

"Just getting some work done," Evan murmured, still staring at his laptop screen.

You're always *getting work done*, she thought grudgingly but didn't say it aloud. Instead, she looked around his study, taking a few tentative steps into the room. Her gaze landed on the serving tray sitting on a rolling cart not far from his desk. It was covered with plates from tonight's dinner.

"You still haven't eaten?" she asked, pointing at the untouched dishes.

"Huh?" he answered distractedly.

"It's almost midnight, and you still haven't touched your food! You didn't eat dinner with us, but I thought you'd at least have your dinner in here."

"I'm not hungry," he muttered.

"You *have* to eat, Ev," she insisted.

He didn't answer her. Leila wasn't sure if he was ignoring her or just hadn't heard her at all. Either way, Evan continued to type. She watched as he paused to flip open a folder and rifle through a few pages before typing again. Her shoulders slumped. She felt dejected and, once again, rejected by her newly minted husband.

Leila stared at Evan's bowed head for a long time. She wanted to tell him so much: that she missed him and needed him, that though he was here with her physically, he might as well be behind prison bars again for how distant he felt from her.

How could Evan not sense her loneliness? Her mother could see it. She had even encouraged Leila to finally reach out to Evan and tell him how she felt.

"That man is your husband, Lee," Diane had lectured only yesterday. "He's Angie's father and might as well be Izzy's father for how her daddy is going to be in jail and away from her for *years*. He needs to be here for you and his family. You need to tell him that!"

But Leila couldn't do that to Evan. She reminded herself of what he was dealing with, of the sword that was dangling over his head. Her purpose was to lighten the burdens, not to make them worse.

There will not be a wife number three, she told herself.

"Well, anyway," she called out, lowering her eyes and stepping back toward the study door, "like I said . . . I just wanted to say good night."

"Good night, Lee," he replied, turning to the folder again.

"Let me know if you need anything. I'm here for you, Ev."

"Thanks," he muttered, still not looking up at her.

She shut the door behind herself and headed back upstairs alone to their bedroom.

Chapter 12

C. J.

"Terry, honey, breakfast is ready!" C. J. called. She removed the two multigrain slices that had popped up from the toaster and tossed them onto his plate, wincing and blowing on her singed fingertips.

"Terry!" she called out again before taking a sip of orange juice from one of the glasses on the kitchen island. "You're going to be late if you don't grab something to eat and head out soon. *Terry?*"

C. J. waited for his voice or the sound of his approaching footsteps but heard neither—just the drone of the flatscreen television in their living room. She grumbled and walked down the hall toward their bedroom in search of her fiancé.

Terrence usually made breakfast, but she was treating him today. It would be his first day as spokesperson for Murdoch Conglomerated, his first stint at a real job in *years*. To say C. J. was proud of him was putting it lightly. Terrence was making such a bold move. He was willing to take on a role he had never considered before, simply be-

cause his brother had asked him to do it. It was awe in-
spiring.

For the past two weeks, C. J. had been giving Terrence
a crash course in media relations, showing him how to in-
teract with reporters and how to answer questions.
Terrence had also been tutored about the company that
had funded his livelihood for decades, but one that he
knew virtually nothing about. Evan and a few of the other
executives and assistants had explained how the company
operated, what its subsidiaries were, the products it sold,
and who were its major competitors. She could tell that
Terrence was overwhelmed with the deluge of information, but, to his credit, he had hidden it well.

Often, she would wake up in the middle of the night to
find his spot on the bed beside her empty, only to wander
into the living room to discover him sitting on the couch,
scanning through binders filled with documents, taking
notes. He had fully dedicated himself to preparing for this,
which was probably why she was more excited than he was
to see him start his new job today. Her stomach was in
knots with nervousness, but she couldn't keep from smiling.

"Terry," she called out as she stepped through the bedroom doorway, "I hope you're not changing your tie again
because the last one was fi—"

Her words and smile faded when she found Terrence
not preening in front of their free-standing mirror, examining his reflection, but sitting on the edge of their bed
with his head bowed. The tie she had mentioned was now
discarded on the wrinkled sheets. His shoes were beside
his bare feet. When she entered the room, he didn't look
up at her.

"Honey, what's wrong? Why aren't you dressed?"

She watched as his shoulders rose then fell as he took a
heavy breath. He slowly raised his head then shook it.

What she saw in his caramel-colored eyes made her uneasy. It was that empty look that he sometimes got when he was in one of his darker moods, when he seemed on the verge of drowning in despair.

"I can't do this," he whispered.

"Can't do what?"

"I can't do *this,* babe. I never should've agreed to do this shit! I told Ev I was probably going to fall flat on my face. Now I'm sure of it! Who the fuck am I to hold a press conference or talk on CNN? Who the fuck am I kidding?"

"Stop, baby," she urged before sitting on the bed beside him. She wrapped an arm around his shoulder. "Just stop! Don't talk about yourself like that. You *deserve* to be there!"

"C. J., come on!" He sucked his teeth and raised his head so that they were face to face, eye to eye. "Be honest. I'm gonna look like a complete fool!"

"You won't look like a fool. You didn't look like a fool the last time you were on camera!"

Terrence closed his eyes and gritted his teeth. "I keep telling y'all that has nothing to do with—"

"You've been preparing for this like crazy! You're ready. I know you are. You're just . . . just nervous, and you're letting the nerves take over, but don't. Evan wouldn't have done this if he didn't believe you could do it. He wouldn't have recruited you if he wasn't—"

"*Desperate? Delusional?* Because that's what he is if he really thinks I can do this job! And obviously it's affecting his judgment. He made a bad decision. Just admit it!"

"Baby, listen to me! Don't—"

"No!" He turned his head away from her and furiously shook it again. "No, C. J., I'm not doing this. I'm not messing up the company any more than it already is. And no amount of bullshit pep talk is going to get me out the door. I'll just call Ev and . . . and tell him I'm sorry, but I can't do it. It's just not me. I'm not Ev, and I sure as hell ain't my dad."

"And no one is asking you to be!"

"I'm the wrong man for this! That's it. I'm done," he said, slicing his hand through the air. "We're not talking about this anymore!"

C. J. gnawed her bottom lip as she gazed at Terrence, scanning the stubborn set of his jaw and the steely look in his eyes. He really was going to quit before he officially started his job. If she was going to get him to change his mind, it was obvious that sweet words and encouragement weren't going to work. She had to change her tactic.

She removed her arm from around him. "Close your eyes."

"*What?*"

"Close your eyes, please."

He groused impatiently. "Why do you want me to close my eyes?"

"Just humor me, okay?" She raised her hand to cover his eyelids. "Now close . . . *them!*"

He closed his eyes, but not before rolling them to the ceiling in exasperation. She lowered her hand and placed it on top of his.

"Now," she said, "I want you to relax. Breathe in through the nose. Breathe out through the mouth."

"C. J.—"

"In through the nose. Out through the mouth. In through the nose. Out through the mouth. Now keep doing that."

She watched as he inhaled and exhaled. Finally, after a minute or two, the stiff muscles in his back and shoulders began to uncoil. He looked like he was starting to relax a bit—to her surprise.

"Now . . . I want you to visualize an office . . . a big office with big windows."

He opened one of his eyes. "Are you serious?"

"*Shsssh!*" she ordered, raising her finger and pressing it to his lips. "Close your eyes and just trust me, dammit."

He did as she ordered and she cleared her throat before speaking again.

"Now visualize an office with big windows with beautiful views. It's one of the offices at Murdoch Conglomerated headquarters. You designed it yourself. Added all your special touches—comfy leather furniture, metal shelves, those ugly, weird knickknacks you like."

Despite himself, he released a rumbling chuckle.

"You're relaxing with your feet up on your desk," C. J. continued. "You've just finished having lunch. You're scanning through your email, and your assistant suddenly calls you to tell you that a group of reporters is waiting for you . . . one from the *New York Times*, another from *Forbes* magazine, and one from *Fast Company*. They want to talk about Murdoch Conglomerated and the problems the company is having."

Terrence's eyes stayed closed, but he tensed ever so slightly, and she squeezed his hand to soothe him.

"You weren't expecting them to come today, but you're prepared anyway. This is what you've trained for. You tell your assistant to let them in. They're pushing and shoving their way through your office door," she said as she released his hand and began to undo the top buttons of his shirt. "They're firing questions at you—asking about how some board members are calling for Evan to be let go as CEO." She lightly placed a kiss on his cheek, then his neck. "Others ask for the company's response to stock prices dropping by as much as forty percent. They want to know if the company will survive."

She rose from the bed, stood in front of him, and slowly dropped to her knees at his bare feet, making him frown. She eased his legs open and knelt between them, gazing up at him. She ran her hands up and down his chest. She kissed him and tugged his bottom lip between her teeth. He reached out for her—wrapped his arms around her waist, pulled her close, and started to kiss her back, but she made a *tsk, tsk* and pulled his hands from around her and lowered them back to his sides.

"Focus, Terry."

She could tell from his facial expression that he was becoming more confused.

"They're firing questions at you one after another," she continued as she reached for his belt and undid the buckle. "You're trying to answer all of them the best you can, but you're starting to feel overwhelmed."

"Babe," he said, cocking an eyebrow as she lowered his pants zipper, "what are you—"

"Stop asking questions and *focus*."

"Okay," he said, holding up his hands and fighting back a smile. "I'm focusing."

"You're wondering if you can do it. If you can pull this off without saying the wrong thing," she whispered before pulling back the elastic waistband of his boxer briefs. "But then you think back to this moment. You think about us alone in our bedroom."

She reached inside, wrapped her hand around his manhood, and began to stroke him. Terrence's facial expression instantly changed. The arched eyebrow fell. His mouth went slack, and his breathing deepened even more.

"You'll remember how good this felt—and you won't care what questions they ask or what quotes they use. You'll be impenetrable, baby," she whispered, "because you won't be there . . . you'll be here. And you'll . . . be feeling . . . *this.*"

She then lowered her head and took him into her mouth as he groaned.

* * *

A little more than an hour later, C. J. arrived in the *Washington Daily*'s chaotic newsroom late but feeling triumphant.

"Hey!" she called to one of the other reporters over the sound of voices and clicking computer keys. She sipped espresso from her insulated coffee mug. "Morning!" she said with a wave as she passed another cubicle.

It may have been a bit manipulative to use sex to get Terrence to finally pull himself together so he could start his first day as director of public affairs at Murdoch Conglomerated, but she didn't regret it. It had worked, hadn't it?

She hoped that he made it through the day with no more crises of confidence. She planned to text him later just to do a friendly check-in with him, though she was wary to come off as a brooding mother hen.

He's a big boy, she reminded herself as she walked through the maze of cubicles toward her desk. *He just flipped out a little this morning, but he can handle it.*

"Morning, Ally!" she said before setting her mug on her desk and removing her satchel from her shoulder. She tossed it into her chair, still grinning. "How are you today?"

"Ralph is looking for you," Allison said grimly, blowing her blond bangs out of her eyes.

C. J.'s smile disappeared. "Looking for me? *Why?* Did he say what it was about?"

Allison shook her head. "No, but he looked pissed. I told him you were running a little late. I told him he could just text you if he had a question on a story. He said he had to talk to you *in person.*"

And just like that, C. J.'s good mood soured. Her stomach twisted into knots. Her editor was pissed and had to speak to her "in person."

Good Lord, what did I do?

Her mind flipped to the stories she had filed yesterday and the day before that. Had she made some grave mistake on one of them? Did she misquote one of the council members? Maybe she had misspelled a source's name entirely.

"Shit," she whispered with a sigh before turning away from her desk.

"Good luck!" Allison called after her as C. J. continued across the newsroom to Ralph Haynes's office, all the while feeling like weights were strapped around her ankles. Maybe she should have done her own "visualization exercise" this morning with Terrence before heading to work.

When she reached the entrance to Ralph's office, she took a deep breath, pushed back her shoulders, and knocked on the metal doorframe.

"Ralph? Hey, I . . . I heard you were looking for me."

He glanced from his laptop and wordlessly waved her inside his office before returning his attention to his screen. She stepped inside, not knowing whether to remain standing or to take a seat—since he hadn't offered her one of the leather chairs facing his desk. She chose to stand. C. J. watched as he typed for another minute or so, then suddenly whipped around from his laptop and faced her. He looked as pissed as Allison had described.

"Did you see the *Washington Post* this morning?" he asked.

C. J. shook her head.

I was a little busy giving my fiancé a motivational blow job so he wouldn't have an anxiety attack, she thought flippantly.

"No, sorry, I . . . I haven't had the chance yet," she said instead.

"Front page of the metro section, below the fold." He tossed the broadsheet onto his desk, motioning for her to read it. "Late breaking version appeared on the web last night. The council voted on that controversial Whitaker bill. It barely squeaked by, but it passed. I want to know why a story about it wasn't in our paper, considering you attended the meeting."

C. J. picked up the newspaper and stared at the headline in disbelief. She had been following the bill for weeks, checking the hearings calendar religiously to see when the council was finally going to vote on it.

"It must have happened after I left the meeting," C. J. murmured, disappointed *and* humiliated. "I'm so sorry!"

She had been eager to leave city hall soon after they finished the first half of the legislative agenda, which was all she had needed for the stories she was supposed to file that day. She had raced out of the council room, down the stone steps, and to the nearby metro station soon after, wanting to rush home to help Terrence prep for his first day at Murdoch Conglomerated.

"This was a big goddamn story—and you missed it, C. J.," Ralph said sternly, peering at her over the rim of his glasses.

"I know but . . . but how could I have known they were going to vote on something that wasn't even listed on the agenda? I couldn't predict something like—"

"And this isn't the first time they've beat you—beat *us*—on a story," he continued. "It happened twice last week! I don't like to get scooped, C. J. I don't like it at all."

"Ralph,"—she lowered the broadsheet to her side—"I just started here barely a couple of months ago. I'm still feeling out the beat and making contacts. It's going to take some time to get . . . to get familiar with everything. Give me a chance! I swear to you. It'll happen."

She watched as Ralph grumbled, tore off his glasses, and roughly tossed them onto his desk. Removing the glasses didn't make his face any softer or more human. His beady gray eyes grew smaller as he squinted at her, and the dark circles and wrinkles on his pale face made him look like Ebenezer Scrooge come to life.

"Look, C. J., someone who works at this paper has to be a go-getter. They have to hustle. I told you in the beginning that's what we needed. At some point there's a question all reporters have to ask themselves. That question is, 'Am I really cut out for this job? Am I the right fit?'"

Her heart sank. She swallowed the lump that had formed in her throat. Was she about to get fired?

"Not everyone is cut out for the metro desk," he continued. "Not everyone is cut out to work at a daily. Maybe it's—"

"Ralph,"—she took a step toward him—"I *am* cut out for this job. Believe me! I'm a damn good reporter. I'm just going through a rough period. Today, it comes to an end, though. I'll . . . I'll . . ."

C. J. thought frantically for a way to assure Ralph that she had just as much right to work at the *Washington Daily* as any of the other reporters outside his door. Even now, he was giving her that incredulous look that he gave whenever he thought a source was lying.

"I'll . . . I'll find a scoop. A . . . a *big* scoop that will put the *Washington Post* to shame." She tossed the newspaper aside and held up her hands. "I promise."

C. J. watched as Ralph slowly leaned back in the chair and interlocked his fingers over his chest. He stared at her a long time, not saying anything. He stared at her so long that when he finally opened his mouth she was prepared to head back to her desk and start packing up her things.

"All right," he said, catching her by surprise and making her release the breath that had been on the verge of bursting from her chest. "Show me what you got."

"I will," she said with a firm nod. "You'll see."

She then scampered out of his office, relieved that she would live to see another day at the *Daily,* but now worried about what her big scoop would be.

Chapter 13

Evan

"Slide over here and raise your glass," Evan ordered, smiling ear to ear, holding his glass aloft.

Terrence chuckled, loosened his silk necktie, and undid one of the buttons on his collar.

At the crowded restaurant, it was standing room only. And all the people around them were vying for the overworked bartender's attention, holding up twenty-dollar bills and shoving for elbow room at the bar, but Evan wasn't moving from his spot. For once he was not sitting in his office or in his study at the mansion. He was going to have celebratory drinks with his brother.

I'm gonna have fun tonight even if it kills me, he thought

"I mean it! Raise your damn glass!" Evan said again, nudging Terrence's elbow.

Ever so slowly, Terrence picked up his glass and raised it into the air, looking amused by his older brother's good mood.

"Terry, I want to congratulate you on doing your first

full press conference and knocking that shit out of the park," Evan said, slapping his brother on the back.

"I didn't knock it out of the park, Ev. I did okay. Don't exaggerate."

"Bull! You handled it like a pro. I'd tell you I was proud of you, but I know you get tired of hearing me tell you that. So instead I'll just say, 'I told you so.'"

The two men then clinked their glasses together before taking a drink.

Terrence had officially been director of public affairs at Murdoch Conglomerated for almost two months now, and he was doing better than even Evan had anticipated. Joe Cannon had been right: Terrence was a natural. And with a little polish and hands-on experience, he was now putting their old director of public affairs to shame. When talking on the phone with reporters or on live television, Terrence was all smiles, charm, and confidence—showing the side of himself that used to win over the beautiful ladies he had wooed before he and C. J. started dating. Of course, it hadn't always been flawless. Occasionally, Evan had seen his brother's debonair mask shift midway during interviews, revealing the real Terrence underneath. Sometimes, at the end of conference calls, Terrence would seem shaken and exhausted from keeping up the façade. It had Evan worried about his little brother in the beginning. Would Terrence really be able to do this? Would the pressure get to him?

But Terrence seemed more relaxed with each interview and each briefing, and his reputation among the media as the handsome face who could provide a few good sound bites was growing. The company had already gotten requests from a few local stations, CNN, MSNBC, and Fox Business News, asking for Terrence to appear on air. Even the Murdoch Conglomerated stock prices were starting to uptick a little. Evan didn't know if he could credit his brother with that one, but he could plainly see Terrence was hitting his stride, and it was having an impact.

Hell, Terrence even dressed differently! It had been months since Evan had seen him in a T-shirt and jeans. Evan took some humor in realizing that despite his protestations, Terrence was firmly a "suit-and-tie" guy now.

"So what do you have lined up tomorrow?" Evan asked, shouting to be heard over the clamor around them.

"Four interviews. They're pretty straightforward. I'm going to sit in the background to monitor but let the executives do most of the talking." Terrence took another sip from his glass, then shook it, making the ice cubes clink together. "I've got a meeting with Ed at one. My new assistant wants me to review a couple of press releases that—"

"Terry," Evan said, lowering his drink to the countertop, "I told you that you don't have to do that stuff!"

"I know I don't have to do it, but it's—"

"You're the face and the voice! That's why we brought you in. All you need to do is—"

"No, all *you* need to do is back off and let me do my job!"

Evan winced at his brother's tone, making Terrence sigh, reach out, and squeeze Evan's shoulder to soften the blow his words might have made.

"Look, I just meant . . . I've got it covered. That's all. I appreciate you guiding me in the beginning. I couldn't have done it without you . . . but I've got it now."

Evan silently gazed at his brother for a long time. Gradually, he nodded and raised his hands in surrender. "Okay, I'll back off and let you do your thing. I wasn't trying to overstep."

"I know you weren't, and I wasn't trying to be an ass about it. I guess I'm just tired. I'm happy the press conference went well, but it's been a long . . ."

Terrence paused midsentence. He frowned, reached into

his suit jacket, and pulled out his buzzing cell phone. When he stared down at the screen, his frown deepened.

"Delete," he said, pressing a few buttons on the glass screen before tucking his cell phone back in his inner pocket.

"Delete what?" Ev asked.

"Just got a text from some chick name Daphne I hooked up with in New York last year."

Evan raised his eyebrows. "You hooked up with someone in New York? You were only up there for like . . . what? . . . a day, weren't you? You're telling me you slept with *a total stranger* while you were there?"

"Yes, Morality Police, I slept with a total stranger. I'm not proud of it! It just happened." He shrugged. "I had just broken up with C. J. I met this chick at a hotel bar when I was feeling sorry for myself. We got drunk, we went up to her hotel room and hooked up. That's it. We never saw each other after that—and I plan to keep it that way." He finished the last of his drink. "I don't even remember giving her my number, but she's been blowing up my phone for the past week."

"So what did she text you for?"

"She told me to give her a call. Said it was important. Blah blah blah." Terrence shrugged again and stepped aside to open a path for a group of diners who were headed to one of the nearby tables.

"*Blah blah blah?* Terry, don't be an asshole. If she said it was important, why not call her back?"

Terrence inclined his head and cocked an eyebrow. "Really, Ev?"

"*What?* Why are you looking at me like I'm stupid? It's a valid question!"

"Ev, these girls *always* say it's important! Do you know how many times one of my exes or past one-night stands have tried to hit me up since C. J. and I got back together?

Do you know how many times they told me they just 'had to talk to me' or 'It's really important! Call me back, Terry!'?" he said in a high-pitched voice, making Evan laugh. "I even relented and finally texted one of them back—this chick named Melissa—because she kept blowing up my phone. You know how she responded? She sent me a pic of herself *butt-ass* naked, holding a tabby with the caption 'The pussies miss you!'"

At that, Evan almost spit out his drink and sprayed the couple sitting on the bar stools next to them. He managed to swallow his scotch only seconds before breaking down into laughter. "Oh, man! That poor cat!"

"That shit's not funny, Ev! I was lucky C. J. didn't see that pic. It could've started World War Three!" he lamented, shaking his head. "She already keeps throwing random shit out there sometimes—'Are you sure you want to get married? Are you sure you're really ready to do this?'—like she's trying to give me an excuse to back out of the wedding. If she'd seen that text, it would've been over! C. J. could've broken up with me—*again!* So, no, thank you. I'm not falling for that shit anymore. As soon as I get a text or voice mail from one of them, I delete it. I've got nothing to say to any of them. I don't want any drama!"

Evan's laughter tapered off. "Okay, sorry I asked."

Terrence glanced at his wristwatch. "Damn, I should probably be heading home."

"Home?" Evan's face fell. "What the hell do you mean you should head home? We just got here! It's not even eight o'clock."

Terrence shrugged again. "And we're both working men who have to be up at six a.m." Terrence reached into his suit jacket pocket and pulled out his wallet. He slapped three twenties on the counter. "That should cover our tab."

"Come on, Terry! Stay a little while longer."

"Ev, my lady's at home waiting for me. She's been bugging me all week to help her finish labeling wedding invitations. And *you've* got a wife who misses you and wants you home, too. Surprise Lee with some romantic shit. I bet she'll appreciate it!"

"I can't! I don't have time for stuff like that. I've got too much work to do!"

"Yet you're standing here telling me to stay and have another drink." Terrence paused and narrowed his eyes at his older brother. "What's going on, Ev?"

"What do you mean, 'What's going on?'"

"I mean why would you rather be in a crowded bar shooting the breeze and drinking with me than at home with your wife and kids? And you don't even like to drink anyway! What's the story?"

Evan stared at his brother, taken aback by the question. "There's no story, Terry. I just wanted to celebrate with you. But if it's really *that* big of a deal, I won't ask you again."

"Come on, man! Don't get pissy! I'm just asking you an honest question. Why don't you want to go home to Lee? Is something up?"

"No . . . no, nothing's up. We're . . . we're fine."

Instead of looking convinced, Terrence eyed his brother even more warily.

"I mean . . . of course there's a little tension because of my court case and everything," Evan explained reluctantly. "I could go away for a long time if I'm found guilty. It doesn't make things easy."

"So while you're here, spend time with her! Spend time with her and the girls! I thought that's what you lived for! I thought that's what you wanted: domesticity . . . nuclear family . . . all that Norman Rockwell shit."

Evan shook his head again.

"Why, Ev?" Terrence persisted. "Tell me why!"

Evan gritted his teeth and tightened his grip around his Scotch glass, now unable to meet his brother's eyes.

His criminal trial was supposed to start at the end of the summer. The possibility of a long prison sentence hung in the distance like a specter. Evan knew that the time he had with the family was precious and could be short-lived, but he still couldn't force himself to cut down his hours at the office and spend more time at home with his family. Terrence wasn't the first person to ask why Evan did this. He had wondered why many times himself—but could never discover the answer. Now he suspected he knew the truth.

"Because . . . because every time I look at Lee," he now said, "I don't think about buying her roses or kissing her anymore. Every time I see the girls, I'm not thinking about taking them to the playground for a father-daughter day or going out for ice cream. I'm thinking about how I have to get everything in place for when I leave them. I'm thinking about how I have to work harder, make more money, make more phone calls, and sign more paperwork. I think of all the shit I have to do to set things in order for them and it makes . . . it makes me tired, Terry. It makes me sad."

"So to avoid all that, you're running away from them," Terrence said, making Evan cringe.

"I wouldn't put it that way!"

"Well, I would, because that's *exactly* what you're doing, Ev. And you have to stop that shit, because you all deserve better." Terrence slapped his brother on the shoulder again. "Look, I'm gonna head home—and you should, too. Spend some time with your family, bruh—regardless of how guilty you may feel. I'll catch you later."

Evan watched as Terrence walked off, pushing his way through the crowd to the restaurant's revolving glass door. He'd never though it would ever be the day that Terrence left a bar before closing, let alone left it before him. Evan also never thought it would be Terrence imparting words of wisdom about family and relationships while Evan felt lost in the dark.

Times certainly had changed.

Evan turned back toward the counter and stared at his half-finished Scotch.

But even though Terrence was trying to help, Evan knew he was wrong.

I'm not running away from my wife and kids, he thought. *I'm not afraid to go home. I just know what's at stake here and I'm behaving accordingly. There's too much I still have to do. Once I do that, I can look Lee in the eyes because I know they'll be taken care of.*

With that, he raised his glass to his lips and finished the rest of his Scotch with one gulp before slamming the glass down.

"This is new. I remember a time when you didn't drink at all," a familiar voice said from over his shoulder.

Evan whipped around from the counter to find his ex-wife gazing at him. He hadn't seen her in months, not since last year. He had heard that she had left Chesterton soon after his release, traveling to the Caribbean with her mother. He'd suspected that she didn't want to be around when their divorce was finalized. She certainly didn't want to be in town when he and Leila finally tied the knot.

Evan let his gaze travel over his ex-wife. Tonight, Charisse wore a shift dress, revealing her tan arms and legs. It looked like a natural tan—not a bronzer from the bottle. Her wavy hair was now cut chin length and was a lighter blond, likely bleached from hours in the island sun, he supposed. She looked lean and healthy and was wearing only a little makeup, letting her natural beauty shine through.

Even though she hadn't wanted their divorce, it seemed to suit her well. She hadn't looked this good in years.

"Charisse, what . . . what are you doing here?"

He watched as his ex-wife threw back her head and laughed. "I'm eating dinner, Ev, just like everyone else in here."

"I know, but . . . but what are you—"

"I was heading to the ladies' room and I saw you standing at the bar. I figured I should come over and say hi." She tilted her head. "How have you been, Ev?"

"As good as can be expected," he answered quietly.

She took another step toward him. "I was worried about you."

He let out a bitter chuckle. "*Really?* Could've fooled me considering I haven't heard from you in five months."

"Counting the months, were we? I didn't think you cared that much!"

"I don't," he answered dryly. "It just so happened that you went silent around the same time that I went to prison. I wouldn't forget something like that, Charisse. You remember who called or sent letters while you were behind bars."

"I didn't reach out to you for a good reason, Ev."

"And that is?"

"We weren't exactly on the best of terms when you were arrested, and as soon as you got out of jail, you were granted the divorce that you kept pestering me about! I thought you were eager to settle in with your new wife and family. Far be it for me to intrude on your happy little home!"

He pursed his lips, deciding not to respond that one.

"How is Leila, by the way?"

"Charisse . . ." he began warningly.

"*What?*" She batted her baby blues and dropped a

hand to her chest, playing innocent. "I was just being polite, Ev! I can't ask how Leila's doing now?"

He eyed his ex-wife.

Evan knew any inquiry Charisse made about Leila was
not made with good intentions. Charisse hated Leila and,
frankly, Leila had grown to hate Charisse, too. Even the
first day, when Evan had introduced the two women at the
Chesterton Country Club—back when Charisse was still
his wife and Leila was just his secretary, not his mistress—
Charisse had instantly taken a dislike to the other woman.
It was an almost visceral reaction, as if she had sniffed the
scent of another female on her turf. The relationship between the two had only gotten worse in the past two years,
and not just because of Evan and Leila's affair. For spite,
Charisse had tried to sully Leila's reputation in town by
lying and telling everyone she was a former coke whore.
He was sure Charisse had gotten a good laugh out of that
one—at Leila's and Isabel's expense. The rumor had caused
Isabel to be bullied at school and had nearly ruined Leila's
stationery business. And then Charisse had invited Evan to
her home under the guise of discussing their divorce and
had kissed him instead. Well, in truth, they had kissed
each other. That kiss had almost destroyed his and Leila's
relationship. It had taken him humbling himself to the
point of tears to finally get Leila back.

"Don't start any shit again," he now ordered, making
Charisse laugh. "I mean it!"

"I'm not starting anything, Evan. Believe me, I've given
up that war. You wanted a divorce and for her to be your
wife. I've accepted it."

He continued to look at Charisse warily as if he were a
fly who had stumbled upon her spider web. She hadn't
come over here just to say hi and have casual conversation
with him. She had some ulterior motive; he just didn't
know what it was.

"I will say, though,"—she glanced down at her manicured nails—"that with the situation you're in, it would've been nice to have someone like me in your corner."

"*My situation?* Do you mean with Dante?"

She nodded, making him shake his head in annoyance.

"You know damn well I didn't shoot that son of a bitch, though honestly, at this point, I wish I fucking had!"

"Of course, I know you didn't shoot him! Any person who would believe you were capable of doing such a thing is a complete moron!" She smirked. "But he's got you in a nice little vise, doesn't he? Someone like me could've kept him from tightening the screws. I could've helped. Now you have to face this on your own, and you are so out of your league, sweetheart!" She shook her head. "You're no match for Dante."

"*And you are?* Is that because you're as devious and petty as he is?"

Her smirk disappeared. For a split second, she actually looked angry, but then she licked her glossy lips and smiled.

"See you around, Evan," she said, patting him on the arm before turning away from him. "Good luck, darling. You'll certainly need it!" she called over her shoulder.

He then watched as she tossed her hair and walked away.

Chapter 14

Dante

"Seventy-one, seventy-two, seventy-three, seventy-four," Kiki counted out, pausing to lick her index finger as she flipped through the wrinkled stack of twenties. "Seventy-five, seventy-six, seventy-seven . . ."

"Do you really have to count out the whole thing? Can't you just give it to me?" Dante asked tiredly, watching his daughter.

"I don't want you to think we cheatin' you," she said, tossing her purple braids over her shoulder. "You said you wanted all your money, right?"

He nodded.

"So shut up and let me count it!" She then returned her attention to the twenty-dollar bills in her hand. "Seventy-eight, seventy-nine . . ."

Dante glanced to his right to find Kiki's girlfriend, Tee, leaning against the kitchen counter. A do-rag was on the young woman's head. Her skinny jeans hung low on her narrow hips. Her birdlike arms were crossed over her flat chest, and she glared at Dante openly, like she was trying her best to intimidate him.

It's not working, honey, he thought, though he was eager to leave this dingy place and head home to his own condo.

The house on Flushing Avenue wasn't haunted by any real ghosts, but it certainly haunted him. Every time he came back here he was reminded of how low things had gotten for him after he had been shot and had to go on the run. Looking at the recliner in the living room made him recall how he used to drink himself into a stupor before falling asleep there. Looking at the mattress on the floor in the upstairs bedroom reminded him of the squalor he had slept in those nights he hadn't passed out in the recliner.

Thank God this isn't my life anymore, he thought as his daughter continued to count aloud and his skin crawled from the heavy air of misery that seemed to hang everywhere around him.

Though he had been reluctant to come here, Dante had stopped by the row house to check on his daughter's budding new private business and to collect the two thousand dollars she owed him for allowing her to use the house as her headquarters. For a fleeting moment he had wondered if it was right to fleece his daughter out of her hard-earned drug money and use it to pay his mortgage and buy more painkillers. But then he realized that this extra income wasn't something he could afford to turn away. His savings were getting increasingly low—to the point that he hadn't checked the account in weeks because he was disheartened at how low the balance was. He also rationalized this was money Kiki rightfully owed him; she was paying for room and board and all the past money he had given her.

So when you really think about it, I'm doing her a favor!

"Ninety-seven, ninety-eight, ninety-nine, one hundred," Kiki said, counting out the last bill before slapping the stack into his open palm. "That's all your money for this week. We good now?"

"We're good," he said, folding the bills and tucking them into his suit jacket's inner pocket. "But if the cops get wind of any of this, I had nothing to do with it, all right?" He pointed at her. "I mean it, Kiki! I better not get called in on—"

"*Yes!* I told you that we wouldn't tell them anything. So stop worrying! We're not gonna get caught. I ain't stupid! I got this!"

"And even if we *do* get caught, why should we be the only ones that go down for it?" Tee asked. "You saying you want our money but don't want any of the risk that comes with it?"

"Little girl, you wouldn't have this much money," Dante argued, gesturing toward the stack of bills still sitting near the stainless steel sink that was also overflowing with dishes, "if it wasn't for the fact that I let you live and work out of my goddamn house! And I can still toss you out!"

"Man,"—Tee pushed herself away from the counter and yanked up the waist of her jeans—"you sure do talk a lot shit for a—"

"Tee," Kiki barked before giving her girlfriend a silencing look. Just then someone's cell phone began to ring, filling the kitchen with a thumping rap tune that made Dante wince. Kiki abruptly yanked her iPhone off the laminated counter.

"Hello!" she yelled after pressing the button to answer. "Yeah, what you got?" she asked before walking out of the kitchen, leaving Dante and Tee alone to stare at each other.

As the duo listened to Kiki talk and laugh on the phone in the next room, an awkward silence fell between them. Dante sighed.

"Well, this was lovely," he muttered. "I guess I'll be heading home now."

"You know," Tee called out as Dante turned to the kitchen entryway, "the high you get from them pills ain't gonna last forever. I bet you barely feel it anymore already."

Dante stopped mid-motion. His spine stiffened at her words. He whipped back around to face her. Tee wasn't glaring at him anymore but smiling openly now, infuriating him.

"What the hell are you talking about?" he snarled, unable to hide his anger that Kiki had revealed his secret to her girlfriend.

To this tiny-ass, do-rag wearing she-him!

"You know what I'm talking about," Tee continued, undaunted, even as he charged toward her. "I'm talking about those pain pills, man! Every junkie thinks—"

"I am *not* a fucking junkie!" He jabbed his finger into her bony chest. "Don't you ever fucking call me that again! Do you hear me?"

The last person who had called him a junkie had ended up with a bloodied mouth. Considering how much lip Tee had given him in the past, she might end up with a lot more.

"I barely touch the stuff," he argued, conveniently forgetting the eighteen pills he had already ingested that day. "Don't put me in the same category as those crackheads on the street, begging for change and sucking strangers' dicks. I'm not one of those meth heads, losing their teeth and pissing themselves."

Tee rolled her brown eyes toward the ceiling and shoved his hand away from her sternum. "Whatever, man. I'm just trying to help you out! I'm telling you that if you keep taking those pills, you gonna run outta cash quick!

But if you wanna get that old high again—faster and cheaper—you're gonna have to move onto somethin' else. It's the truth. *You* know it, and I know it, too."

Dante squinted at her. Though he hated to admit it, even he had to agree that he was finding it harder and harder to "chase the dragon," as it were. Each week his bank account got lower, and it seemed the pills ran out faster. And worse, the doctor who was writing him his prescription was starting to squeeze him. He said the risk of losing his license warranted the high cost of a higher fee for his "labor," but Dante wasn't convinced. It made Dante angry to be so blatantly taken advantage of, but it wasn't like he could go to another doctor and ask him to write multiple prescriptions for Oxy.

He took a step back from Tee, eying her with open suspicion. But he was intrigued now and couldn't hide that, either. "So you're saying that you've got a hook-up then?"

Tee nodded. "Kiki won't sell it," she said, dropping her voice down to a whisper and glancing again at the kitchen entryway where they could still hear Kiki talking on the other side of the yellow-tiled wall, "but I know people who will."

"So what is it? What can they give me?"

"A little bit of that brown sugar, baby," Tee said with a wink, making Dante take another step back, making him frown.

"*Brown sugar?* You mean smack?"

Tee nodded, and he quickly shook his head.

"Oh, hell no! I'm not touching that stuff!"

If he thought crackheads and meth heads were detestable, he was just as repulsed by smack heads. There was no way he would join their ranks.

"I don't know why I even bothered to listen to this shit," he muttered, before turning away again.

"Yeah," Tee said as he walked out of the kitchen and headed toward the front door, "you say that now! Hit me up though when you change your mind, cuz I know you will!"

"Don't count on it!" he shouted over his shoulder before slamming the front door behind him.

A little after midnight, Dante heard a knock at his front door. He raised his head dazedly from the leather couch where he had collapsed. His glass of Hennessy and the open bottle still sat on the coffee table. The television was still on, showing hard-core porn and filling the living room with moans and slapping sounds.

Dante wiped the drool from the side of his face and the corner of his mouth and frowned. The last he remembered he had been reaching for his drink as he grabbed his remote to change the channel. He didn't recall lying down or falling asleep. It was unnerving how often he was having these blackout periods nowadays, but at least it was in a luxe condo in Virginia rather than a run-down house in the ghetto—or at least that's what he told himself.

The person at his front door knocked again, yanking him from his muddled thoughts. He groggily pushed himself to his feet and staggered across the living room, closing his robe and muttering to himself as he went.

"Who the fuck is it?" he barked before peering through his peephole.

When he saw who was standing on his welcome mat, his mouth fell open in shock.

"Who the fuck does it look like?" she answered with a laugh as he quickly undid the lock and swung his front door open.

"Charisse?" Dante murmured, staring at his ex-lover.

"Dante," she said with a wink and a smile before pushing past him into his condo. He watched in bewilderment as she sauntered into his living room as if she had been invited, like she hadn't just shown up at his place in 12:13 in the morning after they hadn't spoken to each other in more than a year.

His gaze followed her as she removed her pashmina shawl and tossed it onto the couch where he had been sleeping only seconds ago. Her four-inch stilettoes left indentations in his rug.

His eyes traced the length of her long, graceful legs, which were clad in thigh-highs. At the sight of those black lace bands skimming only an inch below the hem of her silk shirtdress, Dante involuntarily licked his lips.

In the old days, he had burned hot for Charisse. She had always been easy on the eyes, and the knowledge that fucking her was the same as fucking *over* her then-husband, Evan, had been the ultimate aphrodisiac for him. But her alcoholism and sloppy behavior had been a definite turnoff, one that had gotten harder to ignore over time.

Fortunately, it looked like she was no longer hitting the bottle. Unfortunately for him, that meant he was starting to have lustful thoughts about her again, even though he knew he should be wary of this woman. She wasn't as scheming or as vengeful as he was—but she was damn close!

"Did I catch you at a bad time?" she asked with a smirk, gesturing to the television screen where one buxom blonde was currently going down on another.

He slammed his front door closed. "Why are you here, Charisse?"

"No real reason. I arrived back in town a few weeks ago and just stopped by to say hi." She strolled around his living room, wrinkling her nose at his cluttered coffee table and the general disarray around his condo. "Ever thought of cleaning this place?"

"Oh, we're going to pretend like this is a social call?" He walked out of the entryway hall and joined her in the living room. "I'm surprised you would pay me a visit, considering the last time I saw you, I had you kicked out of my office."

"Well, I've decided to let bygones be bygones—considering I heard that you were fired from the same law offices you had me kicked me out of. Besides, I'm not here to talk about the past, Dante. I'm here to congratulate you! You always had it out for the Murdochs, and you finally managed to land a big win with this trumped-up attempted murder charge against Evan. I'm impressed!"

"It isn't a 'trumped-up attempted murder charge,'" he lied. "Evan tried to kill me. I saw it with my own eyes."

"Bullshit," she said with a laugh, irritating him even more. "You and I both know that isn't true. But who cares! That's not why I'm here."

"So why are you here? You still haven't given me a straight answer! We're not girlfriends who meet up for dinner and drinks."

"I already told you! I'm here," she said with a grin as she began to undo the buttons of her shirtdress, "to congratulate you."

Watching her slowly undress to the sound track of groans and orgasmic screams from his television, Dante began to harden.

"Why would you congratulate me?"

His throat went dry when she shrugged out of her dress, letting it slide over her hips and pool at her feet. She walked toward him topless, wearing only a thong, her thigh-highs, and heels. His eyes drifted down to her perky pale breasts and pert pink nipples before snapping back to her face.

"Because I hate the Murdochs just as much as you do."
She grabbed his chin and leaned forward to give a long,
warm lick on the side of his cheek, then she nibbled his
earlobe. "And I hate Evan even more. I begged him to take
me back. Instead, he chose to marry that tacky fat bitch,
Leila. So to hell with Evan! I don't care if he rots in
prison."

"You don't fool me, Charisse," he said, trying his best
to mask his growing desire for her, but that was a challenge since all she had to do was look down to see his
arousal. He may not have been up to listening to what she
had to say, but his dick was paying full attention. "If you
begged him to take you back, that means you still have
feelings for that motherfucka. You think you can play me,
but you can't, honey. This shit is *all* an act."

She grabbed his hand and tugged it downward, making
him frown in confusion and almost yank his hand back.
She eased his hand past the waistband of her thong and
forced his fingers between her legs.

"Does this feel like an act?" she whispered, staring into
his eyes.

No, it does not, he thought, feeling her slick wetness
against her fingertips. Despite his initial hesitance, he began
to move his fingers and slowly stroke her, making her twist
her hips, making her smile widen as she licked her lips.

"Fuck me, Dante. Do it now," she groaned, and he
couldn't help but oblige her.

He roughly shoved her up against the living room wall
and ripped her flimsy lace thong right off of her. He then
opened his robe and tugged down his sweats and boxer
briefs.

"Just like old times," she gushed before he stood between her legs and hoisted her upward. She wrapped her

legs around his waist only seconds before he plunged inside her.

She reached out for his entertainment center to brace herself for each thrust, sending a series of CDs and DVDs clattering to the floor.

Soon, their moans and yells rivaled those on the television.

Chapter 15

Paulette

"Honey . . . *Honey* . . . look at Mommy! Look at Mommy making funny faces!" Paulette chirped to her son in a high squeaky voice but he had absolutely no interest in what Paulette was doing. Little Nate seemed perfectly content to scream at the top of his lungs, making his little brown face go beet red while tears streamed down his cheeks and chin.

Paulette glanced anxiously at the people in the deli line standing in front and behind her. They all had looks on their faces that conveyed the same message: "Will you shut that kid up?"

"He's teething," she said with a forced smile to the older woman standing behind her.

"Sounds like it," the woman muttered, staring at Little Nate, who was still writhing and yelling in his baby carrier perched in Paulette's shopping cart.

Paulette handed Nate his teething ring, but he shoved it away like it was a funny-smelling canapé at a dinner party. She didn't blame him; the teething ring didn't seem to help much. She glanced down at the number ticket she held, then at the digital display overhead.

"Seventeen," she whispered.

She only had one more number before her order was called. But then Little Nate released another scream, hitting an octave she didn't know was possible for such a little person.

"Okay, maybe Daddy doesn't need roast beef for dinner after all," she mumbled before tossing the number ticket into the small trash can at her feet. She then turned away from the counter, excusing herself as she went. She headed straight to the front of the store to get into one of the checkout lines. With luck, she could be out of here in the next fifteen minutes.

It seemed that all her outings turned into this nowadays—her dragging Nate along and him inevitably having a meltdown. She refused to admit it aloud, but she was actually starting to miss the days when Reina used to babysit him and Paulette could take a few coveted hours for alone time. She'd go to the gym and work out, or get her hair and nails done, or have a lunch date with her sister-in-law, Leila, or another one of her friends. Now she had no time to do that. She and Little Nate had been attached at the hip every hour of every day for the past three and half months.

She had tried to find a babysitter or nanny who could help her occasionally, but she and Antonio had been unable to agree on anyone. Well, that wasn't true. She had found a few she liked, but Antonio had shot down every single candidate.

"She's too old," he had said about sixty-eight-year-old woman who had been taking care of babies for more than forty years and had been recommended by Leila. "She'll probably slip on some applesauce, fall, and break a hip.

Or she'll throw out her back picking up Nate and expect us to pay her hospital bills."

Then there was the woman they interviewed who loved children and had been a teacher before emigrating from Costa Rica.

"I could barely understand what she was saying," he'd told Paulette that night in their bedroom. "Nate would be around her all the time, baby! He's just learning to talk. What if he picked up her thick Spanish accent?"

Then there was the time she had showed Antonio a website listing of a guy she thought was a good candidate.

"There is no way in hell I'm gonna let another grown-ass man take care of my son!" he'd cried in outrage. "What dude would want to be a damn nanny anyway?"

She suspected that unless it was his mother, Antonio would never approve of anyone watching Nathan, but Paulette was growing tired of this. She loved her son, but even perfect moms needed a break occasionally.

Paulette finally reached the front of the grocery store, only to find all the lines had at least four people waiting in them. She grumbled and took one toward the entrance. Meanwhile, Little Nate continued to wail, and she quickly removed him from the cart's front seat and held him against her chest, trying her best to quiet him, to comfort him.

"It's okay, honey. Mommy is almost done. Then we'll go home and we can both go down for a nap," she said with a loud breath that ruffled her bangs.

"Ain't having a good day, is he?" someone asked from behind her.

Paulette turned to find a smiling petite woman with graying dreads peering up at her. Her dark skin shone under the grocery store track lighting. Her bright smile was instantly calming.

"*He's* not having a good day, so I guess you ain't having a good day, either," the woman said with a laugh.

Paulette slowly shook her head. The woman seemed vaguely familiar, but she couldn't quite place her. "No, not really."

"What's his name?" the woman inquired.

"Nathan . . . but his daddy and I call him Nate."

The woman nodded and gazed at Paulette's baby. "So why are you so unhappy, Nate?"

"Well, he's getting a new pair of teeth, and he's in complete agony. I've tried everything to make him feel better—teething rings, teething biscuits, cold wash cloths, and Orajel—but nothing's worked!"

"Is that so?" The woman nodded thoughtfully and gestured for Paulette to follow her. "I think I can help you. Come on over here."

Paulette frowned, glancing at her full cart and the line in front of her.

"Just leave it there, honey. That lady at the counter has about four hundred things she's buying." She motioned to the crowded conveyor belt. "And I bet she has coupons to ring up! Y'all ain't going anywhere anytime soon! Besides, we'll be fast."

Paulette hesitated for only a few more seconds before relenting. If this woman could offer Little Nate something that could finally give him relief from his pain, she was all ears.

"Okay," she said, reaching into her cart to remove her diaper bag. She shifted Nate so that she could toss the bag's strap over her shoulder. "As long as we'll be quick."

She followed the older woman down two aisles and watched as she scanned the store shelves, squinting as if she was looking for something.

"There it is!" she exclaimed, removing a small brown bottle from one of the lower shelves. She held it to Paulette.

"It's an old recipe for toothache. Rub a little on a piece of cloth and let him suck on it."

"You want him to suck on witch hazel?" Paulette stared doubtfully at the bottle. "Is it . . . Is it safe, though?"

The older woman laughed. "They've been using it for hundreds of years and ain't no child's died of it yet! Just try a little bit. Here . . . let me show you." She then reached inside her purse and removed a white handkerchief. She broke the protective seal on the bottle and opened the lid before pouring a little bit on the white cloth. She held it out to Paulette.

"Wrap it around your finger, then let your boy gnaw on it for a little bit. It shouldn't take long to work."

"It's worth a try, I guess," Paulette whispered.

She *did* want Little Nate to feel better. She did as the woman said. It wasn't hard to get her knuckle into Nate's gaping mouth since he was still wailing. He made a face at first when he tasted the witch hazel but after a minute, he clamped down on her index finger and started to gnaw it like one of his favorite snacks. His cries finally tapered off, then stopped entirely.

"Oh, my God!" she shouted in amazement, almost wanting to break into tears herself—in relief. "It worked! I can't believe it worked!"

"I told you it would," the woman said with a smile. She reached up and gently patted Nate's back. "I used it when my boys were babies . . . when they were teething. I used it with all three of them. Well . . ." Her smile disappeared as she suddenly grew somber. "I guess I've only got *two* boys now. One of them died not too long ago."

"Oh, I'm so sorry to hear that!" Paulette cried, grimacing at the woman's admission.

And she wasn't just saying that to be polite. It was horrible to find out that someone who had been so kind to her and Nate had lost one of her children. Worse, it had happened recently. Paulette couldn't imagine ever losing Nate!

The woman nodded. "Thank you for saying so. My baby boy's gone home to live with Jesus now." She took a deep breath, making her shoulders rise then fall. "Well, anyway, I'm glad I could help. You should probably get back in line now if you don't wanna lose your spot."

Paulette glanced again at Nate. He was still gnawing on her finger with vigor, making drool ooze down her hand. "I can't thank you enough for this, Ms. . . . Ms. . . . ."

"Claudia Rhodes. But you can call me Miss Claudia . . . and no thanks needed, honey!" She reached out again and caressed Nate's dark, curly head. "I just hate to see babies in pain! I'm glad to see him feeling better! I told you. He brings back memories of my boys when they were babies." She stared tenderly at Nate. "I babysit my grandkids sometimes, but I miss when they were like this. It's nothing like holding a sweet little one."

"You babysit your grandkids? Do you babysit other children, too?"

The woman paused and lowered her hand from Nate. "Why, yes . . . sometimes. I watch my neighbors' kids when they ask me to. I don't mind. I'm retired. I've got plenty of time on my hands," she said with a chuckle.

Paulette hesitated before she asked her next question. She knew how picky Antonio was when it came to finding someone to take care of Nate, but Miss Claudia seemed like a good candidate. It wasn't just the fact that she had helped Paulette with Nate's teething pain or revealed that she babysat children, but Paulette detected a warmth from this woman that couldn't be faked. She seemed genuinely caring.

"I'm . . . I've been looking for a nanny for Little Nate," she began. "I don't know what your rates are or if you'd be willing to do it. It would require you to come to our house. I wouldn't need it done all the time, but—"

"Like taking care of this one would be a chore! Shoot!" She waved her hands dismissively. "I told you I loved babies. I'd be happy to do it!"

"I would have to check with my husband first," Paulette said quickly. "But could I get your name and number? I'll contact you if he's okay with it. I'll do it as soon as I can."

Miss Claudia nodded. "Of course, honey!"

Later that night, after she had put Nate to sleep in his crib and Antonio was sitting on the edge of their king-size bed watching Sports Center on the flat-screen, Paulette decided to broach the topic of hiring Miss Claudia.

She knew she had to be careful in her approach. If Antonio had no problem turning down women with résumés and references, he might look at her like she was insane if she suggested a woman who had neither of those things babysit their child. This would require some tact, maybe even stealth.

"So how was your day, baby?" she asked as she strolled from the bathroom into their bedroom.

"Fine," he answered distractedly, flipping to another sports channel when a commercial appeared on screen.

"*That's it?* Just fine?" She removed some of their decorative silk pillows and tossed them onto a nearby window seat. She climbed onto the bed and knelt behind him. "No more to tell than that?"

He shrugged. "Pretty much. A client wanted to change one of the spec stats on me and I had to bring in one of the higher-ups for a conference call. It was a pain in ass I didn't need today."

"Oh, poor baby! I'm sorry it stressed you out," she cooed as she began to knead his shoulders and massage his back the way she knew he liked.

"It's okay. We got it taken care of." He closed his eyes,

tilted back his head, and groaned. "That feels good, baby. Can you go lower though?"

She shifted her hands from his shoulder blades and began to knead his lower back through the cotton fabric of his shirt. "So I've been meaning to tell you . . . Leila and I are supposed to meet up later this week . . . maybe for dinner in town."

He moaned again and rolled his shoulders. "A little to the left," he said and she obeyed his orders, hoping that the massage was lulling him into submission, hoping that it would make him more open to hearing what she had to say.

"Are you taking Nate with you?" he asked.

"No, it's a grown-up dinner, honey—no babies allowed. We're supposed to meet at seven, and I should be back by ten at the latest. I was wondering if you could watch Nate for me. It would be Thursday evening. Can you work it into your schedule?"

"Sorry, honey, I can't. You know how my work schedule is. I might not get home until eight some nights."

"Yeah, I understand." She forced a loud sigh. "Well, maybe we could get someone to watch Nate for a couple of hours. See if we can try a babysitter on a trial basis. I met this woman at the grocery store who was wonderful with him! She got him to stop crying, and she's babysat children for years! I bet she'd be willing to do it."

Antonio slowly opened his eyes. He pivoted slightly on the bed so that he could face his wife. "You want someone you met at the grocery store to babysit our son?"

"Don't say it like that, Tony!" Paulette groused, dropping her hands from his back to her sides. "It's not like I found her selling daisies at some intersection! We talked for a while. She even gave me a recipe to help with Nate's teething—and it worked! She seems very reputable."

"Uh-huh." He looked and sounded incredulous. "Baby,

I'm not gonna leave our son with some random stranger who you—"

"But you don't want to leave Nate with anybody!" she shouted, throwing her legs over the edge of the bed and rising to her feet. She stood in front of him. "The only damn people you find acceptable to watch Nate is me and your mama!"

"That's not true. I'd be okay with Leila watching Nate, too . . . sometimes . . . maybe."

"Tony," she began, pacing on the carpet in front of their four-poster bed and clenching her fists at her sides, "I cannot keep doing this! I'm alone in this house *every day* with Nate. I love being a mom, but I need a break every now and then. I'm human! I'm not saying she would have to keep him all day. I just want a little time for—"

"If you want a break, why don't you stop being stubborn and reach out to Mama and tell her you're sorry for what you said?"

"Because I'm not sorry! I meant every damn word!" She pointed at her chest. "Why can't your mother call *me* and apologize to *me* for calling me a whore?"

"She did *not* call you a whore. Stop exaggerating!"

"It isn't what she said outright, but you know damn well that's what she meant. And it wasn't like she was the perfect babysitter, either!"

"But she's my mother—and Nate's grandmother!"

"Oh, *now* she's his grandmother? Funny . . . three months ago she was raising the question if that was even true!"

Antonio gritted his teeth and slowly shook his head. "Dammit, when will you let that shit go? She didn't mean it! She was hurt and angry and she wanted to hurt you, too. But we all need to move on! I know I have!"

"I don't believe that, Tony."

He shot to his feet. "Why the hell not? I have done everything to—"

"Because if you really did move on . . . if you'd let all the stuff go from our past, you would trust me. You would trust me as your wife and you'd trust my judgment! You'd trust me to choose who the hell should watch our son! I wouldn't have to feel like I needed your permission to make a decision on something like this!"

Antonio fell silent. He grimaced. She took a step toward him, clasping her hands in front of her beseechingly.

"*Please* trust me to do this! I swear you won't regret it. If Miss Claudia doesn't seem like a good match for Nate, then we don't have to use her again. I'll . . . I'll even consider asking your mother for help."

She watched as Antonio swallowed, then scratched the back of his head. "Okay."

She blinked. "Okay? *Really?* You mean it?"

"Of course, I mean it! We'll use her this week on a trial basis. After that, we'll see."

Paulette beamed. She then threw her arms around her husband's neck and kissed him.

"Oh, thank you, baby! Thank you so much!"

Chapter 16

Leila

"I'll only be gone thirty minutes . . . forty-five minutes, tops, Mama," Leila said as she cradled her infant daughter's head. The baby was perched in Diane's arms.

Diane smiled and shooed Leila away. "Go on, honey. Enjoy your run. We'll be fine. I'll rock Angie for a bit and then we'll sit on back and watch a Lifetime movie. Won't we, Angel?" Diane tutted to her granddaughter, who was guzzling hungrily from her milk bottle, oblivious to her mother and grandmother.

"Are you going to watch the movie, too, Izzy?" Leila asked her eldest daughter, who was lying on her belly at the foot of Diane's bed. The young girl tore her eyes away from the game she was playing on her iPad. She stared at Leila like Leila had just lost her mind.

"Uh, no, Mom," she answered dryly. "I'm not watching that movie. I'm only a thousand points away from topping my highest score. I have to concentrate." She then returned her attention to the iPad's screen.

Leila chuckled and leaned down to kiss Isabel's dimpled cheek. "Well, good luck with that." She headed to the bedroom doorway. "I'm gonna run, then take a quick shower, then come back here. See you guys in a bit."

A minute later, Leila was walking down the stone steps of Murdoch Mansion. She paused on the asphalt driveway to do her stretches and check the knots in her shoelaces. She then put in her earbuds and began to jog down the driveway toward the tennis courts.

Leila hadn't been running in months, not since Angelica was born. Paulette thought she did it to lose the baby weight.

"Maybe I should start running, too," Paulette had murmured a week ago before glancing down at her curvy hips. "Aunt Ida's right. I am getting a bit thick."

But the truth was, Leila really jogged to clear her head. In the early days, when she had first arrived in Chesterton from San Diego, she used to go jogging around their old neighborhood twice a week. She had jogged to escape her worries about her vengeful ex, her mother's foreclosure, and her ever-growing pile of bills. She no longer had those worries but had developed new ones. She worried about the state of her new marriage. She worried about whether Evan would have to go back to jail and about what would happen to her and the children if he did end up behind bars again. But those worries disappeared as they always did when she ran, as she basked in the warm sunshine.

Leila ran the first mile humming with a few upbeat Beyoncé tunes playing on her iPod. She jogged past the tennis courts then a manmade pond. She took the asphalt path through the clearing into a line of trees. As she did, the world darkened around her. The sun that had been beating down on her head only seconds earlier was now cloaked by the tangled limbs and leaves of the oaks and maples overhead. Leila jogged another quarter mile, enjoying the scenery and the break from the summer heat under the shadows of the forest. As she reached the end of the line of trees and emerged into another clearing, she slowed her pace. She frowned. Even through her headphones she could hear the rhythmic thud of footsteps behind her. She tore her earbuds from her ears.

Is someone following me?

Leila came to a halt and turned in just enough time to see Michael jogging toward her, wearing only a pair of black jogging shorts. His bare chest and arms glistened with sweat. He smiled and waved. When Leila realized it was him, she fought the urge to roll her eyes heavenward.

She had successfully managed to avoid being alone with Michael, at least since that night when he had hugged her and had given her that *look*. The look still unnerved her. He gave it across the dinner table while he sat next to Aunt Ida. He gave her the look when they passed each other in the hall in the morning as she headed to her office in the guesthouse.

It was hard to explain just what she felt when his eyes landed on her: maybe embarrassment mixed with outrage. It angered her that he would look at her like that with her husband and his fiancée sitting only a few feet away. Leila felt violated. She felt like Michael was disrespecting Evan and Aunt Ida. She also got the nagging feeling that he was taunting her, as if he was enjoying her discomfort. She wanted to tell Michael to stop it, but she knew it would only make her look ridiculous, like she was overreacting. So she resolved that she would continue to pretend she didn't notice Michael at all. Unfortunately, she couldn't do that right now with him standing in front of her.

"Hey, Leila!" the young man called out as he drew to a stop in front of her and started jogging in place.

"Hello, Michael," she answered flatly.

"You're on your morning run, too?" He wiped his sweaty brow with the back of his hand. He licked his lips.

There's that look again, she thought. He was gazing at

her like he had just endured a three-day fast and she was the plate of prime ribs he'd just spotted.

Leila turned away from him and stared longingly at Murdoch Mansion, which sat a half mile in the distance. "Yeah, and I was just heading back."

"Maybe we can finish the rest of the run together."

"No thanks. I prefer to run alone. I'm a slowpoke anyway. I wouldn't want to hold you up!" She tucked one of her earbuds back into her right ear. "So I better get—"

She was stopped short when she felt Michael grab her forearm. She instantly yanked her arm out of his grasp.

"Don't do that!" she shouted, feeling panic rise within her.

"Don't do what?"

"Just don't . . . don't grab me like that. Okay?"

"I wasn't grabbing you. I was only trying to get your attention." He reached for her again, but she took a cautious step.

Suddenly, the secluded trees that had offered her cover from the hot sun didn't seem quite so comforting anymore. Leila realized that anything could happen out here. Michael could do anything to her and no one would be the wiser.

"What did I say? Don't touch me! Didn't your mama teach you to keep your hands to yourself?"

His smile widened into a full grin. "My mama taught me a lot of things, honey, but I guess that wasn't one of them."

"Don't call me 'honey,'" she said through clenched teeth.

"Well, excuse me!" He held up his hands in mock innocence. His green eyes twinkled with merriment, only making her angrier. "I didn't mean anything bad by it. I'm just being friendly."

"Yeah, well, maybe I don't want a friend like you. Maybe you need to stay the hell away from me!"

He chuckled.

"What is so goddamn funny?" she snapped.

"You! You and all your huffing and puffing." He looked her up and down. "I love a woman with some fire in her though. I think it's cute!"

Cute?

So he *was* getting off on this, she realized. He was taking pleasure in her uneasiness, but Leila refused to be toyed with.

"Look, I don't know what type of relationship you and Ida may have, but I'm a married woman, okay? I don't—"

"Oh, come on! You can save the speech. You aren't fooling anyone!"

"Excuse me?"

"From what I've heard, wedding vows don't mean much to you." He took a step toward her, making her take another step back. "From what I've heard ... Evan was *already* married when you two hooked up. So were you."

Leila was struck speechless. It took her awhile to regain her voice.

"So you've ... you've been talking about me? *Researching me?*"

He chuckled again and shrugged. "I wouldn't call it research. I just keep my ears open when people are talking. It's a skill I've learned over the years."

Leila slowly shook her head. "Well, I don't care what you've heard or what you *think* you know about me, but you don't know me—and you've got some big balls to presume that you do! Who the hell do you think you are?"

"I'm the man who can help you, Leila. I can be your friend ... your confidant."

"I don't want or need a 'friend' like you. I told you that already!"

"Yes, you do! Because I *know* you, sweetheart. I know you better than you know yourself. I've met a lot of women like you who are sad and lonely. You're no different. I see you with your kids and how you try to smile and look happy, but your face falls when you think no one's looking. I see how you walk up and down the halls at night because you can't sleep. But he doesn't notice any of that, does he?"

She stilled.

"Admit it—that husband of yours doesn't pay you enough attention. He doesn't treasure you like he should—after all that you've done for him, after all that you've sacrificed." He drew close again. "I know what you're thinking. I know what question plays in your mind on an endless loop: 'Does he still want me?' But the question you really should be asking yourself is, 'Do I still want *him?*' "

Her breath caught in her throat. Where had he gotten all of this? Who had told him? She hadn't even shared some of these doubts with her mother.

"You're too good for him, Leila. You know it and I know it."

"I don't . . . I-I never said . . ." she sputtered helplessly.

"You didn't have to say it! He deserves some rich bitch, some prima donna who will spend all his money and doesn't care if she sees him once a week or once a month. But that's not you! You're not a rich bitch, Leila. You weren't born with a silver spoon in your mouth. You've had to fight for everything you've ever gotten. I know it because I'm just like you! You and I are self-starters. We're fighters."

Now there were mere inches between them, but this time she didn't take a step back. She was almost mesmerized by the sound of his words and the intensity of his green eyes.

Michael was giving voice to feelings and worries she was too terrified and even ashamed to say aloud. And now they were all flooding out of his mouth, overwhelming her like a surging tide.

"You're a special woman, Leila. A beautiful, *sexy* woman, who shouldn't be left alone all the time. No, not a treasure like you." He cupped her face. "I can see it, Leila. He can't. But I can."

He then slowly lowered his mouth to hers. Just as their lips were about to touch, Leila jerked back. She furiously shook her head, coming to her senses. Whatever spell she had been under had been broken. She realized what Michael was trying to do, what they *both* had almost done.

She roughly tugged his hands from her face.

"Don't ever touch me again," she ordered, shoving away from him.

She then turned and ran in the direction of the mansion. She kept running, not pausing to look behind her to see if Michael followed.

Later that night, after she had put Angelica down in her crib and Isabel and her mother had fallen asleep, Leila lay awake alone in bed, thinking of what had happened during her morning run. She had almost let that man kiss her—a perfect stranger and a *sleazy* one at that!

What has gotten into your head, girl?

She dropped her face into her hands.

Leila wanted to blame it on momentary insanity, but she knew better. Michael had been right: she *was* lonely and sad and obviously doing a poor job of masking it. She missed Evan's companionship so much that it hurt, but he didn't seem to notice. Her new marriage was starting to look startlingly, eerily like her old one: sitting up in bed at night while she waited for her husband to come home, only to drift off to sleep and wake up alone. Something had to change, or this marriage was doomed to end like the first one. Leila needed to draw up her courage and confront her husband.

A few minutes later, Leila knocked on the study's imposing oak door. The baby monitor was clutched in her hand.

She knew Evan was in here. He was always here when he wasn't back at the office.

"*Yes?*" he called out, and she pushed the door open. She found him sitting at his desk, as usual, and staring at his laptop, as usual. When she entered the room, he didn't look at her.

"Evan," she said, "I know you're busy, but . . . I . . . I think . . . no, I *know* we need to talk."

"Can we do it tomorrow, baby?" he said, not looking up from the laptop screen. "I'm a little busy right now."

"No, we can't do it tomorrow. I need to talk to you *now*, Ev."

He loudly sighed. "Okay, fine," he said as he continued to type on his keyboard. "What do you wanna talk about?"

I want to talk about you phoning in our marriage, she thought. *We waited so long and fought so hard to be together, and now it's like I don't even matter to you anymore! I want to talk about why I can't get more than an hour alone with you. I want you to know I almost kissed another man today.*

But instead, she said, "Can you at least look at me?"

"Huh?" he answered again distractedly, pissing her off even more.

"Goddamnit, look at me, Ev!"

Finally, his dark eyes darted up from the laptop screen. For the first time, he really was looking at her, and he frowned. "Why are you shouting? What's wrong?"

"I'm shouting so that you can finally hear me, since that seems to be the only way to get your attention! And what's wrong is that you stay in this damn study all the time! I feel like I have to make an appointment to see you! You don't talk to me, and when you do, it's only in three-word sentences or monosyllables. You have longer conversations with our infant daughter than you have with me!"

Evan leaned back in his desk chair and pursed his lips. "Are we really doing this? Are you really trying to pick a fight with me knowing all the shit that I have on my plate right now, Lee?"

At those words, she felt her first pang of guilt, but she told herself not to back down. They needed to do this. For the sake of their marriage, she had to do this.

"I'm not . . . I'm not trying to pick a fight. I'm just telling you that—"

"*That I'm ignoring you? That I'm not giving you enough time and attention?*" he finished for her. He now looked just as angry as she felt. He shoved his laptop aside and shot to his feet. "Lee, in two and half months, I'm going on trial for attempted murder. You hear that? *Attempted murder!*"

"I *know* that, Evan!"

"And my company is falling apart. So I'm sorry that I can't wine and dine you and take you out to dinner! I'm sorry I can't—"

"Dammit, that's not what I'm saying and you know it!" She slammed the study door behind her and marched toward his desk, so frustrated that she could punch him. She set the baby monitor on the edge of his desk, stood squarely in front of Evan, and glared up at him. "I'm not asking you to take me to a fucking restaurant. I'm not even going to bring up the fact that we haven't made love in . . . in *weeks!*"

"You just did," he said tightly.

"I'm asking you to talk to me, Ev! Just *talk* to me! That's what married couples do. That's what best friends do. You're supposed to confide in me! I'm supposed to be the one that you turn to at times like this! But instead, you're shutting me out—literally! You keep leaving a door between us, and I don't . . ." Her eyes flooded with tears. Her throat went dry. "I don't know why."

Evan grimaced. All the anger had left his face. He slowly shook his head. "I'm not trying to shut you out, baby. I'm just trying to handle this the best way I know how. I'm trying to set this right. I hate that I've dragged you and the girls into this mess as much as I already have. This isn't the life I wanted for us!"

"You didn't drag me into anything. I *wanted* to be here," she whispered, raising her hand to his cheek. She trailed her thumb over his bottom lip. She was openly crying now. "I love you! Where you go, I go. That's what you told me, right? I want to be with you. I want to help you any way I can."

She then stood on the balls of her feet and kissed him. He wrapped his arms around her waist and fiercely kissed her back. She sank into him, longing for his warmth and his touch, missing the sensation of his full lips against her own and his tongue inside her mouth. She wrenched her lips away, wrapped her arms around his neck, and gazed lovingly into her husband's eyes.

"I told you before that I'm not a china doll, Evan Murdoch. I guess I'll have to show you again that I won't break," she said with an alluring smile before rubbing her pelvis against his groin and raising her mouth back to his.

The second kiss was even deeper. The longing Leila felt was quickly replaced with overwhelming desire, one that left her panting and tugging at the buttons of his dress shirt. It left her fumbling as she frantically pulled down the zipper of his slacks.

Evan was just as eager. It was as if she had awakened a spark inside him that had been dormant for a while, but it was a raging fire tonight.

He undid the belt of her robe and ripped the panels

open before lifting her and lowering her back onto his desk. As he did, the folders and stacks of papers he had been meticulously examining only minutes earlier all tumbled to the study floor in a raining flutter like New Year's Eve confetti. He shoved her nightgown up her calves, then her thighs, and finally to her waist. As he did it, she wrenched her arms out of the robe sleeves and tore the straps of her nightgown off her shoulders, eagerly baring her breasts to him.

He stood between her legs and cradled one of her breasts, toying with the dark, hardened nipple before hungrily kissing her again. Leila wrapped her legs around his waist and pulled him close as their tongues danced, feeling his erection press against the crotch of her panties. She pressed her breast into his hand. He raised his other hand to her chin and slowly ran his thumb over her bottom lip, and she took it into her mouth. She sucked on his finger before biting down on it hard.

"Oww," he said, tugging his hand back. "What was that about?"

"Punishment for making me wait so long to have you," she whispered saucily before kissing him again, flicking her tongue along the rim of his mouth.

Leila was not only flooded with carnal delight at having her man back in her arms, but also memories. This moment reminded her of when her love affair with Evan began, when he was still trapped in an empty, name-only marriage to Charisse and she was recovering from the heartbreak of failed marriage and impending divorce from Bradley, when Evan was her boss and she was his assistant at Murdoch Conglomerated. They would wait until after most of the twelfth floor had cleared out for the day and make love on his office sofa or his conference table or his desk. She'd try futilely to stifle her moans and shouts, but ended up yelling out his name despite her best efforts. But it wasn't just those nightly trysts that she had longed for but the love and reassurance she felt when she was with him. They had sought solace in each other's arms and found strength in each other's embrace. Her recollections of those clandestine nights would never fade.

"I've missed you, baby," she now whispered against his lips as he shifted the crotch of her panties aside.

He rubbed her between her legs, making her grow wet. She closed her eyes, threw back her head, and groaned. He massaged her clit with slow, steady strokes, and she urged him onward by leaning back and arching her hips. He then pulled his hand away, and her eyes flashed open.

"I missed you, too," he said as he lowered the waist-band of his boxer briefs. He pulled out his manhood, cen-tered himself between her legs, and entered her with one swift thrust that made her shout out in the cavernous study.

Leila unwound her arms from around his neck and grabbed the edge of the mahogany desk to brace herself as he plunged into her over and over again. He steadied her by holding her ass and her hips. As the rhythm of their lovemaking increased, Evan's grunts grew more guttural and her tortured moans turned into yells. After a few min-utes, she couldn't match the tempo anymore. She couldn't brace herself so she fell back against the desk and let him take over. He continued at the same fervent pace, un-heeded.

"Oh, God! Oh, God!" she yelled as the tremors over-took her. Her back arched. Her legs tightened around him before going slack.

He shouted out her name and collapsed on her a minute later, and she cradled him close, staring at the coffered ceiling with a contented smile on her face.

Just then she heard Angelica wail on the monitor, and she sighed.

"Sounds like somebody's awake," she said, patting Evan on the back. "I have to head back upstairs to get her."

He raised his head and pushed himself off of her. "I can help."

"Are you sure?" she asked, pulling the straps of her nightgown back on.

He nodded and raised his pants back to his waist. "The work will still be here tomorrow. I can head to bed."

She leaned forward and kissed him. "It's good to have you back, baby," she whispered.

He smiled. "It's good to be back."

Chapter 17

Paulette

"Happy birthday to you! Happy birthday to you!" they all sang, filling the living room with their shouts. "Happy birthday to Nathan! Happy birthday to you!"

"Now blow out the candle, honey," Paulette cooed as the room fell silent with the exception of a few toots from noisemakers.

Paulette stood on one side of her son. Antonio stood on the other, holding up his cell phone and making a video of the joyous occasion. They were surrounded by both friends and family who were sprawled on the living room sofa and loveseat. A few stood near the windows.

"Go on! Blow out the candle," Paulette urged again.

Nathan turned in his high chair and stared at his mother blankly.

"Okay, Mommy will help you." She then leaned forward, holding back her long hair over one shoulder. She blew out the solitary candle on the cake, making all those in the room break into applause.

Not to be outdone, Nathan plunged face-first into his toy train birthday cake. Everyone in the room burst into laughter. He gave a triumphant grin that his father promptly caught on camera.

Reina rushed across the living room with napkins in hand. "Oh, poor baby! Just look at this mess!"

"Babies make messes," Miss Claudia said, stepping forward and wiping gobs of icing and cake from Nathan's face, chest, and hands with a paper towel. "He'll survive."

The gesture and her words stopped Reina in her tracks. The older woman drew herself up to her full height and glared at Miss Claudia. Paulette stood back, hiding her smile, amused for once to not be the one battling it out with Reina.

"Well, where I come from we don't let babies roll around getting filthy like hogs in a pen," Reina snapped.

"And where I come from, we don't, either," Miss Claudia replied, cocking an eyebrow at Reina, not looking remotely intimidated, "which is why I'm gonna take this beautiful baby upstairs to wash up and change his clothes." She paused to turn and look at Paulette. "That is, if it's okay with you."

Paulette nodded. "It's perfectly fine, Miss Claudia. Go right ahead."

With that, Miss Claudia undid the straps on Nathan's high chair. "Let's get you cleaned up, honey," she said before kissing his plump cheek and ushering him out the living room and toward the stairs.

"Humph," Reina breathed through her flared nostrils while dropping her hands to her wide hips. Her eyes followed Nathan and Miss Claudia as the duo climbed the stairs to the second floor. "So just who is the mother around here, I ask you!"

"Mama," Antonio whispered in a beseeching voice as he removed the party hat from his head, "come on. Don't start this today!"

"No, Tony, the way that woman is acting, you'd think

that she was Nate's mother. Not this one over here!" She pointed at Paulette with a derisive sneer. "You better watch out—or that woman is going to take over."

"Jealousy doesn't become you, Reina," Paulette said with a chuckle as she removed what was left of Nathan's cake from his plastic tray.

Luckily, she had another cake waiting in the kitchen for the rest of the partygoers to sample.

"Oh, it's funny now!" Reina shouted, making Antonio groan. "But it won't be funny when that boy starts calling her 'mama'!"

Paulette headed to the kitchen, ignoring Reina's baiting.

She didn't care what Reina said—she liked Miss Claudia, and Nathan liked her, too. Paulette no longer felt like she was on the verge of going crazy from being stuck at home with the baby all day. She now got a few coveted hours of alone time per week to center herself. She could work out at the gym or go shopping for a few hours unhindered by a wailing infant, a diaper bag, and a stroller. She would return home to a babbling baby and a nanny who had already made lunch and cleaned the living room and kitchen.

Paulette's good mood and new outlook had done wonders for her and Antonio's marriage. They were intimate at least three times a week now—something that Antonio definitely loved.

Miss Claudia was a godsend! Paulette could understand why someone like Reina would be easily intimidated by her, but Miss Claudia was here to stay. She didn't care what Reina said.

Paulette lowered the cake plate into the sink and then headed to the counter where an identical cake sat, waiting to be sliced.

"Hey, sis, where should I put this?" Terrence asked as he poked his head through the doorway.

"Put what?"

"This!" He held up the platter covered with the cupcakes that Reina had brought to the party.

Paulette shook her head. "I told her she didn't have to bring those. I had it covered."

"Yeah, I thought so, too, but your mother-in-law cornered me while Tony was doing something else, I guess. I got *explicit* instructions from her to give this to you and make sure everyone at the party got at least one. She said she didn't care that you already had a cake."

Paulette closed her eyes. Reina just would not let up, but Paulette refused to let anything dampen her mood today.

"Thanks, Terry. You can sit it down over there." She inclined her head in direction of the cluttered kitchen table.

"No prob." Terrence elbowed aside a jar of jelly beans and stack of plastic cups so that he could set down the platter while she opened a nearby drawer and removed a knife to cut the birthday cake.

"Can you grab some plates for me, too, Terry? They're in the cabinet by the window."

He nodded before reaching up to open the cabinet and pull out a stack of ceramic plates.

"I can't believe Little Nate is already one year old!" Terrence mused as he walked toward her and set the plates on the counter at her elbow. "It seems like he was born just yesterday. Time went by so fast."

Paulette smiled wistfully. "If you feel like it went fast for you, imagine how it feels for me. I remember giving birth to him like it happened just yesterday! Now he's already toddling around the living room. It's only been a year, but I can't imagine my life without him. I love him so much!"

"I know you do." He leaned on the counter and watched as she began to cut into the cake and place a slice on each plate. "I see you and Tony with Little Nate and it makes me think about having kids with C. J. someday . . . something I never would've considered a couple of years ago."

Paulette paused midway in licking blue icing off her thumb.

"I've started imagining myself pushing a stroller and changing diapers and it doesn't . . . it doesn't scare me anymore, you know," he confided, reaching for one of the cake plates and a fork. "I never really wanted to be a dad because I didn't think it was me . . . that I could handle that type of thing. But I can see it with her. It doesn't seem so scary anymore."

Paulette hesitated. She didn't want to broach the topic of Terrence's engagement, especially because she believed in her heart that her brother was making a big mistake by marrying this girl. She didn't want to start a fight with her brother, either, which she knew would happen if she told him how she really felt. Today was her son's first birthday party. This was not the time for such a weighty discussion. But then Paulette considered that she rarely if ever had time alone with Terrence anymore. Now was probably as good a time as any to talk to him. And maybe he wouldn't be as hostile to her advice as she suspected. Maybe he'd realize she was coming from a good place.

"Terry," she began, "are you really sure you're . . . you're ready for . . . all of this?"

He chuckled as he shoved a piece of cake into his mouth. "Well, maybe not completely, but we're not talking about having kids tomorrow," he said between chews. "We've got time."

"No, I mean . . . I mean do you *really* think you're ready to get married?"

He lowered the fork from his mouth. "I hope so, since we're supposed to do that shit in four weeks!"

Paulette set aside the knife she held. Terrence liked to joke and be casual about everything, but she wouldn't let his easygoing attitude make her shy away from telling him the truth. Not today. She turned to face her brother.

"Look, Terry," she said, placing a soothing hand on his forearm, "all I want is for you to be happy. I want you to find the right person and settle down someday. But . . ." Her words drifted off.

"But *what?*" he asked, furrowing his brows.

"I just . . . I just don't think this is the right time for . . . for you to get married."

The kitchen fell silent. The furrow only deepened in Terrence's brow.

"Why don't you think it's the right time for me to get married?"

"Because you've only known C. J. for about a year—and you guys have already broken up once!"

He shrugged. "*So what?* People break up then get back together. Plenty of couples do it. It doesn't mean a damn thing!"

"Yes, it does mean something! It means that you guys could just as easily break up again a few months from now, but by then, you'll be legally married and financially shackled to this girl! I mean . . . are you even making her sign a prenup?"

His face twisted as he snatched his arm out of her grasp. "Why in the hell would I make her sign a prenup?"

"Because it would be irresponsible not to! Especially when you're worth millions of dollars."

"*Irresponsible?*" He cocked an eyebrow. "Did you make Tony sign one?"

"No . . . but Tony didn't lie to me like she lied to you."

"She never lied to me!" he boomed.

Paulette immediately brought a finger to her lips and made a shushing motion.

"No! Hell no! Don't try to quiet me down when you're

lying about my girl like that! This shit is out of line, Paulette!"

"You know damn well that I'm not lying! She didn't tell you when she first met you that she wrote all those stories about Evan or the family company."

"Because none of that shit mattered!"

"She didn't tell you about that day she lied to try to interview you at the hospital after your accident! How can you just shrug that off? How do you know she's being totally honest with you now? Just be smart about this! That's all I'm saying!"

"I don't think you're one to give relationship advice, okay? And you sure as hell don't have any room to talk about honesty! Don't project your fucked up marriage shit onto my relationship with C. J., okay?"

She flinched. Terrence knew about the trials and tribulations she and Antonio had endured in their marriage, how they had come close to the edge more than once.

"Have you always been honest with your husband?" he charged, dropping his cake plate into her farm sink with a clatter. "Has he always been straight up with you? Hell, no! So don't go lecturing people about telling the truth, all right, Miss Perfect?"

She slowly shook her head. "Dammit, I'm only trying to help, Terry! I'm just trying to save you from heartbreak, but you're too stupid and pigheaded to see that!"

"Yeah, well, I don't need your help or your advice! And if you really feel the way about me getting married, you don't have to show up to the fucking wedding! Stay your ass at home!"

"*What* is happening in here?" Evan called out.

Terrence and Paulette turned to the kitchen entryway to find Evan staring at them, looking aghast.

"What is going on? We're at a kid's birthday party and

you two are cussing each other out at the top of your lungs!" he said in a harsh whisper as he walked toward them, looking every bit like the overbearing older brother from their childhood. "Stop it right now! The both of you! This isn't the time or the place."

"Don't worry. I was just leaving," Terrence said as he shoved past her and stomped out of the kitchen.

"What the hell was that?" Evan asked, and Paulette gritted her teeth, too frustrated to answer him.

Chapter 18

Leila

"What do you mean Paulette isn't coming to Terry's wedding? *Why?*" Leila asked as Evan drove their Range Rover from Paulette's house.

Isabel was in the backseat, engrossed with the pages of her book and listening to music through her earbuds, ignoring her mother and stepfather. Baby Angelica was slumbering contentedly in her car seat beside her.

"She and Terrence had a big blow-up before he stormed out of Little Nate's birthday party," he explained as he pulled onto the main road leading to Murdoch Mansion. "I have no idea what it was about. I couldn't get a straight answer out of her. I just know she's not coming to the wedding now."

Leila gnawed the inside of her mouth.

Oh, hell, she thought as she gazed out the windshield. Had Paulette finally divulged to Terrence how she really felt about his fiancée?

I hope not!

"What's with that look? Do *you* know what they were fighting about?"

"N-no," Leila lied, "why . . . why do you think I would know?"

Evan eyed his wife as he drove. "Lee, baby, tell me the truth. Do you know what they were fighting about?"

She loudly groused and leaned her head back against the leather headrest. "Not exactly. But I know that . . . that Paulette doesn't want Terry to marry C. J. She thinks he can do better. She doesn't trust her."

"*What?* She doesn't trust her?" Evan cried as they turned onto their driveway. "Why doesn't she trust her?"

"I don't know, honey. You know your sister! She has her own logic that you can't always follow."

He slowly shook his head. "I just don't get why she would do this now!"

"What do you mean?"

"I mean I could be going away for a long time, Lee," he whispered as he drew to a stop in front of the stone steps leading up to the mansion. He glanced up at the rearview mirror to check to see if Isabel was listening. She wasn't. She was still reading her book. "If I'm going to be in jail for twenty years, I'd at least like to go in knowing my brother and sister are on speaking terms."

She placed a hand on his knee and gave it a squeeze. "It'll be all right, baby."

She then watched as Evan shifted the car into park and removed his key from the ignition. His face clouded over as he stared down at the steering wheel. "Sure, it will," he said, though he didn't look very convinced.

A minute later, the entire family stepped through the mansion's double doors. Angelica was nestled on her mother's shoulder. Isabel beelined for the center staircase.

"If I hurry I can catch the last twenty minutes of my show," she said over her shoulder. "See you guys later."

Evan frowned. "What show?"

"Who knows!" Leila said with a shrug. "Okay, I'll check in with you before bedtime, honey," she called to her daughter's receding back as Isabel took the stairs two at a time. Leila then turned back to Evan. "I was just going to put Angie down in the nursery if you wanted to hang out for a bit. Maybe grab a glass of wine and de-stress."

"That sounds good, baby. But give me an hour, okay? I need to get something done in my office, then I'll head up-stairs."

She nodded as Evan walked across the foyer to the east wing with his head bowed and his brow wrinkled, like he was muddling something over.

He's still worried about Terry and Paulette, she thought, which is the last thing he needed to concern himself with right now.

It irritated her that Paulette would cause this last-minute drama, but she should've expected as much from her sister-in-law. In the last few years, Paulette attracted drama like a magnet. Unfortunately, it seemed to have a domino effect on her siblings. Evan was usually the one to intercede in situations like this, but Leila figured it would probably be better for her to take over this one.

"Ev!" she called out to him, making him pause midstride. "Really, honey, don't worry, because everything's gonna be okay. I'll . . . I'll make sure of it."

He nodded absently. "See you in an hour. Keep the mer-lot waiting for me." He then pushed open his study door and shut it.

Leila turned back toward the center staircase and climbed the stairs, holding her sleeping baby in her arms. When she turned to her right to head to the west wing, she halted. Michael was standing a few feet in front of her, casually leaning against the cream-colored wall.

"What's Evan worried about?" he asked, cocking his thumb into the pockets of jeans that were so tight she could almost tell whether he was circumcised.

"Do you do anything besides skulking and eavesdropping?" she snapped, then walked past him toward the nursery. "Doesn't Ida have some errand for you to run?"

He chuckled as he trailed behind her. "No, she's busy getting a mani-pedi in D.C. right now, but this morning she sent me to Nordstrom's to get her more panty hose."

"Well, there you go," she murmured as she continued walking. When she realized he was still trailing behind her, she sucked her teeth in irritation. "Please stop following me."

"Or what?"

"Or I'll tell my husband everything that you've said and done. And trust me, he'll make sure that you get tossed out of here on your ass."

She drew to a stop near the nursery's entrance, and he halted beside her.

"Let's be real, Leila. If you were going to tell Evan all that, you would've done it by now." He leaned against the door frame. "But you haven't—which says something."

"Yeah, it says that he has enough on his plate without having to worry about you—or your pitiful attempts to seduce me."

Michael laughed. "Oh, I'm pitiful, am I?"

"Yes, you are! You may have some game with the senior citizens, but you aren't as appealing to women below the age of sixty. Sorry to disappoint you!"

"Believe me, sweetheart, if you decide to pass this up, *you're* the one who's gonna be disappointed."

"I think I'll survive," she said dryly before stepping into the nursery and shutting the door behind her, leaving him alone in the corridor.

* * *

"Thank you for coming today," Leila said as she squeezed a slice of lemon into her water glass and took a sip.

C. J. shrugged. "No problem!"

She and C. J. sat at a table toward the back of the restaurant, in a secluded spot where Leila hoped they wouldn't attract much attention from the other patrons or the waitstaff if they raised their voices.

Though I really hope that doesn't happen, Leila thought as her eyes drifted to the restaurant's glass front door. She expected the third attendee of today's lunch to step through the doorway at any moment, and once she did, Leila knew the proverbial sparks would fly.

She had orchestrated this lunch with C. J. and Paulette after Terrence outright refused to attend himself, even when Leila tried for a good hour to convince him. He said he didn't have anything else to say to his sister until *she* apologized for what she had said about C. J.

Thankfully, C. J. wasn't as stubborn as her fiancé. She had agreed to meet with Paulette on the condition that the conversation remain civil.

"I'm not gonna be bullied again by her, Leila," C. J. had warned her over the phone. "If the conversation goes left, I'm leaving!"

Leila hoped it wouldn't come to that.

"I'm willing to try to help, though I'm not sure if I really can," C. J. now said as she shook out her dinner napkin and tossed it onto her lap. "This whole conflict seems to be between Terry and Paulette—not Paulette and me."

"It's between Terry and Paulette—but the crux of this whole blow-up is about *you*, C. J. You know that."

C. J. lowered her eyes to the white linen tablecloth and nodded grudgingly.

"Plus, Terry is refusing to talk to Paulette."

C. J. nodded again. "Yeah, he's dug his heels in with

this one. I've tried to get him to cave a little, but he won't listen to me. He told me not to bother defending her, that she wasn't worth it."

Leila's shoulders sank.

"I didn't even tell him that I was coming here today to meet her for lunch. I didn't know how he would respond. I made up a lie about meeting friends."

Leila anxiously gnawed her bottom lip. "I had to lie, too."

"Lie about what?"

"I . . . I didn't tell Paulette you would be here today."

C. J.'s mouth fell open.

"She thinks she and I are the only ones meeting up for lunch."

"What? *Are you serious?* You mean she doesn't even know I'm here? But you told me—"

"I know! I know! And I'm sorry for doing this. But I knew if I told you the truth, you wouldn't do it. You'd think we were ambushing her."

"Because we are!"

"And if I told Paulette the real reason for today's meeting, I knew she wouldn't show up, either. She . . . she kind of blames you for all of this."

"But that's ridiculous! I didn't do anything wrong!"

Leila closed her eyes. "*I* know that. *You* know that. And I'm hoping that today's meeting will finally make Paulette realize that, too. She's being stubborn and obnoxious and only making—"

"What's this about me being stubborn and obnoxious?" Paulette asked.

Leila's eyes flashed open. She gazed up at her sister-in-law, who was now fixing her with a cold glare over the top of her Chloe sunglasses.

"Oh," Leila said, anxiously shifting in her chair. "I didn't . . . I didn't know you were here."

"Yeah, I could tell," Paulette said dryly. "So it looks like we're not alone for our little girls' date." She gave a contemptuous glance at C. J. "You're just full of surprises today, aren't you, Lee?"

C. J. didn't comment but only looked at Leila, letting her take the lead on this one.

You created this mess, the look said. *You've got to fix it!*

"Paulette, honey, please . . . just have a seat," Leila urged.

Paulette didn't budge, making Leila let out a huff.

"Come on, girl! It's just lunch! You came all this way. You might as well eat a salad and hear us out. You can be pissed at me later!"

Finally, ever so slowly, Paulette pulled out one of the chairs at their table. She tossed her crocodile clutch near her bread plate before flopping back into her chair.

"Fine," she said succinctly before yanking off her sunglasses and glowering across the table at Leila and C. J. "I'll stay."

Thank God, Leila thought. At least she'd won that skirmish, but she knew that soon the real battle would begin.

The waiter appeared seconds later to refill their water glasses and to take their orders. After he walked away, their table quieted again. The tension between the women returned.

"So you said you wanted to talk," Paulette said, breaking the strained silence. "So talk!"

Leila took a deep breath. *Here it goes.*

"Look, I didn't want to get involved in this, but—"

"But you did anyway," Paulette finished for her, adjusting the knife and fork near her plate.

"I did it for *Evan's* sake," Leila quickly clarified, "and for your family's sake. I've known you guys for *years*, Paulette, and it's painful to watch you fight like this. This is such an important time. Evan is going through a lot, and we don't know how much time we all still have together as a family! Do you really want to waste that time bickering?"

Paulette's hard visage softened.

"I mean . . . won't it hurt not to go to your brother's wedding?" Leila persisted.

"Of course it will! But I didn't choose not to go to his wedding. Terry *rescinded* my invitation, and he did it because he couldn't stand to hear the truth!"

"The truth about what?" Leila asked.

"The truth about *her*," Paulette said, fluttering her fingers in C. J.'s direction, making the other woman narrow her eyes.

"If you're going to talk about me, can you at least address me like I'm sitting at the table with the rest of you," C. J. said.

"Fine. I will!" They watched as Paulette pivoted in her chair to look squarely at C. J. "I reminded Terry of all the stuff he'd conveniently forgotten—like the fact that *you lied* to him when you first met. You didn't tell him that you sneaked into the hospital that day to interview him. You didn't tell him that—"

"Oh, my God!" C. J. threw back her head and slammed her hands on the table. "That was over *a year ago!* He confronted me about it. I apologized for not being honest with him. We sorted it out and put it behind us! If he can forgive me, then why can't you?"

"Because my brother is more forgiving than I ever will be!"

"Obviously!" C. J. snapped back.

Leila looked uneasily between the two women. They were getting louder. The other restaurant patrons were now turning in their chairs and looking in their direction. This was going left—fast.

"Let me tell you something, C. J. If Tony ever broke my

heart the way you broke Terry's, I would've never, *ever* forgiven him! I can't believe you would just . . . just dump my brother and waltz back to your ex like—"

"I didn't 'waltz back' to my ex! That's not how it happened!"

"But you started dating him again, didn't you?"

"Yes, I did—and Terry started dating again, too, while we were broken up. What's your point?"

"My point is that you could've driven my brother into another depression with your . . . your petty selfishness!"

"*Selfishness?*" C. J. squeaked. "Selfishness?"

"You could've ruined him. But he made it through despite how badly you treated him—and just when he started to bounce back, you *swooped* in to mess with his head all over again! He never had a chance!"

"Are you serious? Terry *asked* me to take him back! Because he loves me and I love him. We didn't—"

"But I'll be damned," Paulette continued as if she hadn't heard her, "if I quietly sit by and let you—"

"Stop!" Leila shouted, holding up her hands again. She just couldn't take any more of this bickering back and forth. "Ladies, just . . . just stop, please . . . before we get kicked out of the restaurant."

Both women immediately fell silent. C. J. looked supremely pissed and on the verge of getting up and walking away from the table. Paulette looked smugly proud of herself.

"Look, I didn't bring you guys here for this. I brought you here to resolve your issues—not to make it worse."

"I get that, Leila, and I appreciate it . . . but it looks like it's a lost cause," C. J. said, removing her napkin from her lap and dropping it to the tablecloth.

Paulette snorted before taking a sip from her water glass. "I couldn't agree more."

Leila watched helplessly as C. J. shoved her chair back from the table and rose to her feet.

"Like I said before, I love Terry and he knows that," C. J. argued. "My feelings for him are real, and I don't have to prove a goddamn thing to you, Paulette . . . to *any* of you, for that matter!"

"Wait, don't go! Not yet!" Leila pled. "We know how you feel about Terry. We know you love him!"

"No, *we* don't," Paulette sneered.

"Dammit," Leila shouted, finally losing her cool, "can you stop being a bitch just for one second? You're acting like a child, and it's going to—"

"*I'm acting like a child?*" Paulette raised brows and pointed at her chest. "I'm acting like a child because I want to protect my family from yet another user . . . from yet another *liar* who could ruin my brother's life?

"Remember how we let Dante into the family with open arms? Huh? Remember . . . remember how we . . . we didn't ask any questions and just accepted him? And what did that get us?" she barked, making both Leila and C. J. go still. "Remember Marques and what he did to me . . . what he did to my marriage, to my entire life? I will never forget that shit!" Her voice cracked. Tears welled in her eyes. "I'm not going to be that stupid, naïve girl anymore! I'm not letting it happen again!"

Paulette lowered her head and began to weep. She grabbed her dinner napkin and wiped her eyes, smearing her mascara as she sobbed.

C. J. stood awkwardly by her chair, twisting the strap of her satchel. Leila reached across the table and squeezed Paulette's hand.

"Honey, what they did to you . . . what they did to *all of us* was wrong. There's no denying that! But C. J. isn't Dante. She isn't Marques, either. You're judging her based on what other people have done, and it's not fair."

Paulette finally raised her reddened eyes to look at Leila.

"She's a good person, and Terry loves her. He *loves* her! I mean . . . let's be honest. Did you ever think something like this would happen? I would have bet hell would freeze over first before Terrence Murdoch would want to marry someone."

Despite her tears, Paulette let out a burst of laughter. She wiped her runny nose.

"And he wants to start a life with her. He wants his brother and his sister to stand by him and support him when he does it. Can you do that? Can you try to make this right?"

Paulette pursed her lips. Ever so slowly, she nodded. "Okay," she whispered.

"Really? You mean it?"

Paulette nodded again.

Leila then turned to C. J.

"I know she's been the biggest bitch to you, but—"

"Hey!" Paulette cried, looking annoyed.

"Paulette, it's true! You *have* been the biggest bitch and, frankly, she may not want to forgive you and start all over again, but . . ." Leila looked up at C. J. "I hope she does."

C. J. chuckled before shaking her head ruefully. "If you want to meet a real bitch, I should introduce you to my brother, Victor. He's a lot scarier than this one," she said, casting a glance at Paulette. "But yeah, I'm willing to start fresh if everyone else is. I'll let bygones be bygones." She then sat down in her chair and slid back up to the table.

"Good. That's so good," Leila said, grinning. "And you'll talk to Terry so that Paulette can come to the wedding?"

C. J. nodded. "I'll let him know we're cool now. He may still be a little mad but . . . I'll talk to him for the next week. And if talking doesn't work, I'll try . . . something else."

"*Something else?*" Paulette frowned. "What . . . what does that mean?"

C. J. smirked as she placed her dinner napkin on her lap again. "What do you think it means?"

Paulette closed her eyes and cringed. "Oh, God!" she groaned as the waiter arrived at the table with their dishes. "I can't believe I walked into that one. That reminds me of the time I stumbled in on Terry and one of his girlfriends by the pool house back in the late nineties! I was so mortified!"

C. J. and Leila giggled and began to dig into their salads.

"*You ran in on him?* Terry never told me that story!" C. J. said.

"I don't know why. He thought it was hilarious at the time! Meanwhile, I'm nine years old and I had no idea what the hell was going on. I yelled at him, 'Stop it, Terry! Dad said we're not supposed to wrestle by the pool. You're gonna get in trouble!' "

C. J. threw back her head and laughed at that one.

Leila gazed at the two women who had been at each other's throats only minutes ago and marveled at how they were now joking with each other. She sighed contently and patted herself on the back for this one.

Chapter 19

Dante

Dante grunted, pushed himself up onto his elbows, then flopped onto his back on the mattress. He bounced on the bedsprings and closed his eyes as his heartbeat slowly returned to its regular pace.

"Damn, that was a good one," he exhaled as he stared at the ceiling, watching the ceiling fan go around and around. Staring at the blades was almost mesmerizing and surprisingly calming. His eyelids grew heavier and heavier. His breathing deepened.

"Don't nod off," Charisse ordered, making him open his eyes again. He had just realized he had been snoring. "I might want a second round in a couple of minutes."

He laughed. "I wasn't nodding off. Just catching my breath. Don't worry about me, sweetheart."

"Uh-huh," she murmured, looking incredulous. She then ruffled her blond hair—hair he had looped through his fingers and pulled like the reins of a horse only minutes earlier, making the skin along her hairline turn stark white.

Charisse had cried out in pain when he did it, but he

didn't stop. He knew Charisse liked it rough; she always had. It got her wetter faster than anything else.

They had been hooking up almost daily for the past few weeks, and it was just as hot and heavy as old times. He had forgotten how freaky she could be, how kinks that seemed to intimidate other women were worth at least one try when it came to Charisse. He always got the distinct feeling that her sexual adventurousness wasn't just because she was open-minded. Something dark lurked behind the mask of a pristine, rich blonde. But he never asked about it. He wasn't her shrink and, frankly, he didn't care why she liked to be slapped or let him wrap his hands around her throat during sex. As long as *he* was having a good time, what did it matter?

Charisse flipped onto her back beside him and reached for the pack of cigarettes and the lighter sitting on his night table.

"Smoking helps to bring me down after a bout like that," she said before shoving one of the cigarettes into her mouth. "The one habit I still can't kick."

Dante watched as she smoked. He could use something to take the edge off, too. The sex high had already begun to fade. Now he needed another. He slid across his bed and rose to his feet. He walked across the room naked, heading to the bathroom.

"Where are you going?" she shouted to him before taking another drag from her cigarette and shooting a plume of smoke into the air.

"Don't worry about it. I'll be right back," he called over his shoulder. He then shut the door behind him.

Dante slipped off his condom, knotted it, and tossed it into a nearby trash can. He peed, opened his medicine cabinet, and grabbed a bottle of Oxy. He shook two into his palm, then tossed them into his mouth, swallowing them without water. He looked again at the bottle and shook another into his hand. He had just tossed the third into his mouth when the bathroom door swung open. He barely managed to swallow the pill without choking.

"Fuck!" he yelled as he angrily turned toward Charisse, who stood in the doorway. "Do you knock?"

She laughed. "Since when did you get so prissy?"

He didn't answer her but instead closed the lid on his pill bottle, placed the bottle on the cabinet shelf, and slammed the medicine cabinet closed.

"What was that?" she asked, leaning against the door frame. "What were you taking?"

"None of your goddamn business!"

"It definitely wasn't just Motrin from the way you're acting." She eyed him silently for several seconds, looking him up and down. "What are you on?"

"What?"

She grinned. "An addict knows another addict, Dante. What are you on?"

"I don't know what the fuck you're talking about!"

"Yes, you do!" She tilted her head and raised her brows. "Xanax? Adderall? *Demerol?*"

He didn't answer her. He started to shove his way past her and out of the bathroom just as she reached around him and yanked the medicine cabinet door open. She snatched the bottle off the shelf.

"OxyContin!" she yelled gleefully, reading the label. Her blue eyes went wide. "So *that's* your drug of choice!"

"Give it back," he ordered as he grabbed her forearm and wrenched the bottle out of her hands, "or I'll snap your arm in two. I will fucking kill you!"

"Oh, no, you won't!" she chided playfully. She puckered her plump lips. "You're all bluster, honey. You don't fool me. But there's no need to be so defensive."

"Fuck you," he spat as he stomped back into his bedroom.

"You just did . . . six ways from Sunday! *Remember?*"

"Yeah, I remember. And now you can get the fuck out!"

He slammed the bottle on his night table, torn between fury and humiliation at her discovery. How dare she invade his space and his privacy like that! Who did she think she was? He never should have hooked up with her again. It was a mistake, a huge mistake!

Despite his obvious fury, she didn't budge.

"I said *get out!*" he yelled again. He pointed toward the door, making her loudly sigh.

"I told you . . . don't be so defensive. Believe me, I don't have room to judge. I've been in rehab twice. I'll be an addict for the rest of my life! That's the fun little takeaway they teach you in counseling."

At that, he stilled.

"So you see . . . we're just alike." She slowly walked across the bedroom toward him before looping her arms around his neck and kissing him. He allowed her to do it, wrestling her tongue with his own. She dragged his bottom lip between her teeth and bit down, making him wince and harden at the same time. She pulled her head back to gaze up at him.

"I get you, Dante. Better than I get anybody else—even my own husband."

"*Ex*-husband," he corrected. "Remember . . . you aren't a Murdoch anymore."

"Yeah, well, I forget that on occasion. But then I'm reminded that he's married to that bitch now. I'm old news. I see him walk around with her on his arm around town and I want to scratch her eyes out." She ran a finger over Dante's bottom lip. "But thanks to you, I won't have to see them together much longer, will I?"

"What do you mean?"

"What do you think I mean? You're the one who made up the story about him shooting you! Now Evan could go away for a long, *long* time." She chuckled. "Serves him right!"

"I told you, I didn't make it up."

She gave him that knowing look again, and he couldn't hold up his façade any longer. He couldn't help but smile.

"Come on," she said, nudging him. "Who really shot you, Dante?"

He hesitated for a second longer, wondering if he should divulge the truth to Charisse of all people. But she was right: they were a lot alike. Most would be appalled by what he was doing to Evan, but not someone like her. She despised Evan just as much as he did.

"Some bitch I fucked for a while. She was pissed when I moved on. Didn't take rejection well."

"So she shot you?" She chuckled. "Can't say I blame her. When you tossed me out, I wanted to shoot you, too! But how do you know she won't pop up again and ruin the case the prosecution's built against Evan?"

"Because she's dead," he answered bluntly. "She's not popping up anywhere."

"How do you know she's dead? Did *you* have anything to do with that?"

"What do you take me for, Charisse?" he asked with feigned innocence, making her eye him again.

"Well, it looks like you've covered all your bases. Let's hope for your sake you're a convincing liar on the stand ... that the jury will believe your account of what happened that night."

He barked out a laugh as he looped his arms around her waist. "I've never had a problem convincing people in the past. I've been a lawyer for fifteen years, Charisse. I know how to work a courtroom. Jurors are bigger dupes than most! Put on a good enough performance and they'll believe anything. Trust me, once I'm done with my testimony, Evan won't stand a chance."

"Aren't we full of ourselves!"

"I've got no reason not to be."

"Well, keep talking, big boy," she said as she wrapped her hand around his dick and began to stroke him. "I love a man with confidence."

"Is that all you love?" he asked as he reached for one of her breasts and began to fondle her nipple.

"Nope." She released him and pulled out of his grasp so she could flop back onto his bed. She leaned back and spread her legs wide and welcoming. "It's just one of many things. Maybe it's about time you remind me of the rest."

Dante couldn't resist her offer. He walked the remaining few feet and climbed on top of her to give her exactly what she asked for.

Chapter 20

Evan

Evan glanced up from his laptop when he heard a knock at the door. He knew instantly who was knocking. His wife was checking on him again. He chuckled and shook his head ruefully.

"I know I said I'd be upstairs a half hour ago, baby. I'm almost done," he called out to Leila as he typed. "Start running the bubble bath and I'll be upstairs by the time you climb in. I swear!"

The door slowly swung open.

"Well, well!" Aunt Ida cried with a smile as she leaned against the door jamb. "A hot bubble bath, huh? Someone has some fun planned for tonight!"

Evan stifled a groan.

His aunt was the last person he expected to see walking into his study. She usually spent most of her time sitting by their Olympic pool while her boy toy, Michael, swam laps, or she spent her days getting facials or shopping in downtown D.C. She rarely made it to this part of the mansion. She certainly hadn't visited Evan in his study before, but he supposed that was how Aunt Ida operated. She had rudely barged back into his life to supervise how he was handling the family company, so now she was barging into his office.

"Can I help you, Aunt Ida? Did you need anything?" he asked, forcing himself to be polite.

She didn't respond. Instead, she strolled toward one of the polished mahogany bookshelves on the other side of the room, scanning the titles on the leather spines of the many books. She removed one of the books and began to randomly flip pages.

"No," she finally answered, "I don't need anything. I just decided to see the old study." She returned the book to its shelf. "I remember when Daddy built it back in sixty-two. He modeled it after the study at Glen Dale mansion up the road—the one on the old Hughes plantation."

"I know which one you're talking about," Evan said, though he hadn't been aware of the connection.

"Our family used to be slaves on that planation. Did you know that?" she asked, picking up another book.

Evan slowly shook his head.

"House niggers, of course," she continued. "We didn't have the temperament for the fields, I guess. Anyway, from what I understand, my great-great-great grandmother was one of the house girls. She got knocked up by Master Murdoch Hughes. She had a son named John who the master doted on, even if he was a slave. He treated him like he was his own, making sure he had a trade he could use to earn his own money if he wanted to. When emancipation came, John used the money from ol' master to buy this very property. He built the first Murdoch homestead here . . . naming it after his daddy. My father built the second one, and of course George expanded and redecorated the place when he took over." She returned the book to its shelf and looked around her again. "I thought you would do the same, but it doesn't look like you made any changes in here."

"No, I pretty much left it as is," Evan answered as he watched her walk toward the other side of the room.

Evan wasn't fooled; he knew his aunt wasn't in his study to just give him a family history lesson or to see if he had changed the velvet curtains his father had installed in 1995. There was an ulterior motive for why she was here tonight. Unfortunately, he had no idea what it was—yet.

"But I'm of the opinion that sometimes changes need to be made," she said. "For instance, what do you plan to do to fix the mess Murdoch Conglomerated is in? I've been here for five months now and I've yet to see anything happen."

Bingo! There it is, Evan thought.

"Aunt Ida, the problems that Murdoch Conglomerated faces can't be changed overnight. We have an uphill battle that we're waging, but I and the other officers have a strategic plan that we're—"

"Don't give me some speech that you would give to your investors, honey! I don't have an MBA from Harvard, but I'm not some simp off the street, okay?"

Evan's jaw tightened. "I wasn't implying that—"

"As I see it," she began, speaking over him as she opened a cabinet a few feet away from his desk, revealing his liquor stash, "the fate of the family company is tied with yours. So you can do all the 'strategic planning' and hire all the consultants you want, but as long as *your* life is a mess, the family company stays a mess!" She removed a crystal tumbler from one of the shelves then the lid from one of his brandy decanters. *"Comprende?"*

"My life is not a mess."

"Could've fooled me!"

He forced himself to take a deep breath and count to ten. He was doing that a lot nowadays. "Look, if you're alluding to my criminal charges, I have no control over that," he began calmly. "All I can do is hire a strong team of defense lawyers to help—"

"No, that isn't all you can do! You can do *a lot* more!" She began to pour brandy into her glass, filling two thirds of it. "But you haven't. You're just letting that Dante fellow ruin your life, legacy, and livelihood." She smacked her teeth and whipped around to face him. "Boy, stop dancing around that man and stomp him like the cockroach that he is!"

"I'm not dancing around him—and I'm certainly not letting him do anything! I told you ... I'm fighting this with everything I've got!"

She walked toward one of the wingback chairs facing his desk. "You're fighting it with every *legal* means you have, but more than that may be called for in this situation, honey. It's certainly what your father would do!"

Evan rubbed his brows in frustration. He was so tired of hearing about how his father would handle this. Suddenly, everyone had become the authority on the great George Murdoch. The man had been blown up to almost mythical proportions since his death.

"You don't know what he would've done! You just assume that he—"

"I'm not *assuming* anything! I know! I was there."

"What are you talking about?"

"Have a drink and let me tell you another family story," she said before dropping into the chair. She shook her tumbler and nodded toward the opened doors of the liquor cabinet. "And you might wanna make it a double."

"I don't want a drink."

But he *did* want her to leave his office so that he could finish the last of his work and head upstairs. He glanced at the clock on his monitor. At this point, Leila was probably taking her bubble bath. If Aunt Ida kept talking, his goal would have to change from some sexual healing in their sunken tub to just getting upstairs before Leila drifted off to sleep. He had made a promise to her that, from now on, he would be there by the time she closed her eyes at night.

"Fine," Aunt Ida said, slouching back into her chair, "suit yourself! Hear the story sober, though I'm warning you . . . you probably want a little bit of liquor when I tell you this one."

"I'll survive," he deadpanned and continued to type on his laptop. "What's the story about anyway?"

"About how your father killed our brother."

Evan's eyes snapped up from his screen. He stared at his aunt, dumbfounded. "You're joking, right?"

"Do I look like I'm joking? Everyone thinks Theo died in a car crash, which he did. But they also think the car crash was an accident, which it wasn't. George caused it. I *know* he did!"

"Dad told me about that crash, Ida. It *was* an accident! He suffered some injuries in it, too. You can't just throw around allegations like that! If someone else heard you, they'd—"

"Oh, no one would care!" she drawled, waving off his warning with a flutter of French-tipped fingernails. "Theo's dead. George is dead. Life moves on! No one but me knows what really happened. I don't even think George was aware I knew the truth!"

"Why on earth would my father want to kill his brother?"

"Because he hated him," she answered plainly. "Well . . . I guess they hated each other. They always had since they were little boys! Our parents started it. Theo was the first-born. The chosen one. He was the one who was supposed to continue the family legacy. Mama and Daddy acted like the sun rose and set over Theo's hind parts! He must have thought so, too, because he was a shameless asshole to everybody. Always had his nose in the air. He used to pick on George when they were younger. He called George names, told him that he was weak . . . that he was stupid. Mama and Daddy ignored it. The bullying only made George work harder to prove himself. He did well in school and made top grades. He tried harder in sports and went all varsity. He got into Harvard. But all that drive . . . it changed him." She frowned. "George was never what you would call warm or sweet, but he was sensitive. He could even be kind sometimes, especially when we were little. He used to stand up for me when the kids picked on me at school: the portly high-yella rich girl with the buck teeth and four eyes."

Evan squinted. The only version of his father that he had seen most of his life was the shrewd businessman, philandering husband, and household dictator. He would've never described his dad as sensitive, let alone kind. Just the idea sounded so foreign to Evan that he started to wonder if Aunt Ida was talking about a different person.

"But over the years . . . over the years, George got tougher," she continued. "His wounds started to callus over and the soft part of George just . . . well, it just disappeared. He got nastier. Not on the outside," she quickly added before taking another drink from her glass. "He wasn't like Theo, who was meaner than a rattlesnake. But George was sneakier. He would smile in your face and lie through his teeth. He'd say anything to get what he wanted. But if you were smart, you knew never to cross him or he'd make you pay for it. He'd make you pay for it bad."

Now *that* was the George Murdoch Evan remembered!

"Look, I'll admit Dad wasn't perfect," Evan conceded. "I'll even accept that he may have hated his brother. But that doesn't mean that he murdered him!"

"Will you let me finish telling my story? You think I'm

lying, and I'm not! George killed him. I'm trying to explain to you *why* he did it."

Evan loudly grumbled. "Fine," he said, closing his laptop, knowing that any attempt to get more work done at this point was absolutely pointless. "Finish your story."

"Well, anyway . . . I think George was willing to put up with Theo for the sake of family—at least he was willing to do it for a while. Even after Daddy made Theo the head of the company, which was a mistake."

Evan had known that his now deceased uncle Theo had been the first CEO of Murdoch Conglomerated, but his tenure had only lasted two years thanks to his death.

"I knew George would've been a much better fit, but again . . . he wasn't first born. He wasn't Theo! Murdoch Conglomerated had a shaky start. It wasn't doing as well as Daddy had hoped, but he refused to ask Theo to step down. That made George angry, but he stayed. He worked in the shadows and continued to deal with all the crap Theo dished out—that is, until Angela came along."

At the mention of his mother's name, Evan started listening again.

"You may not believe it, but your daddy really did love that woman, Evan. Don't let how he treated her by the time you children came fool you! He adored her. She was sweet. She was beautiful. Angela Newberry could turn some heads, honey—even though she was as dark as bark!"

"My mom being dark-skinned is irrelevant to this conversation," Evan said, annoyed at having his beloved mother talked about that way.

"Well, it wasn't 'irrelevant' back then! Angela was pretty, but I don't think she really ever thought she was. That girl never had any real confidence! It worked to George's advantage, because he got a woman that was, quite frankly, a bit out of his league. But it worked to George's disadvantage when Theo set his sights on her. He was more handsome than George. He could even be charming when he wanted to be. Angela didn't stand a chance!"

Evan stilled.

"Oh, Theo didn't really want her. He only wanted her because George had her . . . because he was married to her. He couldn't stand for George to have something he didn't. So he went after her. George found out what they'd done and . . . well . . . he lost it. He—"

"Are you trying to tell me that my mother had an affair with my uncle?" Evan chuckled in exasperation and shoved himself up from his chair. "I'm sorry, but I'm not . . . I am *not* listening to any more of this. I'm going upstairs. Close the liquor cabinet and the door when you're done."

"You don't wanna hear the rest because I'm telling you the truth? Because I'm ruining the perfect image you have of your precious mama?"

"No, because I know you're full of shit!" He rushed toward her. "My mother would never, *ever* do that!"

Angela Murdoch had always been the saint to George's sinner, the angel to his devil. She endured her husband's philandering and verbal abuse silently with a stoic resolve that left Evan speechless to this day. How dare Aunt Ida speak ill of her now! The old woman was obviously drunk.

"In all the years that Dad cheated on Mom with countless women, she never once stepped out of her marriage! She stayed true to her wedding vows! She didn't—"

"But why didn't she cheat? Why didn't she ever try to get back at him? Why did she put up with his nonsense all those years? Just *think* about it, boy! Because she was ashamed of what she did!" she shouted. "Because George always reminded her of how she broke his heart and betrayed him—and how he'd forgiven her. He held it over her head like a sword all the years of their marriage. He wouldn't let her forget what she'd done!"

Evan fell silent.

"And he wouldn't let Theo forget it, either. I was there when they had their big fight. It was right here in this study," she said, pointing to the floor and looking around the room. Her eyes scanned the bookshelves and coffered ceiling. "Angela and I tried to pull them apart, but George just kept punching him and kicking him. That was the night he threatened to kill Theo. He screamed it like some crazy person. I thought he had just said it in a fit of anger. I didn't know he really meant it! But he did." She furrowed her brows. "He waited until almost two years later . . . when we thought the dust had settled. I thought he had forgiven Angela . . . forgiven Theo. But that was George's way, wasn't it? Wait until you got comfortable. Wait until you thought he had moved on, and then he'd pounce.

"It was Christmas. George was all smiles that night. He seemed like he was in good spirits. Theo got so drunk that he couldn't drive himself home, and George offered to do it. I watched them walk out together. I watched them from one of the foyer windows. Theo had his arm looped around George's neck as they were walking down the driveway. Then when they got near George's car, George's face changed. His smile disappeared. He had this . . . this look in his eyes. I watched him shove Theo in the car so rough that it looked like it hurt, and I just had this . . . this *feeling.*"

She lowered her eyes to gaze into her tumbler. A chill went down Evan's spine.

"I knew something was going to happen that night. So when I got the call the next morning that Theo had died in a car crash and George had survived, I wasn't surprised. I knew . . . I *knew* George did it on purpose. Theo's body was so beat up and bruised that the coroner asked if Theo had been in a fight that night before the crash. I can't prove it, but I think George gave Theo the worst beating of this life then crashed the car to make it look like it was all part of the accident. He killed his own brother without having to go to jail for it."

She took another drink, and the silence stretched in his study. All you could hear was the tick of the grandfather clock.

"With Theo gone, George became CEO of Murdoch Conglomerated. He never had to worry about Theo going after his wife again. George won the battle in the end."

Evan studied his aunt for several seconds before speaking again. "You don't sound too sad about what happened to Theo. My dad murdered his own brother, according to you."

"Of course, I was sad." She paused to down the rest of her drink then set down the empty glass on his desk. "But even I could admit it was for the best. No one wants to kill their brother, but Theo left George with no choice!"

"So what are you telling me? What was the point of that whole story? Are you saying I should kill my brother just like my father killed his?"

"Yes," she answered without hesitation. "Yes, that's *exactly* what I'm saying. Don't tell me you haven't thought about it."

"Of course I have! But taking a life isn't something I consider lightly—even if it's the life of a son of a bitch like Dante!"

She closed her eyes and shook her head. "Boy scouts like you make me so tired sometimes."

"Then you should go to bed," he muttered before turning back toward his study door. "I'll see you tomorrow, Ida."

"You think you're too good to do what needs to be done . . . to protect what's yours?" she called out to him as he neared the study's entrance, stopping him in his tracks. She pivoted in her chair to face him. "You think you're too noble to take the necessary steps? But sometimes to get things done, you do *all* that is necessary, Evan. Sometimes you're left with no other choice!"

"There's *always* another choice, Ida. Good night," he said as he turned back around and stepped into the hall, trying to shut her story and warning from his mind.

Chapter 21

C. J.

"Enough," Terrence said before snatching C. J.'s iPhone out of her hand.

C. J. blinked in astonishment at her now empty palm. She turned to her fiancé to find him tucking her cell into his suit pocket as they strolled across their condominium's parking lot.

"Stop playing, Terry! Give that back!" she whined, reaching for her phone, only to have him grab her hand and hold it. He shook his head and smiled.

"Babe, it's bad enough you were on that thing the whole damn time we were at dinner tonight and driving back to our place. It's ten o'clock! Who the hell are you emailing?"

"D-d-different people. It was ... it was all wedding related, though," she lied, hoping the excuse would work, but Terrence side-eyed her knowingly before stepping forward to open the building's glass door.

"No, it wasn't," he said as she stepped into the condominium's marble-tiled foyer and he walked in behind her.

"Okay, it was for a story, if you must know! But I've been trying to track down this source all week."

"C. J., I've got work I could be doing, too, but this is our time together. You don't see me answering press phone calls or checking my email, do you?"

"No, but Ralph has been on my ass all week for—"

"Ralph is *always* on your ass! You've been working there for damn near six months now and working pretty damn hard, I might add. He still keeps hammering at you! When are you going to accept that there's no pleasing him?"

C. J. pursed her lips as they walked toward the elevators at the end of the hall, deciding not to respond to that one.

The longer she stayed at the *Washington Daily*, the less enamored Terrence seemed with her job and her editor. He thought Ralph was too hard on her, and he hated the long hours she spent in the newsroom. He could see how Ralph's exacting standards had shaken her confidence, how it made her question whether she was even worthy of calling herself a real reporter.

She now watched as Terrence pressed the up elevator button. "You're too good for this shit, babe. Look, maybe . . . maybe you should consider . . . I don't know . . . going back to the *Chesterton Times*."

C. J. instantly shook her head. "No, Terry."

"I'm sure your editor would be more than happy to give you your old spot back!"

"That's not even possible! They've already hired another reporter for my old position, and I'm not going to give up on the metro desk at the *Daily*. Do you know how hard I've worked to get here? Almost my entire career! This is important to me!"

"I know it's important to you, but—"

He was stopped midsentence when she raised her hand

to his mouth, shushing his words. "I can handle it, baby. I'm tough."

He kissed her palm before lowering her hand from his mouth. "I know." He then handed her back her phone.

Just then the elevator doors opened and they boarded. He pressed the number eight, and C. J. turned to face him. She wrapped her arms around his waist and gazed into his eyes.

"Let's not talk about work anymore," she said as the elevator ascended floors. "We've got bigger things to worry about—like our wedding! I cannot believe that in *two* weeks we will be husband and wife."

"Getting cold feet?" he asked as he pulled her even closer.

"Nope. *You?*"

"Hell, no! I'm ready to get that ass on lockdown," he whispered before reaching down and cupping her bottom with both hands.

"Why, what a romantic way to refer to getting married!" she cried sarcastically, then laughed.

He lowered his mouth to hers for a soul-stirring kiss that made her dizzy, that made her moan. Just then, the elevator dinged, signifying they were now on their condominium floor. She whimpered when he pulled his lips away from hers.

"I wish these elevator rides were a lot longer!" she lamented.

"Don't worry." He gave her rear end a firm squeeze and then bestowed her mouth with another quick peck. "We'll continue this inside, Miss Aston. You won't be sorry for the wait."

She poked out her bottom lip, making him smile. The elevator doors opened a second later. When they did, C. J. winced at the ear-piercing scream that rocketed down the corridor and sliced through her ear canal.

They stepped off the elevator onto the eighth floor and turned the corner. When they did, they saw the source of the screaming: a redheaded woman standing near their front door, pacing back and forth, holding a wailing baby in her arms. The infant was writhing in its blanket, pumping its tiny fists. Its face was almost as red as the hair of the woman who held it. She looked disheveled, frazzled, and almost near tears herself.

"What in the hell . . ." C. J. whispered, staring at her.

"Terry!" the woman shouted, looking relieved when she saw him. She rushed down the hall toward them, bouncing the crying baby up and down as she did it. "You're finally home. I've been ringing your doorbell over and over again. I thought I'd have to wait for you all night!"

At that, C. J. squinted in confusion. *Waiting for him?*

"Terry, do you know her?" C. J. asked, pointing at the woman and the baby, turning to look up at her fiancé to get a clue as to what was going on.

His face had gone slack and looked ashen. His mouth hung agape. He seemed to be rooted in the spot where he stood.

"Didn't you get my text messages? My voice mails?" the woman persisted. "Why didn't you ever respond, Terry? I said I needed to talk to you! It was important! I had to track you down!"

"What's . . . what is going on?" C. J. asked, staring uneasily between the two. "What's happening?"

Shaken from his daze, Terrence finally looked down at C. J. again, as if he had suddenly remembered she was standing there beside him.

"I d-don't know," he stuttered before turning back to face the woman again. "Daphne, what are you doing here?"

"I told you that I had to talk to you! Look, I didn't want

to do it this way," Daphne continued, "but you've left me with no choice. Duncan and I have nowhere else to go!"

"Duncan . . . who's . . . who the hell is Duncan?" Terrence asked.

"*Who's Duncan? What do you mean, who's Duncan? Our* baby," Daphne said, holding the wailing infant aloft, "*your* son!"

At those words, C. J. felt light-headed. The room began to darken, and she thought she might faint—crumble right there to the hallway floor. She reached out for the wall to steady herself and gulped for air as the woman, Daphne, continued talking, then yelling, at Terrence. Now she was in tears, too. Terrence was yelling right back at her. The baby continued to scream at the top of its lungs.

It was too much—the sounds, the emotions, and the chaotic atmosphere.

C. J. rushed past Daphne to their front door. With shaky hands, she inserted her key, opened the lock, and ran inside, slamming the door shut behind her.

She staggered across the darkened living room into their kitchen, bracing her hands on the kitchen counter, still struggling to breathe and calm her racing heart. Tears flooded her eyes as the realization of what had just happened sank into her.

Terry cheated on me. He had a baby with someone else. He cheated on me!

But she should have known this would happen. Terrence was never built for monogamy—not the high-flying playboy whose bed had once been filled with a revolving door of girlfriends and one-night stands. It wasn't until his car accident that he had been willing to slow down to even notice a girl like her. Why had she believed he would ever be truly willing to settle down?

Because he told me he was.

He had claimed he was ready, though she had secretly

worried that Terrence wasn't the commitment type. A part of her had suspected that he would one day realize that monogamy wasn't all it was cracked up to be. But she'd never thought he'd hurt her on this grand a scale, in this big of a way.

And Paulette was worried that I'd be the one to hurt him, she now thought bitterly.

Why had Terrence convinced her to come back if he was going to do this? He could have left her alone, allowed her to return to her work and the independent life she'd had before they'd met. Instead, he had asked her— no, *begged* her—to take him back, only to break her heart all over again, but this time worse than before.

C. J. didn't know how long she had been standing in their kitchen, staring down at the brown-and-black granite countertop, before Terrence finally walked through the front door, shutting it behind him. He turned on the overhead lights and rushed toward her.

"Baby, I'm so sorry that happened that way. I never would've—"

"Don't." She held up her hand, stopping him. "Don't do it. I don't need your apologies or excuses, Terry." She raised her eyes to glare at him. "Whatever shit you're trying to feed me, you can fuckin' eat it yourself!"

"I know what you're thinking, but I didn't cheat on you! I hooked up with Daphne when we weren't together. It happened while we were broken up, when I went up to New York. I didn't—"

"While you were in New York?" she repeated, frowning.

She remembered now that he had told her that a woman from his brief trip to New York had been trying to contact him.

"I think it's someone from the modeling agency. I guess they can't take the hint that I'm not interested," he had explained casually when she asked him about a text on his

phone screen one day. He had deleted it, and she hadn't asked him any more questions. She hadn't given it a second thought.

Because I was dumb enough to believe him, she now thought angrily, shoving back from the counter.

"So you hooked up with someone at the modeling agency? . . . Is that what you're telling me? You made up that bullshit story about how she was trying to contact you to get you modeling again when she was really trying to tell you that you're her baby daddy?"

He lowered his head, shamefaced. "I didn't . . . I didn't meet her at the modeling agency. I met her at . . ." He exhaled. "I met her at a bar in Midtown."

C. J. stared at him, struck mute all over again. "Wait . . . *Wait!* You're telling me she was some random chick you met at a bar?"

"I was . . . I was in a dark place, C. J. I was depressed and acting out. We'd . . . We'd had that fight and you had kicked me out of your apartment. I didn't know—"

"Don't you dare . . . don't you fucking *dare* blame this shit on me!" she screamed, unable to control herself any longer.

She charged out of the kitchen toward him with tears pouring out of her eyes and down her cheeks. She shoved him with all her might, sending him back several feet, making him bump into the back of the leather sectional.

"Don't you dare blame me, Terry!" She pounded at his chest. "Fuck you! Fuck you for not keeping your dick in your pants! Fuck you for being a liar, you son of a bitch! You son of a bitch!" she screeched.

She slapped him across one cheek then the other. He didn't raise a hand to defend himself. Instead, he grabbed her wind-milling arms and held them at her sides. He held her against his chest, and she soaked his shirt and tie with her tears. When he wrapped his arms around her and rested his head on top of hers, she violently shoved back from him.

"Don't touch me!" she sobbed. "Don't touch me, god-damnit!"

"Baby, I'm sorry. I would—"

"Stop it with that 'baby' shit!" She wrenched free of his grasp. "Don't try to placate me with any more of your 'babe, baby, honey' bullshit!"

He fell silent.

"You accused me of hooking up with Shaun and I didn't. I stayed true to you even when you doubted me, Terry! And while we were broken up, I didn't fuck anybody else. I didn't get pregnant! And I damn sure didn't dump something like this on you *weeks* before our wedding! I never . . . I would *never* do this to you!"

He slowly shook his head, still unable to look her in the eyes. "I'm sorry. I'm sorry. I am so sorry," he kept mumbling.

She bit down hard on her bottom lip. "I'm sorry, too—because I can't do this shit anymore."

C. J. grabbed her purse from where she had thrown it on the sofa and headed toward the front door. She didn't know where she was going, where she would stay, but there was no way she was sleeping in the condo tonight.

"Wait! Wait, goddamnit!" he shouted, running after her, grabbing her arm.

"Let go of me." She tried to wrench her arm out of his grasp but he held firm this time.

"No! No, I can't lose you over this! We're supposed to get married in two weeks, C. J. We can work this out!"

"No, we can't."

His face crumpled. Watching him, he looked like he was physically in pain, but the pain she felt was worse. C. J. felt like she was being ripped apart at the seams, like her limbs were being yanked in all directions.

"Dammit, I didn't cheat on you! I'm not lying! I've told you everything. I . . . I know I fucked up! I made a mistake, a *big* mistake, but that doesn't change the fact that I want to spend my life with you. It doesn't change how I feel about you!"

"But it changes how I feel about *you!* Don't you get that?"

"Look, cuss me out all you want," he charged, firing words at her, tightening his grip even as she tried once again pull away from him. "Call me every damn name in the book! I can take it. I'll accept it!"

C. J. closed her eyes again.

"Hell, hit me! Slap me twenty more times if it makes you feel better—but don't . . . *don't* leave me! Don't walk out like this! Don't give up on us!"

It would be so easy to do as he asked, to take out her frustrations on him. She'd tearfully punch Terrence a few times and slap him silly. He'd let her weep before holding her and wiping away her tears. They'd kiss and the kiss would eventually turn into passionate makeup sex against the living room wall or on the sofa.

Yeah, that's how it'll probably play out, she thought with disgust.

But after the makeup sex was over . . . after they fell asleep and woke up in each other's arms, she would have to face the reality of what had happened tonight. She would have to face the fact that Terrence was telling her the truth now, but he had lied to her all along about the Daphne woman who had been trying to contact him. She'd also have to accept that if Daphne was telling the truth and Terrence was the father of Daphne's baby—he would have one messy drama on his hands.

This is not how C. J. had planned to start off their marriage. This isn't what she had envisioned, and because life had thrown her this curve ball, she had to step back and seriously consider her next step. She had to take some time and space for herself even if it hurt him—and her—to do so.

"I didn't say I was giving up," she whispered. "But you do need to let me go."

After some seconds, he finally did that—with great reluctance.

She then threw her satchel strap over her shoulder and headed to the front door.

"C. J.," he called after her, "tell me what I have to do. What do I have to do to make this right?"

"You really wanna know what you can do, Terry?" she asked as she opened the front door. "Just leave me the hell alone!"

He grimaced just as she slammed the door shut.

Chapter 22

Evan

Evan knocked on the closed office door. He waited a beat for a response. When he heard nothing, he knocked again.

"Come in," Terrence finally called out, and Evan pushed the door open.

Terrence had occupied the office three doors down from Evan's own for only four months, but he'd already given the room his personal touch. While Evan's C-suite office was all glass, chrome, and clean lines—reflecting his no-nonsense approach to business—Terrence's office was filled with chocolate leather sofas and ebony desks and bookshelves—reflecting Terrence's laid-back, masculine style. The accents were simple but contemporary. The lighting was warm. Evan felt the same way when he walked into this room as he did whenever he had a heart-to-heart with his brother. He felt comforted.

Evan strolled across the throw rug to Terrence's desk. Terrence's back was toward him; he was staring out the floor-to-ceiling windows at the Potomac River.

"So what's this I hear from your boy Max about you

canceling your bachelor party next week? He said he got a text from you saying to cancel it and you won't call him back. I thought you were all geared up to . . ."

His words faded when Terrence turned around to face him. He cringed.

Terrence looked horrible! Bags were under his eyes and he looked like he hadn't shaved in days. He wasn't wearing a necktie. His shirt looked wrinkled, like he hadn't bothered to iron it.

"What the hell happened to you? Are you sick?"

"No, I'm not sick."

"Well, you look like shit! Is that why you canceled the bachelor party?" Evan asked as he lowered himself into one of the chairs facing Terrence's desk.

Terrence slowly shook his head, looking dazed.

"Then what the hell happened? Talk to me!"

Terrence closed his eyes then opened them. He took a deep breath. "C. J. . . . . C. J. left me, man."

"*What?*" Evan cried. He stared at his brother, completely shocked. "You're kidding, right? When did she leave you? When did that happen?"

"Friday night." Evan watched as Terrence dropped his elbows onto his desk and lowered his head into his hands. The younger man tiredly scrubbed his face. "And I've been thinking about this shit all weekend. I can't focus on anything else," he said into his palms.

"Why would she leave you? You guys are only *days* away from walking down the aisle! Why would she—"

"Because I got somebody pregnant! Okay?" Terrence said, dropping his hands to his desk.

Evan went mute. His stomach dropped to his shoes.

"That chick who I hooked up with in New York . . . who had been calling me and calling me . . . I finally found out why she was calling." He leaned back in his chair and sighed. "She had the baby two months ago. His name is Duncan. She showed up at my place Friday night to give me the news in person since I wasn't returning her messages."

Evan gritted his teeth. "Goddamnit," he spat. "Goddamnit, Terry! How could you do this? How could you be so . . . so fucking irresponsible?"

"Look, the *last* thing I need is a lecture from you, Ev," he said tightly, glaring at his older brother. "All right?"

"Why would you hook up with a stranger like that? Why didn't you wear a damn condom? You know—"

"I thought I did! But I told you . . . I was drunk. So was Daphne! I guess my memory of that night isn't as good as I thought it was."

"So you might have worn one, then? Then the baby might not be yours?"

"Maybe," Terrence conceded with a lazy shrug. "We're doing a DNA swab test later this week. It should take a few days for the results. But none of that shit matters! C. J. thinks I was trying to cover it up. She thinks I lied to her and . . . and . . . now I don't know what's going to happen with us. She won't return my phone calls or texts. I don't even know where she's staying! She told me to leave her the hell alone . . . to let her . . . let her do her own thing. I guess she needs time alone to figure this out, but . . ." He clenched his hands into fists then released them. "But I can't! I can't, Ev!"

"I'm sorry, but you're going to have to do it, Terry."

"But what if she decides to leave me?" he shouted. "What if she cancels the wedding and—"

"Then she cancels it," Evan answered solemnly, "and you'll have to respect her decision."

Terrence's face went slack. He looked close to breaking into tears.

"Look, I've been where you are, okay?" Evan rushed out, gazing into Terrence's hollow eyes.

Evan had also been at the mercy of the woman he loved, hoping desperately that she would take him back. Miraculously, Leila had done it. She had forgiven him, but C. J. may not do the same.

"I had to wait. I had to pour out my heart and let Lee decide what she wanted to do . . . and you'll have to do it, too, with C. J. You can't force this, Terry."

Terrence lowered his head again.

"Besides, it sounds like you have an even bigger issue to deal with now."

Terrence looked up at him. He frowned. "Which is?"

"That you could be a father! You've got a little guy who'll have to depend on you. That's a lifetime commitment. You've got to be there for him!"

Terrence gradually nodded. "You're right. I know you're right."

Evan rose from his chair. "It's going to be okay . . . whatever happens."

Terrence didn't respond.

"I have to head back to my office for a meeting, but if you need to talk some more, I can—"

"I'm good." Terrence held up his hand. "I'll work through it. That's what therapy is for, right?"

Evan laughed sadly. "Exactly."

A minute later, Evan walked back down the corridor to his office, his mind now sluggish with worry.

Just when it seemed like things had finally settled down with his family, something else popped up. Unrest and upheaval were painful and consistent realities for the Murdochs. They couldn't get away from it! He hoped, for Terrence's sake, that this latest bout with C. J. would rectify itself, though he knew they both were in for major drama if Terrence turned out to be the baby's father. Something like that could have a huge impact on their lives and future marriage. He hoped Terrence was prepared.

As Evan neared his office, he slowed to a stop.

He saw his assistant, Adrienne, talking to a woman standing near her desk. Though he couldn't see her face from this angle through the glass enclosure, he knew instantly who the woman was. He would know that lean frame in a pink pencil skirt and the sun-kissed blond hair anywhere. Maybe she'd felt his eyes upon her, because as he drew closer, Charisse turned to face him. She grinned as he stepped through the doorway.

"Why, hello, Evan! Your secretary said I had just missed you. Glad you're back!"

He warily eyed his ex-wife. "What the hell are you doing here, Charisse?"

In response, she raised her eyebrows and barked out a laugh. "*That's* how you greet the woman you were married to for five and a half years? I can't get a 'Hello, Charisse! How are you, Charisse?'"

He glanced at Adrienne, who had returned her attention to her laptop screen and was pretending not to overhear their conversation, but he could tell that she was listening.

"Look," he said, dropping his voice down to a whisper, "I have a very busy schedule today, and I don't have time for your bullshit, so if you have something to tell me, say it quickly."

"Fine. I was going to give it to you in your office privately, but I guess I'll just do it out here, then," she said as she shoved her hand into her snakeskin hobo bag.

"Do what?"

He watched as she pulled out her cell phone. She then pressed a button, and a voice erupted from the phone's speaker, filling Adrienne's office.

"Well, it looks like you've covered all your bases. Let's hope for your sake you're a convincing liar on the stand . . . that the jury will believe your account of what happened that night," he heard Charisse say.

"I've never had a problem convincing people in the past," Dante said before breaking into laughter.

At the sound of his half brother's voice, Evan stilled.

"I've been a lawyer for fifteen years, Charisse. I know how to work a courtroom. Jurors are bigger dupes than most! Put on a good enough performance and they'll believe anything. Trust me, once I'm done with my testimony, Evan won't stand a chance."

Evan watched as Charisse pressed the stop button on the phone screen.

"How . . . how the hell did you . . ." Evan sputtered before falling silent, absolutely stunned.

She grinned. "Got time for me now?"

Chapter 23

Dante

"What the hell do you mean, you're dropping the charges?" Dante yelled as he slammed his fist on the conference table, making a pitcher and tray of cups rattle. "Are you shitting me? You can't do this! I want Evan Murdoch tried and put in jail! Do you hear me?"

The commonwealth's attorney looked up from shuffling papers in his manila folder and gazed at Dante blandly. He then adjusted his wire-framed glasses, which were sliding down the bridge of his nose. "Yes, I heard you quite clearly, Mr. Turner, and I will ask you to lower your voice."

"I can't believe you guys are doing this. This is just . . . just outrageous!" Dante bellowed, ignoring his request. "It's a travesty of the justice system!"

"It's not a travesty. We simply were presented with new information and, therefore, are no longer able to move forward with the charges against Mr. Murdoch."

"Bullshit! Bullshit!" Dante felt a vein throb along his forehead as pain radiated across his skull. The overhead lights felt too bright. He was having a hard time seeing straight. He narrowed his eyes and pointed at the balding, frumpy man sitting across the table from him. "The Murdochs got to you, didn't they? Threw some money at you to get you to back down, and you just—"

"If you are suggesting that Evan Murdoch bribed me into dropping the case against him, I can assure you that is not what happened. I did it strictly based upon the new evidence that was presented . . . previous information that was not disclosed. I made my decision accordingly."

"What new evidence? What the fuck are you talking about?"

He watched, bewildered, as the attorney pulled a sheet of paper from the stack in the manila folder. The attorney stared down at the paper as he spoke. "Prior to telling Detective Morris that Evan Murdoch was the person who shot you the night of July the eighteenth, did you provide him with another name for the possible shooter?"

Dante stilled. He frowned uneasily. "What . . . what do you mean?"

"I meant exactly what I said, Mr. Turner." The prosecutor then leaned his elbows against the table and interlocked his stubby fingers. He peered into Dante's eyes. "Did you or did you not provide the detective with a different name? Did you initially claim that someone else had shot you?"

Dante's throat went dry. His palms began to sweat. "I don't . . . I don't recall."

"You don't recall?" The prosecutor raised his brows. "Fair enough. Let me see if I can refresh your memory." He stared down at his papers again. "According to a deposition provided by the defense, you told Detective Morris in September that a former romantic acquaintance . . . a Renee Upton . . . yes, that's her name. You claimed it was *she* who shot you. You claimed that Ms. Upton did it for revenge after you dumped her. But by December, you told the detective that it was really Mr. Murdoch who shot you." He looked at Dante again. "Why did you change your story?"

"I didn't . . . I didn't change it!" Dante sputtered. "I just . . . I j-j-just better remembered what . . . what happened. That's all!"

"I see. So one month you believed the shooter to be a five-foot-three-inch, one-hundred-fifteen-pound woman, and a few months later you believed that same shooter to be a six-foot-one-inch, hundred-eighty-five-pound man."

"It was dark that night," Dante explained feebly. "The garage was poorly lit. I could barely see anything in there! Forgive me if I made a mistake at first."

He watched as the prosecutor pushed himself back from the table. The other man sighed tiredly. "Please don't play games with me, Mr. Turner."

"I'm not playing games with you!"

"You knew you provided the detective with false information," the attorney charged. His pale, wrinkled face was grim. "That was bad enough. But you were actually willing to commit perjury on the stand. You tried to make a mockery of this case and send an innocent man to prison. As an attorney yourself, I would think you'd know better. You could get disbarred for something like this!"

Dante gave a cold chuckle. "Now I know for sure that you're on the Murdochs' payroll. That's the only reason you're spouting this bullshit."

The prosecutor closed his folder.

"Besides, you can't prove that I lied! This is all conjecture! This is all stuff you pulled out of your ass! You have no—"

"*Evidence?*" the prosecutor asked, raising his gray brows. "Oh, to the contrary, Mr. Turner . . . I do." He then turned toward the conference room's glass door. "Ryan, could you come in here please?"

A few seconds later, the door swung open revealing a bookish-looking young man holding a laptop.

"Thanks, Ryan," the prosecutor said as the young man set the open laptop beside him on the table. Ryan nodded, then walked back toward the open doorway, shutting the door behind him.

"What the fuck is this?" Dante snapped as he watched the attorney type a few keys.

"It's the evidence you claimed I didn't have. Again, provided by the defense," the attorney said before clicking the mousepad.

When the media player clicked on, voices filled the conference room. Dante blanched. He literally felt sick to his stomach, had the overwhelming urge to vomit right there on the linoleum table. But that nausea was quickly squelched and replaced with fury.

That bitch, he thought as he listened to Charisse's recorded laughter. *That fucking bitch!*

She had recorded him while they were in bed together. He knew he never should have trusted her. Oh, he was going to make her pay for this one, if it was the last thing he did.

"Open up!" he yelled as he pounded his fist on the front door of Charisse's condo hours later. "Open the goddamn door, you bitch!"

Soon after he'd left the prosecutor's office, Dante began calling and texting Charisse, screaming into the phone and threatening to kill her as soon as he got his hands on her. Of course, she didn't answer his texts or return his phone calls. But she couldn't avoid him now when he was standing in front of her door, screaming at the top of his lungs.

"I know you're in there, Charisse! I know why you're hiding, you sneaky, double-crossing cunt! Open the god-

damn door or I'll go up and down this hall telling everyone what a whore you are!" he shouted, kicking the door
with his foot and wincing at the pain in his toes. "I'll . . .
I'll tell them how you sucked my dick and let me fuck you
in the ass just so that you could—"

He stopped when he heard the sound of a lock being
turned. A few seconds later, her door opened by a few
inches. He could see Charisse's big baby blues peering
back at him through the gold chain.

"I have called the police," she said primly, looking every
bit like the rich, entitled, blond pampered princess that she
was. "I suggest that you leave the premises, or you will be
arrested."

"Fuck you!"

She smirked, looking like she was holding back a laugh.
"This is a nice neighborhood, Dante. It won't take long
for the cops to get here. With a big, hulking *black* man like
you pounding on my door, it won't look good. It won't
look good at all."

"Yeah, well, before they drag my ass outta here, I'll
make sure I choke the shit out of you first!"

"I'm absolutely terrified," she deadpanned. "Look, just
give it up! I told you that you and I were more alike than
you realize. You chose not to listen to me when I said it. I
did to you exactly what you did to me! You got what you
deserved, Dante. Move on!"

"Move on? *Move on?* You're one to talk, you stupid
bitch! You did *all* this to win back a man who doesn't even
want you! If you were on fire, Evan wouldn't piss on you
to put out the flames! He couldn't give a shit about you,
Charisse! *Why?* Because you're one tenth of the woman
Lee is!"

At his words, Charisse's aloof veneer faltered. She genuinely looked hurt, maybe even angry about what he'd said, which only spurred him on more. He smiled maniacally.

"Lee never embarrassed him by being a drunken whore he had to hide from everybody! And she gave him the baby that you couldn't!" he shouted, slicing into her like a razor. "She may not be his wife forever, but he certainly isn't going to trade her in for you. You're damaged goods, Charisse! Trying to win him back is a lost cause."

She didn't immediately respond to that. Instead, she blinked like she was fighting back tears.

Oh, look! She's going to cry, he thought with amusement. It was a small victory that he was happy to take. But to his surprise, Charisse didn't cry. She sniffed and pushed back her shoulders before staring at him evenly.

"You're right. Evan will probably never take me back . . . but what I did to you wasn't just about Evan. It was about *us*, Dante! When I was at my lowest, you deserted me. You threw me out of your office like I was a piece of trash," she hissed. "And now you're at your lowest. Once again, some grand scheme of yours has fallen through! Evan will move on to bigger and better things—and your life will continue to be the steaming shit pile that it is now. You are a worthless, pill-popping junkie who is a joke of a lawyer and, frankly, a joke of a man. So don't think you can—"

She didn't get to finish.

"I'm a joke? A fucking *junkie?*" he yelled as he slammed his shoulder into her door with all his might, causing her to scream in alarm. She stumbled back into her foyer. "I'll show you what I am, you fucking bitch! I'll show you!"

Dante felt like Jack Nicholson in the film *The Shining*. If he'd had an axe at that moment, he probably would have hacked the door down. But he didn't have an axe, so he had to settle for slamming his body into the door over and over again instead. He was propelled by rage, by blind fury. Charisse's screams for him to stop only made it worse. With one more shoulder slam, he heard the gold chain of the top lock snap. The door swung wildly and slammed against the adjacent wall. Charisse continue to screech and backed against her foyer wall.

"Stay back!" she shouted, holding up her hands. "I mean it, Dante!"

But he stalked toward her anyway.

She had betrayed him and ridiculed him. With her lies and manipulation, she had handed Evan yet another victory. He couldn't let this go unpunished; Charisse would pay the price tonight. And she had to pay the price for *all* the others—Evan, Leila, Terrence, and Paulette—who had thwarted him at every turn.

As he walked toward her, he imagined wrapping his hands around Evan's neck and choking the life out of his brother. He envisioned watching Leila gag and claw at his hands as he squeezed, much like Charisse would be doing a few seconds from now. In Charisse's face, in her look of horror and fright, he saw all of them.

This bitch is gonna die tonight, he thought as he lunged for her. But his fingers latched onto air, not her slender neck. He felt someone grip him around the shoulders.

"Nuh-uh, fella! I don't think so," the cop yelled as he yanked Dante back into the hall where another office waited, holding out handcuffs.

"Let go of me! You fucking let go of me!" he shouted while the officers slammed him to the ground.

"Stop resisting! Stop resisting!"

"Fuck you!" Dante yelled again as she tried to shove them off of him, as he tried to rise to his feet.

Meanwhile, Charisse stood in the doorway, watching them almost with fascination.

"I said stay down, goddamnit!" the other officer ordered.

But Dante managed to slip out of his grasp. He got to his knees and leaped forward, causing Charisse to jump back.

"That's it," the one with the handcuffs muttered before taking his Taser out of its holster and zapping Dante with forty thousand volts of electricity, wracking Dante's body with paralyzing pain, making him shout in agony.

Chapter 24

Paulette

"I'm finished cleaning up, so I guess I'll head out now, Mrs. Williams," Miss Claudia called out to Paulette as she walked out of the kitchen into the living room.

Paulette sat on the couch, scanning a magazine, while Little Nate played with his plastic blocks on the Afghan rug to the sound track of *Dora the Explorer*.

Paulette closed her magazine, looked up, and smiled. "I told you that you don't have to clean up. I can do that myself."

Miss Claudia waved her off and grinned. She stretched her arms. "Oh, Little Nate and I made a big ol' mess today making those chocolate chip cookies. I didn't want to leave you with it. Any mess I make, I clean up myself! That's what everybody should do!"

Paulette shook her head in awe. "I swear you're the best, Miss Claudia!"

The older woman shrugged as she walked toward Little Nate and scooped him into her arms. She planted a kiss on his plump brown cheek. "It's nothing, honey!"

"No, I mean it! You really are amazing! Thank you so much for taking care of Nathan."

She had been working for them only for a couple of months now, and Paulette couldn't imagine their lives without her. She had such a calming presence in the house-hold—unlike Reina. Even Antonio had finally admitted that Miss Claudia was a much better fit for them, since she caused less friction. And it went without saying that Little Nate adored her. Paulette would smile whenever Miss Claudia entered the door, knowing she was leaving her son in good hands.

"Oh, I like watching over him!" she said, kissing his cheek again. He wriggled restlessly in her arms, so she lowered him back to the floor. He toddled a few feet away, back toward his building blocks. "Being around him brings joy to my heart. He reminds me so much of my boy when he was his age."

Paulette watched as Miss Claudia's face changed. Her wide grin disappeared, and her brow wrinkled. She grew solemn as her eyes stayed locked on Little Nate while he began to bang two blocks together. "It would've been my son's birthday last week."

"Oh, my . . . I . . . I'm so sorry to hear that!"

Miss Claudia suddenly turned to look at her. "Sorry to hear what?"

"That your son's birthday was last week and I didn't know. That must have been a hard week for you. I would've . . . I would've . . ." Paulette's words trailed off.

"You would've done what?"

Paulette went through the catalog of things Miss Claudia had done the previous week—from cleaning up Little Nate's vomit on his high chair and the kitchen floor to taking out the trash with her when she went home at the end of the day. Paulette *never* would have let her do those things if she had known she was wrestling with the memory of her dead son. But Paulette couldn't say that. So instead she said, "You could've taken the week off. Really . . . we would've understood."

"Why would I take time off when I told you I feel good just being around him? Just looking at that beautiful face brings me so much joy . . . joy that I haven't had since my son was killed."

"*Killed?*" Paulette breathed in sharply. "B-but you said he . . . he died. I didn't know he was murdered!"

Miss Claudia shrugged. "Well, it ain't exactly something you advertise, is it?"

"I . . . I guess not. But I just thought—"

"I didn't tell you because my son did some . . . well, he did some illegal things when he was alive. The police say that those things might be the reason why he was killed, but I don't think it was. I told them I think I know who did it, but they wouldn't believe me!" She sighed. "My boy didn't deserve to die. He wasn't perfect, but he . . ." Her voice trembled a little. She lowered her head and sniffed. "He didn't deserve what happened to him."

Paulette leaped from the couch and walked toward the crying woman. She wrapped her in her arms. "I'm so sorry," she whispered.

She felt Miss Claudia ease back, and she immediately released her. Miss Claudia looked at her and nodded.

"It's all right, honey. God will see it through. I know he will. The good get their just reward . . . and the bad won't go unpunished. I have faith that the Lord will make it right!"

I'm not so sure of that, Paulette thought as she pursed her lips, though she didn't voice it aloud.

It had been her past experience that sometimes cruel, conniving people went unpunished. For every Marques Whitney who finally got his just desserts for his evil deeds, there was a person like her half-brother Dante who continued to operate in the vengeful, reckless way he always did with no repercussions.

"Working with Nate brings me peace. It brings back all the good memories I had when my son was little." Miss Claudia's eyes drifted to Little Nate again. "He looks so much like my boy."

"I've always thought Nate looks a lot like his dad," Paulette ventured hesitantly.

"Of course, he does! Why wouldn't he?"

At those words, Paulette dropped a hand to her chest. She felt a wave of relief that settled into her core and almost made her burst into tears. She still remembered how Reina had said Nathan didn't look a thing like his father. It always left Paulette with the worry that everyone else could see what Reina claimed to know: that it was all a farce. No matter how good a father Antonio was to Nate, it was as clear as day that Nate wasn't his son—in the world's eyes. She worried that people were silently going *tsk-tsk* or snickering behind her and Antonio's back, something that her husband didn't deserve. It made her paranoid and ashamed.

"I'm so happy you said that," she gushed. "Someone . . . someone once told me that he didn't."

"Who on earth would say that to you?" Miss Claudia asked, scrunching up her nose.

My mother-in-law . . . also known as the biggest bitch on the Eastern seaboard, she thought.

"A . . . a relative," she mumbled.

"But why would your relative say that?"

Paulette hesitated again. Though she liked Miss Claudia, she hadn't known her for that long. A confession like this was highly inappropriate and risky. But the older woman radiated so much warmth. The look on her face was of beatific understanding, not hostility or judgment. And Leila had been the only person to whom Paulette had ever revealed all that had happened in the first year of her marriage. Now that Leila was a mother of a new baby, starting a new business, and remarried, she had her own life to focus on and couldn't always be a sounding board for Paulette.

I don't have anyone to talk to anymore.

She opened her mouth, closed it, then opened it again. "When . . . when Tony and I first got married, things were . . . were a little rough. I was lonely. I was scared. I made . . . I made lots of mistakes and I—"

"You cheated on him," Miss Claudia blurted out, gazing at Paulette evenly.

Paulette closed her eyes and nodded.

"So you *really* don't know for sure who's Little Nate's father?" she asked, looking genuinely surprised.

Paulette slowly nodded again.

"Well, the answer is pretty plain to me, but I guess you can only know for sure if you get the baby tested. Any reason why you haven't done it?"

Paulette opened her eyes. "Because Tony says it doesn't matter to him, so I—

"But it *does* matter! It does matter to you, at least, or you wouldn't be this upset about it! You wouldn't be talking about it with me." She tilted her head. "Seems to me that it's about time you found out the truth, don't you think?"

Paulette didn't respond. Instead, she watched as Miss Claudia leaned down and grabbed her purse from where it sat near the couch.

"Well, I better head out if I want to get home in enough time to watch my shows. You give the little one a kiss for me when you put him down for the night. All right?"

Paulette dumbly nodded as Miss Claudia walked out of the living room into the foyer. She opened the front door and waved. "See you Monday!" she said, before closing the door behind her.

Paulette stared at the closed door.

"Mama!" Little Nate shouted, snapping her out of her malaise.

"Yes, honey," she said before turning toward her son.

The next morning, soon after breakfast, Paulette took Little Nate on a field trip to the local drug store. She made a furtive glance around her as she pushed the stroller through the store's entrance, though it wasn't necessary. No one but her knew why she was here today.

"Anything I can help you with, ma'am?" a salesgirl asked with a smile. "Looking for anything in particular?"

Paulette quickly shook her head. "Uh . . . no . . . no, I'm fine. Thank you." She then pointed the stroller toward her left. Little Nate continued his baby chatter as they made their way across the store's linoleum.

While she walked, scanning signs over each aisle, Paulette thought back to last night's conversation with Miss Claudia. Miss Claudia was right: It *was* eating at Paulette that she still didn't know whether Antonio was Nathan's father. That's why no matter how good things were in her life and their marriage, she always felt something lurking in the background like an ominous sound in the distance. If she found out the truth about Nate's paternity, all her worries and inner turmoil would go away. She could have her answer. She could finally be the happy wife and mother that she'd always wanted to be.

Paulette approached the second to last aisle and found the boxed test kit within seconds, hanging next to the sealed packages of fertility tests and the assortment of condoms. She reached for the box, then paused.

What if the test says Tony isn't Nate's father?

She slowly lowered her hand from the shelf.

If that was true, then she would be hiding yet another secret from Antonio, and she had promised that she would never do that to him again. They had promised to each other that there would be no more lies and subterfuge in their relationship.

But Tony said he doesn't care either way, she told herself. *He said when Nate was born that he accepts him as his son no matter what. I'm the one who wants to know . . . who has to know!*

With that resolved, she quickly grabbed the box and beelined to one of the checkout counters at the front of the store.

Getting a DNA sample from Little Nate had been a little challenging, but she had managed. Nate had tried more than once to swat Paulette's hand away, whimpering in protest as she swabbed the inside of his cheek. But she rewarded him immediately after with his favorite strawberry Jell-O, and his mother's offense was quickly forgotten. But Paulette knew getting a sample from Antonio wouldn't be as easy.

She waited until late at night to do it, almost an hour after Antonio had fallen asleep. When his snores were loud enough to fill their bedroom suite, she slowly pulled back the covers on her side of their four-poster bed and eased to the hardwood floor. She walked toward the bathroom, pausing midway when his snores abruptly stopped.

Shit! He woke up, she thought.

She halted and whipped around only to find that her husband had flipped onto his side. The snores resumed, and she breathed a sigh of relief.

Paulette finally made it into the bathroom and retrieved the test kit, which she had stashed under her side of the bathroom sink. She turned off the bathroom light and returned to the bedroom, holding the swab brush in the air.

She crept back across the room, stopping at the foot of the bed. She squinted at her husband in the darkened room.

Antonio was still asleep—thankfully. But his lips were only parted, not cocked open—as she'd hoped they would be.

Dammit, she thought. Her shoulders slumped.

But she still had to try. If she wanted answers, she *had* to do this!

Paulette climbed back into the bed and inched toward her husband, holding her breath as she did it. She leaned over him, peering down at his face. She eased the swab forward centimeter by centimeter, finally drawing close to his lips. She plunged the tip forward, quickly swabbing the inside of his mouth with a few quick strokes.

Antonio began to snort and cough and she instantly jumped back, tossing the swab stick over her shoulder. His eyes fluttered open as he turned to face her. He stared up at his wife uneasily.

"What the hell were you doin'?"

"Nothing," she said, forcing a smile.

"It didn't feel like nothing." Antonio smacked and licked his lips. "It . . . it felt like you put something in my mouth."

"Honey, what are you talking about?" She tittered nervously. "You must've been dreaming! I was just . . . just adjusting your pillow. *See?*" She shifted the pillow underneath his head. "Maybe that's what you felt. You were snoring so loud that I thought if I raised your head a little, it might help."

He didn't respond. Instead, he continued to squint up at her.

"I told you that you should consider getting one of those breathing thingies, Tony! All that snoring is keeping me up at night!"

He raised a hand to his cheek. She could see him licking the inside of his mouth where she had done the swab test. She held her breath again. Finally, he closed his eyes and rolled back onto his side.

"Sorry," he murmured, "I'll try to keep it down."

Despite his promise, it took less than five minutes for Antonio to start snoring again. Paulette felt around her pillow and her bedsheets in the dark, in search of the swab. She found it on the edge of the bed, near the headboard. When she did, she said a prayer of thanks.

She tucked the swab back into its container, placed the container in her night table drawer, closed her eyes, and drifted to sleep.

Chapter 25

C. J.

C. J. yawned, stretched, and winced at the popping sounds in her lower back.

She hadn't had a good night's sleep in almost a week, unable to get comfortable on her newsroom buddy Allison's lumpy pull-out couch. More than once she had been woken up in the middle of the night with the eerie sensation that someone was watching her, only to open her eyes and find Allison's cat, Eddie, inches away from her face. She'd yelp, and Eddie would hiss before scurrying down the hall with his tail whipping behind him.

I miss my bed, C. J. thought as she stared tiredly at her laptop screen, working up the will to type her news story.

And if she were honest with herself, she would admit that she also missed the man who usually slept in that bed.

C. J. hadn't spoken to Terrence in almost a week, not since she had walked out of their condo that painful night. It wasn't that she hadn't felt the urge to talk to him, but a little voice in her head would utter, "Don't do it, girl!" whenever she found herself dialing his phone number or driving toward their condo.

She had already been through the full grief cycle. Her initial fury at what Terrence had done had faded days ago and was now replaced with a dull acceptance. Terrence had gotten someone pregnant, but it had happened while they were broken up—according to him, anyway, which seemed plausible considering how young the baby was. Either way, Terrence was now a father, and if she married him, that would make her the baby's stepmother.

"A stepmother," she mumbled as she typed a few more sentences and shook her head.

And there went her dreams of her and Terrence starting a family together, of holding their newborn in her arms.

You can still do that, she told herself. *You guys can still have a family of your own. None of that has to change!*

But it wouldn't be special for Terrence as it would be for her. She had already accepted that she was one in a long list of girlfriends he'd had over the years. Now she would be just another one of his baby mamas.

C. J. lowered her elbow onto her desk, dropped her head into her hands, and closed her eyes.

But even with the heartache and disappointment, she couldn't deny that she still loved him. She couldn't see herself walking away from him forever.

"C. J.!" her editor, Ralph, barked.

At the sound of his voice, her eyes flashed open and she snapped to attention, sitting upright in her chair.

Shit! I must have nodded off.

She peered over the top of her computer screen at Ralph, who was staring at her sternly. "Yes? Wha-what?"

"I need to see you in my office—*now.*" He gestured to his open office door before stalking inside.

C. J. nodded and slowly rose to her feet. She walked out of her cubicle and then the few feet leading to Ralph's office. When she entered, he was already sitting at his desk with his fingers laced behind his head.

"I'm filing the city planning piece in like an hour," she rushed out. "I'm just waiting on—"

"So how is the wedding planning going?" he suddenly asked, catching her off guard.

"W-w-wedding planning?"

In all the months she had worked at the *Daily*, Ralph hadn't once asked her about her personal life, let alone her engagement. Why was he doing it today?

"Uh, it's . . . it's okay," she lied.

He reached for one of the pencils sitting on his desk and began to twirl it around and around, all while gazing at her. "You know you've never spoken about your fiancé—not to me, not to the other reporters. It seems awfully odd."

She frowned. "Why does it seem odd?"

"Because I would think anyone marrying into the Murdoch family would want to plaster it on a wall."

C. J's stomach clenched.

"Or name-drop a few times, at least," Ralph said with a chuckle, leaning back in his chair again. "Enough people have heard of them that it's pretty noteworthy."

"How . . . how did you know that—"

"You work at a newspaper filled with investigative reporters, C. J. One of them is working on a story about your soon-to-be brother-in-law's attempted murder trial, and he found that interesting nugget of information about you."

She was at a loss for words. What exactly was she supposed to say to this?

"But our reporter got word today that the prosecutor decided to drop all charges against him. Just made the announcement out of the blue."

"Oh, my God!" C. J. clamped a hand over her mouth. "They . . . they dropped all the charges against Evan?" She lowered her hand and grinned. She took another step toward Ralph's desk. "That's . . . that's *amazing!* Terry was so worried about his brother! I know he'll—"

"Yeah, they dropped the charges, but we don't know why they did it," Ralph said, narrowing his eyes at her. "Which is why *you're* here, C. J."

Her elation disappeared. "What? What do you mean?"

"I mean you have connections to the Murdochs that our other reporters don't have. I need you to talk to Evan. Find out what happened. Maybe his lawyers have spoken to the prosecutor. I bet *he* knows what's going on."

She shook her head. "I can't . . . I can't do that, Ralph. Like you said . . . Evan Murdoch is my soon-to-be brother-in-law. It's not ethical for me to get involved in a story about him. Besides, I've written stories about the Murdochs in the past, and it only caused friction. I promised Terry that I wouldn't do it again!"

Ralph tossed his pencil onto his desk.

"Look, I'll work on any other story you want, Ralph. Just not this one! The Murdochs are practically family to me!"

She watched as Ralph abruptly pushed back his chair and shot to his feet. "C. J., do you want to work here?"

"Of course I do!"

"*Really?* Well, you could've fooled me!" He began to pace behind his desk. "Because I'm not seeing it. I'm not seeing any growth. Your stories aren't getting any better. Frankly, you're a subpar reporter."

"I am not a subpar reporter, Ralph! Just because I won't—"

"You promised me scoops! You promised me that you would up your game, and the shit never happened, C. J.! You're all talk!"

Her cheeks warmed with humiliation as she lowered her eyes to the office floor.

"I'm asking you to finally prove yourself as a member of the *Washington Daily* team, and you're refusing to do it. That leaves me with a major problem. I'm not sure what decision I should make at this point."

"*When are you going to accept that there's no pleasing him?*" Terrence had asked her. "*You're too good for this shit, babe.*"

C. J. raised her eyes. "I don't know what decision you should make, Ralph, but I know which one *I'm* going to make—and it's one I should've made a while ago." She then turned and headed toward his office door. "I quit," she said over her shoulder.

C. J. hesitated when the elevator doors opened, wondering if she should step out or just ride back to the first floor.

"This is probably a bad idea," she muttered as she stepped into the carpeted corridor and the metal doors closed behind her.

She longed to see Terrence but had no idea what situation she would be walking into by showing up at his place without warning at eight o'clock at night.

Had he fallen back into depression; would he be splayed out drunk and sullen on his couch, in no mood to open his door let alone talk to her about their future? Or had he decided to seek solace in another woman's arms instead of the liquor bottle? Would she stumble on him in bed with some model type?

That gave her enough pause to halt her in her steps. She didn't think she could take it if she found him with another woman, especially so soon after she had walked out on him. But C. J. forced herself to start walking again. She had been mulling this over since she'd left the *Washington*

Daily's office earlier today. Once she resolved what to do after hours of inner debate, she couldn't backtrack from her decision to come here. She would just have to accept whatever awaited her on the other side of Terrence's door. *She* was the one who had told Terrence to stay away from her. Whatever way he chose to deal with her absence was something she would have to accept.

As she drew closer to his condo, she heard a sound she hadn't expected: a baby wailing.

"Aww, what's wrong? Come on, li'l man, it's not that bad!" she heard Terrence pleading over the baby's screams. "Mama will be back soon, all right?"

C. J. inserted her key into the door and shoved it open. When she did, she was met by the sight of Terrence cradling a crying infant against his chest, bouncing it up and down as he paced back and forth on the living room's hardwood floor. He paused when he saw her standing in the doorway.

"C. J.?" he said, looking surprised.

They both stared at each other for several seconds while the baby continued to scream at the top of its lungs.

"What are you doing?" she asked, and he blinked, snapping out of his stupor. His face hardened.

"What the hell does it look like I'm doing?" He started pacing again. "I'm trying to get him to stop crying. I've been trying for the past hour, pretty much since Daphne left him here. I've fed him. I've changed his diaper—and that took about four tries before I could get the damn thing on! I've rocked him. I don't know what else to do." He peered down at the baby again, who seemed to have gotten louder, whose tiny face was one tight red little ball. "It's okay, buddy. Come on, it can't be that serious."

She shut the door behind her, removed her satchel, and set it on the floor. "How did you get stuck babysitting?"

Terrence stopped and glared at her. "It's not babysitting if it's your kid."

"You're right . . . I just meant . . . well, never mind." She walked toward them, removing her sweater and tossing it onto the sofa as she did. "Give the baby to me. Let me try."

Terrence seemed to hesitate.

"I just wanna help, Terry."

Finally, he lowered the baby from his chest and held him out to her. "Fine. Whatever," he murmured.

Don't act so grateful, she thought sarcastically as she scooped the wriggling infant into her arms. She was struck by how light he was. When she lowered him to her shoulder, she felt his warmth, and despite his screaming at the top of his lungs, it had an almost calming effect on her.

"Do you miss your mommy, honey—or is it something else?" she whispered into the baby's ear. She placed a hand on his forehead.

"You don't seem like you have a fever," she said as she peered into the infant's big brown eyes. She then gently patted his back. "Did you burp him?"

"*What?*" Terrence asked, squinting again.

"Did you burp him after you fed him?"

He shook his head.

"Okay, I think I know what's wrong," she said, patting the baby on the back again. She did it a few more times, and then suddenly the infant released a loud, rumbling burp that made her grin.

"There you go!" she said, still gently patting his back. She then lowered herself onto the sofa. The baby's strangled sobs had ceased. He now let out a few whimpers and gurgles but for the most part was quiet.

"How'd you learn to do that?" Terrence asked, taking the spot on the sectional across from her.

"I used to babysit for some of the kids in my church when I was a teen, and then Victor Junior when he was a baby. I haven't done it in quite a while, but there are some skills you don't forget, I guess."

Terrence nodded. "Well, you look good doing it . . . holding a baby, I mean. It looks . . . natural."

"Maybe." She switched from patting the baby's back to gently rubbing it. "I didn't expect to be doing it again this soon, though."

Terrence sat forward on the sofa cushions, lowered his gaze to the floor, and sighed. "Look, C. J., I can say sorry one million times, but it doesn't mean anything if you don't believe it. So I can't keep apologizing. I didn't intend for this to happen, but . . . it happened. Duncan's my son."

"And you know that for sure now?"

He nodded again. "Took a DNA test on Tuesday. Ninety-nine point five percent chance that he's mine."

She closed her eyes at the news and involuntarily rested her cheek on the baby's crown. Duncan's lids were growing heavier and heavier. He looked like he was finally drifting off to sleep.

"I should've used a condom," Terrence continued. "I thought I did, but . . . but both of us were pretty drunk that night. Maybe the condom broke. Either way, it wasn't good decision making on my part. I know that. But I was just so hurt and pissed off after I caught you with that son of a . . ."

She raised her eyes to glare at him, stopping him mid-sentence.

"Which I know *now* that you two weren't hooking up," he said, quickly correcting himself, "but I didn't know it at the time, is what I mean. Well, anyway, I thought it would be a one-night stand with Daphne that would make me feel better. But it didn't. Then Daphne got pregnant." He stared at his hands. "She said she reached out to me not just because I was Duncan's father but because she had nowhere else to go. She didn't tell me at the time but she's . . . she's married. When she found out she was pregnant with Duncan, she thought it was her husband's baby—until he was born. Then she could see her son wasn't his. They *both* could," he said, gesturing to the curly-haired, café au lait baby C. J. held. "The shit really hit the fan, and her husband kicked her out of the house."

C. J.'s hand stilled on the baby's back. "Oh, God!"

"It gets worse." He sighed. "She told me her family are conservative Mormons and don't believe in that shit. They didn't like the fact that she cheated, and she thinks they liked it even less that she cheated with some black dude. They told her to forget their numbers, to pretend like they never existed."

"They cast her out," C. J. whispered, feeling sympathy for Daphne that she didn't want to feel.

C. J. knew what it was like to be excommunicated from her family. Daphne had lied and cheated on her husband, but had that warranted her mother and father turning their backs on her completely—especially now that she was alone and a new mom?

"She and Duncan need my help. She doesn't have any more money saved and no real place to live. She's been hopping from friends' houses to hotels, but that's not a way to raise a baby. I'm putting them up in an apartment. I'm giving her money now to take care of Duncan. I don't know how you . . . you feel about that, but it's . . ." He took a shaky breath. "It's not something I can compromise on. I *have* to take care of my son!"

"And I wouldn't expect any less of you," she answered softly.

"So if you . . . if you decided to take me back, that

would be the situation we'd be facing. It would mean having me—and Duncan. We're a package deal now. You need to know that."

The room fell quiet. All C. J. could hear was Duncan's soft breaths against her ear.

"Duncan's asleep," she whispered. "Do you have somewhere that I can lay him?"

"Yeah . . . uh . . . Daphne brought one of those . . . uh . . . bassinet thingies. I set it up in the bedroom."

She gradually rose to her feet and crept toward the bedroom. Terrence trailed behind her. When they reached the bedroom entryway, he walked around her and turned on one of the night table lamps. She laid the baby on his back in yellow bassinet. It was hard to believe he had been screaming his head off only minutes ago. He looked so peaceful. His round face looked almost angelic.

She and Terrence walked back into the hall.

"We should check on him every fifteen minutes or so," C. J. whispered over her shoulder as she eased the bedroom door shut, "to make sure he doesn't—"

"*We?* So you're staying?"

"Sure! I'll stay to help you with Duncan if you—"

"You know that's not what I meant. Are you *staying*, C. J.? Are you coming back?"

C. J. winced. So they were now back to the reason she had come to his condo in the first place.

"I need to know, baby," Terrence pleaded. He clasped her shoulders and squeezed them tight. When she looked up, she saw pure desperation in his eyes. "Just *tell* me! You can't keep me in limbo forever."

Grudgingly, she nodded. "I know . . . and I wasn't trying to."

"Our wedding is in a week," he argued. "*A week*, C. J.!

You didn't call it off, so I held out hope you'd take me back . . . that you'd still want to get married. But . . . but I don't know what to think."

She glanced down at her engagement ring, running her finger over the solitaire diamond. She exhaled and looked up at him again. "I know. I just—"

"I mean . . . Should we start making phone calls? *Sending back gifts?* We have people flying in for our wedding. I don't want them to show up to the venue and no one's there!"

"I *know*, Terry. Like, I said . . . I wasn't trying to—"

"The only person I told the truth about what happened was Ev, but even my friends are starting to suspect something's up, C. J.," he rambled on. "I canceled the bachelor party because I wasn't in the mood to get drunk and smoke cigars when I didn't even know if the woman I love more than . . . more than *anything* still loved me!"

"Terry . . ." she began patiently.

"You wouldn't call me back. You wouldn't see me! I know I fucked up, but . . . but you're killing me! You're straight up killing me, babe!"

She closed her eyes. His words were increasing in speed and intensity. It was as if he believed that if he kept talking and made his case, it increased his chances of winning her over. "Look, Terry, I—"

"Ev said I had to give you space. I had to give you time to decide what you wanted to do. I can't force your hand. I know that! But, babe, I'm begging you to give me another chance. I will drop to my damn knees right here in the hallway and do it if I have to!" he said, pointing down to the hardwood floor. "And I know I asked you to forgive me before, only to fuck up again, but I swear this time I—"

"Terry, stop! Just stop, okay?" She held up her hands. "Let me talk for a second."

He instantly quieted. She pursed her lips, not knowing where to start.

I guess the best starting point is at the beginning, she thought. She swallowed.

"When I . . . when I was a little girl," she began, "I had this . . . this dream of what my wedding day would be like. I'd wear my mom's old wedding gown. My dad would walk me down the aisle. And I'd be marrying a man who was basically the . . . the black version of Prince Charming. He'd sweep me off my feet. Say and do all the right things. He would be perfect . . . absolutely perfect. That entire day would be perfect!"

A tear trickled onto her cheek at those memories. She sniffed.

"But none of that's happening. I'm not wearing my mother's wedding gown. My dad isn't walking me down the aisle. And though you're fine as hell, you are no Prince Charming, Terry."

He grimaced.

"But I'm no deluded princess, either. I don't *want* Prince Charming. I don't want perfection. I just . . . I just want to spend my life with you. And I don't ca—"

She didn't get to finish. She didn't *need* to finish. She'd already said the part he'd been waiting to hear.

Terrence clasped both sides of her face and lowered his mouth to hers. They kissed, and relief flooded over her. He pressed her back against the wall, and the kiss deepened. They started panting as they clung to each other, and C. J. had to force herself to pull back, to tear her lips away from his.

"I missed you, too," she whispered, "but there's a baby five feet away. Keep it PG—at least until he goes home with his mommy."

Terrence nodded, still gazing down at her. He smirked.

"So that's the other up side of parenting? *Getting cock-blocked?*" His smirk suddenly disappeared. His face went somber. "I was worried that telling you the truth about Duncan . . . about how I've decided to accept him and make a place for him in my life would be the final thing to push you away."

"Oh, Terry," C. J. raised a hand to his cheek and shook her head, "you don't know me at all, do you? Baby . . . that was the thing that convinced me to *stay*."

At that, he leaned his forehead against hers, closed his eyes, and embraced her.

Chapter 26

Evan

Evan gazed into his closet mirror, adjusted his silk necktie, and smiled.

Free at last. Free at last. Thank God almighty, I am free at last, he thought.

He had gotten word from his lawyer yesterday that the commonwealth attorney had filed the paperwork and officially dropped all charges against him. And tonight, he and Leila were celebrating his freedom with a romantic dinner in Chesterton. Evan had already shared the good news with Terrence and Paulette. Terrence had, in turn, shared some good news of his own.

"She took me back," he had told Evan by phone. "C. J. forgave me, Ev. She still wants to get married despite all the shit I've put her through, and I'm . . . I'm amazed, man. I'm so lucky to have her back in my life!"

Evan concurred. They were all extremely lucky that their lives were turning out for the better. Terrence would walk down the aisle with the love of his life, and Evan wouldn't have to worry anymore about being taken away from his wife or his family. He could remain CEO of Murdoch Conglomerated rather than release control of their father's legacy to a stranger. Now that the family and the family business was no longer on the brink of catastrophe, Aunt Ida had announced that she and Michael would be leaving Murdoch Mansion and returning to her apartment on L'Avenue de Ségur in Paris.

"I know you all will be so sad to see me go," she had joked.

The dust was finally starting to settle, and life was returning to normal.

"Let's hope it stays that way," Evan muttered aloud before giving his reflection one last examination. He then turned to the closet doorway.

"Lee?" Evan called as he adjusted the lapels of his suit jacket. "Lee, are you almost ready, baby?"

He walked into their bedroom and found her standing next to their bed with the zipper at the back of her dress half open and her shawl tossed on the footstool. Her back was facing him, but he could see that she was staring down at something in her hand.

"Baby, what are you doing? I thought you were getting dressed!" He walked toward her and wrapped his arm around her waist. He lightly kissed her neck, inhaling the scent of jasmine and vanilla, before peering over her shoulder. "We better get going if we're going to make our reserva—"

His words faded when he saw what she was staring at—his cell phone screen.

"Don't mention it, Ev. I was happy to do it for you," Leila read aloud in a theatrical breathy voice. "To the world, I may not be Mrs. Murdoch anymore, but I . . ." Leila's voice faltered. She audibly swallowed. "I will always be in my heart."

He dropped his arm from around Leila as she turned to face him and brandished his cell phone, showing him the text message from Charisse.

He had sent her a text earlier today to thank her for all that she had done for him. He guessed she had finally responded to his message. Unfortunately, it looked like Leila had seen the text before he had.

His brow knitted together. He snatched his cell out of her hand. "Since when did you start checking my phone messages?"

"Since you started lying to me," she spat, crossing her arms over her chest. "You told me you weren't ever going to talk to her anymore!"

"I never said that, Lee."

"You told me that you guys were done!"

"We *are* done!"

"Then why is she still texting you? What the hell kind of message was that?"

He fell silent, forcing himself to remain calm. He could feed into her fury with his own anger, but it would accomplish nothing.

"Baby, please . . . *please* don't do this."

"Don't do this? *Don't do this?*" she yelled.

"We're in a good place. Things are finally getting better. Look, let's just forget about this. Table it for now. Let's go out and—"

"I found out that you're sending texts back and forth with your *ex-wife* and you expect me to 'table it'? You want me to shrug it off and just go out to dinner with you? Are you fucking out of your mind?"

"But it's not what it looks like! It's—"

"I love you, Evan, and I've put up with a lot because of it. Your wife has spread rumors about me around town. She had kids bullying Izzy at school because of it! I wanted to march to her house and beat the shit out of her, but did I do it? No! I held back. Because I thought it was the right thing to do. You *kissed* her, for God's sake, and I forgave you!"

He grimaced and lowered his eyes to the carpeted floor.

"I forgave you because I wanted to try to make it work. I've accepted all your excuses and your explanations, but not anymore. I've been pushed as far as I'm gonna go with this bitch! She isn't even your wife anymore, Ev! *I am,*" she said, pointing to her chest. "You don't have children together! You're not in business together! I don't want anything to do with her. I don't want *you* to have anything to with her, either!"

He shook his head again. "It wasn't like that, Lee. I sent her a text message thanking her for something she did . . . something big. She sent a message back! That doesn't mean I want her and me to get back together! I love you. I want you! I made one mistake and I admitted it. Are you always going to question me?"

"No more phone calls. No more texts," she continued, like she hadn't heard him. "I don't want her to even send a fucking birthday card to this house! I want her out of our lives! Do you hear me?"

"She's my ex-wife, Lee, but we live in the same town! I can't completely avoid her. That's not realistic!"

He watched as she lowered the zipper of her dress down her back. He guessed they wouldn't be going out to dinner tonight after all.

"No, Ev, what's not realistic is that you're still friendly with a woman who cheated on you, who tried to destroy me and turn everyone in town against me! I've been a good fucking wife to you, Evan Murdoch! I deserve your allegiance. Not that bitch!"

"Lee, she saved my ass!" he argued, making her suck her teeth. "Believe it or not, I'm standing here with you right now because of what Charisse did! I could be sitting in a courtroom on trial for attempted murder or in jail if she hadn't seduced Dante and duped him into spilling his guts. *She* was the one who told the prosecutor the truth about what happened! All right? She recorded their conversations and got the case thrown out. She didn't have to do that!"

"So she seduces Dante and earns your undying loyalty?" Leila let out a caustic laugh. "Well, if that's the case, then maybe I should've fucked him, too, when I had the chance! Stupid me . . . All I did was jerk him off! But I guess I didn't count on you being so *appreciative*," she snarled.

Evan blinked. All the blood drained from his head. The overhead lights in their bedroom seemed to dim then flare up again. He stared at her for several seconds, struck dumb. He watched as Leila turned away from him.

"W-wh-what . . . what did you say?" he finally stuttered.

"You heard me!" she snapped as she pushed her dress off her shoulders and down her torso. She removed the diamond teardrop earrings that he had given her on their wedding day. She walked toward her dresser and hurled the earrings onto the mahogany dresser top with contempt.

"So it . . . it was true. What . . . what Dante said you did . . . all that shit he was talking? You *really* did it? You lied to me, Lee!"

She turned back around to face him. Her expression was cold and remote, almost smug. The look conveyed that she didn't give a damn how much she was hurting him, how her words were ripping him apart limb from limb.

This wasn't the Leila that he had adored and loved since childhood. She had morphed into someone else—a person he didn't recognize.

She shrugged. "So what if I did lie, Evan? I wouldn't be the first person in this family to lie, now would I?"

She then turned back around and continued to remove her jewelry.

After she said that, everything seemed to speed up and slow down simultaneously. Evan didn't have any cohesive thoughts as he marched around the footstool and grabbed her arm, making her shout out in alarm.

"Let go of me!" she yelled.

But he didn't let go. Instead, he grabbed her other arm and shook her like a rag doll.

"What the fuck do you mean you lied? I trusted you, Lee, and you lied to me? You let that motherfucka touch you!" he bellowed, curling his lips in disgust. "How could you do that shit to me? I loved you! I trusted you!"

The wrath had come over him so quickly, like a bomb had been set off inside him and his actions were the resulting explosion.

She tried to shove away from him and instead fell back onto the bed. He pounced on her, even as she tried to crawl away. He grabbed her dress and pulled, ripping the seam, shredding the hem. He grabbed her ankle and dragged her back across the bedsheets, making her scream.

"Why him, huh? Why him, Lee?"

She slapped and kicked to get him off of her, but he was the stronger of the two. He pinned her down to the mattress, pressing his full weight on top of her as she pled for him to stop, to let her go.

"You wanted to get back at me for that shit with Charisse? Is that it?" he hissed. His vision had gone completely red. "Why the fuck would you do this to me?"

What else had she lied about? What else had Leila done while he was stuck in a prison cell dreaming of her every night? Suddenly, Evan was flooded with lurid visions of his wife with Dante, with all the things they'd done in that hotel room.

Unable to get away from Evan, Leila turned her head

instead, squeezing her eyes shut as she whimpered and cried. He knew at that moment he seemed utterly terrifying. He was certainly scaring himself. But he wouldn't stop. He *couldn't* stop. He would make her pay for this betrayal. Tears wouldn't work. Screams wouldn't, either. There was no way she would escape this.

"You're going to fucking answer me," he said, even as she continued to sob and babble incoherently. "And you're going to look at me. If you're going to stab me in the chest, at least have the fucking balls to look at me while you're doing it! You hear me?"

He squeezed her chin and wrenched her head around so that she faced him, making her shout out in pain. "Look at me, Lee! You fuckin' open your eyes and look at me!"

Ever so slowly, she did as he ordered. Her eyes were bright red and pooling with tears. Her mascara streamed down her cheeks and chin. Snot ran from her nose as she gulped for air.

"Why did you do it? Why did you do it, dammit? Just tell me! To get even with me? *To hurt me?*"

"No! No, I did it to *help* you!" she screamed up at him, choking on her own sobs, making Evan go still. "Just like she did . . . I did it to help you! He said that's what I had to do to get you out . . . out of jail! I-I-I didn't wanna do it, but I had no other choice!"

He loosened his grip around her arms and let go of her face.

"I didn't wanna do it! I didn't wanna do it!" she kept repeating while furiously shaking her head.

And just like that, the fury disappeared. The red veil of rage had been lifted, and he could see it all so clearly now. She had morphed back into the Leila he knew—the Leila who had sacrificed for him, who would do almost anything to put a smile on his face. Except she wasn't smiling now. She was sniveling and trembling with fear, and he had been the one who made her this way. He had done this to her. This time, *she* was looking at him as if she didn't recognize him.

Oh, God, he thought as he sat back on his shins. Evan stared down at his wife, at the mother of his child, at the woman he loved more than anything. He had attacked her—something he would never have imagined himself doing in a million years.

All because of Dante.

He could practically hear that son of a bitch cackling in his head. Dante knew how to hit him where it hurt. He knew how to sully what was most sacred to Evan. He had tried to take away his freedom and livelihood—and failed. But now he had ruined the one thing that Evan had treasured the most: the bond he and Leila shared. Their relationship wouldn't be the same after this; they could never go back again.

"I'm gonna kill him," Evan whispered with a shaky breath and unshed tears in his eyes.

He climbed off of Leila, who was still hiccupping and crying. She turned to the side and buried her face in their duvet.

"I'm gonna kill him," Evan said again as he strode across their bedroom, swung open the door, and slammed it closed behind him.

He strode down the corridor of the west wing and the staircase to the first floor, lost in a daze. He passed Diane and his housekeeper as he went. Both women shrank back from him like he was some monster stalking through the mansion hallways.

And he *was* a monster. He could feel it happening all along, during all these months, and now he had finally turned into his father: flying into a rage, yelling and abusing his wife. And Evan was about to do what his father had done: kill his brother. The Murdoch family legacy was coming full circle. History was about to repeat itself.

He threw open the French doors and jogged down the stone steps to the Lincoln Town Car where his driver, Bill, was waiting with a ready smile. He held open the door for Evan.

"Mrs. Murdoch is running a little late, I guess?" Bill asked. "Still beautifying?"

"She isn't coming," Evan answered succinctly before climbing inside the car.

Bill looked at him quizzically as he shut the door behind him but didn't comment.

Evan sat in the backseat, his muscles rigid and his pulse racing. Perspiration was on his brow and pooling under his armpits. He was breathing like he had just finished a five-mile jog.

"Did you still want to head to the restaurant?" Bill asked, shifting the car into drive.

"No." Evan slowly shook his head as the Town Car glided out of the mansion's circular driveway. "I want to go to seven-oh-eight Mason Avenue in Reston."

"*That far?* That's quite a drive, sir!" Bill leaned over to stare at Evan in the rearview mirror. "What in the world is out there at this late hour?"

"The son of a bitch who I'm going to kill tonight."

"Excuse me, sir?"

"I've had enough of it, Bill," Evan continued, feeling the words flood out of his mouth like a broken dam. "I've had enough of all his shit."

He probably shouldn't be confessing this to his driver, but he didn't care. He would be arrested soon after he did what he had to do tonight anyway.

"He's ruined my life. He ruined us. Lee will probably

never forgive me for what I did tonight, and she has every right not to. But I'll be damned if he gets away with this shit yet again! I didn't try to kill him last time, but I will this time. That motherfucka's nine lives are up."

Bill squinted as he pulled onto a roadway. "You aren't talking about that Turner fella, are you, sir? Your half brother?"

"Yes," Evan answered, glaring out the passenger window.

"Well, now . . . I can't let you do that, Mr. Murdoch."

"If you won't take me to his place, then take me back to the house. I'll drive there my goddamn self."

"No, sir," Bill said, shaking his gray head as he turned the wheel onto another street. "I'll keep driving until you really have a chance to think about this . . . to think about what you're doin'. Your wife may be mad at you now but she depends on you. Those children depend on you. You can't afford to go back to jail. You know that."

Evan turned away from window and stared down at his lap.

"You've done right by me, Mr. Murdoch. You've done right by my wife and my kids. I'm able to pay for my oldest to go through college because of you. She's studying to be a teacher. I'm grateful for what you've done, and I wouldn't be showing how grateful I was if I just sat back and let you send yourself down the river again." He paused. "I served time when I was a young man. You remember that, don't you?"

Yes, he knew that Bill had been to prison. He had seen Bill's prison record when he applied for the job as family driver several years ago. He had been shocked that the polite, gregarious older man had served more than a decade behind bars for robbery and theft. It had given Evan pause until he realized Bill had been charged when he was only nineteen years old. Though he'd worried he was making a huge mistake, Evan had decided to hire Bill anyway based on the man's glowing recommendations. Now he was glad he had; Bill had been an exemplary driver who had served him well.

"I remember what it's like in there. You and I both know, you don't wanna go back, sir," Bill insisted.

Evan closed his eyes and took a shuddering breath. "I don't . . . but at this point, they all may be better off without me."

"Don't say that," Bill ordered with an icy firmness, surprising Evan with his tone. "Don't you dare say that, because you know it isn't true!" Bill braked at a light and gazed at Evan in his rearview mirror. "I spent seven years in prison. I missed birthdays, graduations . . . I even missed my grandmother's funeral. I spent seven years feeling sorry for myself until I realized when I finally got out that my wife, my daughter—they had missed me, too. Can you believe it?"

Evan didn't respond.

"Me—a man who had disappointed them and embarrassed them by getting locked up in the first place! I was a drunk. I was a junkie. I robbed houses and stole cars to pay for my habit—and they still missed me. They still wanted me back. After I realized that, I made it my mission to prove to them I was a man worth waiting seven years for."

Evan pursed his lips. He finally unclenched his hands.

"So no, I'm not taking you to Reston tonight," Bill said. "We'll just keep driving around until we figure this out. We'll drive until dawn if we have to. If you change your mind . . . good. I think you're making the right decision. You're doing right by yourself and your family. If you don't change your mind and you decide you still want him dead, you're a grown man. I won't drive you there, but I know in the end I can't stop you if you want to do it badly enough. I just want you to make sure this is really what you want. I want you to understand what's really at stake. All right?"

Evan gradually nodded. "All right."

Chapter 27

Leila

Leila awoke to the smell of baby powder and the soft drone of a humidifier. She opened her puffy eyes and squinted against the bright light streaming through the plantation blinds of a nearby window. She felt disoriented, wondering exactly how and why she was here. She slowly sat upright, stretched, and looked around her.

Now I remember, she thought with a shudder.

Leila had fallen asleep in the nursery, having fled here soon after Evan had left their bedroom last night. She hadn't wanted to be in the bedroom when he returned—*if* he returned. He had stalked out of there, mumbling about killing someone. She didn't know who. He'd looked unhinged—his face was a billboard of anger, utter humiliation, and pain. She didn't know if Evan would ever come back. Either way, she didn't want to be there if he did.

She'd crept down the hall to seek the comfort of her baby's company and the quiet of this serene space. As she sat in the dark, replaying a mental video of what had happened that night on an endless loop, she'd started to cry all over again. She wept silently for who knows how long before finally tumbling into a restless sleep in the pink glider next to her daughter's crib.

Leila now glanced to her side and saw that Angelica was still slumbering on her back. One little arm was up in a permanent wave, as if she were saying "Hello" to someone in her dreams. Her tiny lips were parted. She whizzed softly.

Leila eased to her feet, careful not to make so much noise that she'd wake Angelica. She leaned over the crib and gazed at her daughter.

Mommy messed up, honey, she thought forlornly. *I messed up so bad!*

That night with Dante in his hotel room hadn't been done out of spite or revenge, despite Evan's angry insistence. Leila had been willing to do almost anything to get Evan out of jail, including have sex with a man whom she utterly despised. But Charisse—Evan's conniving ex-wife—had beaten her to the punch. She'd spread her legs for the likes of Dante and gotten Evan off the attempted murder charge, something Leila, regretfully, had been unable to do. Charisse's devotion had earned Evan's forgiveness and unwavering loyalty, despite what Charisse had done to both him and Leila in the past. Meanwhile, Leila's devotion remained ignored.

She had wanted to hurt Evan like she'd been hurt when she found the text message from Charisse. She wanted to make him feel the same agony she'd felt for the past seven months, wondering what would happen to him and their family. The hateful words had leaped from her lips without a thought.

"I should've fucked him, too, when I had the chance! Stupid me . . . All I did was jerk him off!"

Even now, she cringed at the memory.

Leila wished she could take it all back: what she'd said to Evan and what had happened after it. But she couldn't take it back; mistakes like that were irrevocable. Now her marriage and her life were in shambles.

She reluctantly turned away from the crib, tiptoed across the room, and opened the nursery's door. She couldn't hide in here forever. She had to face the reality of what she'd done.

Leila quietly stepped into the hall and closed the door behind her.

"Hey, you're up early!" someone shouted, almost making her jump out of her skin.

She turned and found Michael striding toward her.

"Glad I caught you! Ida and I were just packing up the last of our stuff, and we were wondering if we could . . ." He paused when he drew closer. He narrowed his green eyes at her. "Damn! What the hell happened to you?"

"Nothing," she answered quickly, pushing back her tangled, matted hair. "N-nothing happened."

He was still looking her up and down. She knew she probably looked horrible. She was still wearing her dress from last night, though it was now wrinkled and soiled with her sweat and tears. She hadn't seen herself, but she was certain her lipstick was smeared and she had a bad case of raccoon eyes.

Still, she felt no need to explain her appearance—especially to the likes of Michael. It was her business.

"Doesn't look like nothing." He slowly shook his head. "You look like you just stumbled out of an earthquake," he said.

Leila didn't answer him but instead shoved past him and headed back down the hall to her bedroom.

"Being the replacement wife of a rich guy isn't all you thought it would be," he called after her, making her come to a stop and whip around to face him. "Are you starting to wonder now if you should've taken me up on my offer?"

"You mean your bullshit offer of friendship?"

"It wasn't bullshit, Leila. I don't offer friendship to just anybody. I'm very particular about who I let into my inner circle. You should be flattered."

"Well, I'm not. And no, I don't regret rejecting you! Even if my marriage was on its last leg, which it isn't," she hastily added, "I'd rather be alone for the rest of my life and never have sex again than be 'friends' with you."

He shrugged as she turned to head back down the hall. "Your loss."

"Go back to trolling the nursing homes for your hook-ups, asshole," she said, making him laugh.

She then heard him open the door leading to Ida's bed-room. "I'm back, baby!" he called out to Aunt Ida. "I couldn't find the thing you wanted, but I'll try again later," he said before shutting the door behind him.

Leila peeked into her bedroom door a minute later to find their bedroom empty and in the same chaotic state she had left it the night before. She quickly redid the bed-sheets and removed the pillows from the floor. She re-turned her shawl to the closet and took off her torn and shredded dress before tossing it into the wastebasket. She then entered the shower and washed the sweat and tears of last night off her skin.

When she returned to her bedroom twenty minutes later, she felt clean, though not renewed. She glanced at the clock on her dresser table. It was after eight a.m. and Evan still had not returned. She dressed, careful this time to wear an outfit that covered her bruises, and went back to Isabel's bedroom to wake her up, then the nursery to wake up Angelica. For the rest of the morning, even as she spooned oatmeal into Angelica's mouth and admonished Isabel to clean up her room, she kept an eye out for Evan. She was nervous at the prospect of another volatile or even strained encounter with her husband, but eager to get it over with.

Couples fight, she told herself. *Couples sometimes even say and do awful things to each other that they are ashamed about later, but it doesn't mean we can't make this better.*

She could humble herself, and so could Evan. They could even go to counseling if need be! She loved him enough to be willing to try to make it work.

But she didn't run into Evan that morning or that afternoon. She checked his study and didn't find him there. She checked the Olympic-size pool in the east wing where he sometimes swam when he was under stress, but he wasn't there, either. She even checked the guesthouse, but Evan was nowhere to be found. She tried calling him, but he didn't answer. She hung up before the phone line went to voice mail.

By dinnertime, Evan still wasn't back at the mansion. She was really starting to worry.

"He's probably just at the office," her mother said in between bites of shrimp and couscous. "You know how he is."

"I *called* the office, Mama," Leila said tightly as she wiped the puréed carrots from Angelica's chubby chin. "He didn't answer."

Her mother shrugged and ate another spoonful.

She knew Leila was worried about Evan, but she didn't know why. She hadn't told Diane about what had happened last night—and she didn't plan to tell her, either.

"He's probably just up to his eyeballs in work, honey. I wouldn't worry so much." She glanced at Leila's sweater. "You're probably so anxious because you're hot! Don't you know it's ninety degrees outside? Just looking at you is making me sweat!"

Leila didn't reply, only adjusted her sweater on her shoulders. She wouldn't take it off. It was the only thing she could find in her summer wardrobe that covered her bruises.

By the time she had kissed Isabel good night and put Angelica to bed, she was sure her newly minted marriage was over. Maybe Evan had gone to Charisse's condo. Maybe he had sought the comfort of his ex-wife now that his new marriage had turned into such a catastrophe.

No, she told herself, *Evan wouldn't do that.*

But a lot had happened lately that she'd never expected. She couldn't say anything for sure anymore.

Leila walked into her bedroom, feeling miserable and at a loss for what to do next. She raised her head as she shut the door behind her and began to remove her sweater. She halted mid-motion.

"Ev!" she shouted in surprise.

He was sitting on the edge of the bed with his head bowed and his hands linked in front of him, as if he had been patiently waiting there for her this whole time. When he heard her voice, he looked up. She rushed across the bedroom toward him.

"Where have you been, baby?" she cried. Her yearning for him was quickly replaced with relief. "I haven't seen you all day! I was so worried about you!"

She fell to her knees in front of him and wrapped her arms around his shoulders. The anxiety of the day and anguish of yesterday finally overwhelmed her and she started to weep.

He didn't respond at first to her tears or her touch. Gradually, Evan turned to her and wrapped his arms around her, letting her cry on his shoulder. "It's okay, honey. It's okay," he whispered against her ear.

But was it okay? Could they go back to what they had been before what had happened last night? She could tell by his demeanor and body language that something had changed. She eased back, slowly raised her head, and gazed into his eyes. "I was . . . I was so scared you weren't coming back. I thought I'd pushed you too far. I'm so sorry, Evan!"

"No, I'm sorry for what I did to you . . . for how I hurt you. I couldn't stand to look at myself. I had to get out of here."

"Where'd you go?"

He took a deep breath and broke her gaze. He stared at the dresser in front of him, but she could tell he was looking past it. He was lost in thought.

"Where'd you go, Ev?" she asked again, bracing herself for what she considered the worst answer: that he had spent the night with Charisse, that Leila's anger and deception had pushed him into his ex-wife's arms. But he didn't give her the answer she'd expected.

"I went to kill Dante," he said bluntly. "I went to kill him with my bare hands."

Her blood ran cold. "What?" She didn't know she had pushed him *that* far. She slowly shook her head. "You don't mean that. You wouldn't . . . you wouldn't do that. That's not you!"

"Yes, it is. It's always been me, Lee. Like father, like son. I have the same capability to hurt and to kill just like Dad did. I'm not going to deny it anymore." He held up his hand to stop her when she began to disagree. "Let me finish! I have the capability to do it, but it doesn't mean I *have* to do it. I realized that last night."

He released her and held her hands in his own. He squeezed them tight.

"I wanted to end him, Lee. I wanted to finally end this shit between him and me once and for all—and I would have . . . until Bill stopped me. He told me the truth: that I wouldn't just be ending Dante's life but throwing away mine, too . . . everything I've ever wanted, that I ever had.

I would be giving up on myself and on us. So I had to think about it . . . really think about it. I told him to drive me to my office, and I spent most of the night awake, thinking about everything that's happened in the past three years. I thought about how Dante and I have been circling each other like fighters in a ring. He punches. I punch back. And we dance and we dance, round after round." He shook his head. "He's tried over and over again to destroy me, and I thought last night he'd finally done it, but then I'd realized that the only person who was capable of destroying me is me.

"He cheated with Charisse and put the final nail in the coffin that was my marriage, but he freed me to finally be with you. He lied and had me sent to prison. That month away from all of you reminded me just how important you are to me. You were willing to have sex with a man you despised just to get me out of jail."

At that she flinched. She tried to pull away, but he held on tighter to her.

"I know you weren't betraying me, Lee. You thought you were proving your devotion. I get it now. I get so many things I didn't realize before, baby. I'm not angry at Dante anymore. That shit is wasted energy. I pity him because he's so blind with rage that he can't see the time he's wasting, but I can. I'm not going to waste my time anymore. I love you. I love our family. If it means putting this feud with Dante behind me, I will. If it means cutting off ties with Charisse, so be it. I am devoted to you and . . . and I want to be with you—if you'll still have me."

She started to weep again, this time with relief. She threw her arms around his neck. "Of course, baby! Of course!"

Chapter 28

Dante

Goddamnit, Dante thought, gritting his teeth. He listened to the pounding that was either inside his head or on the other side of the bedroom wall. He didn't know which, but it was driving him crazy.

"Shut up! Shut up! Shut up!" he kept muttering. He had to concentrate.

He tried to steady the lighter under the spoon, watching as the brown substance inside the spoon liquefied then bubbled. But his hands were shaking. He had waited too long for his next hit, and now he had the jitters. It had taken less than a week of doing smack and he already craved it.

He reached for the syringe on the night table beside him, but his trembling fingers were clumsy. The syringe fell to the floor beside the mattress, almost getting lost in the dingy shag carpet. He leaned down, nearly dropping the spoon to the floor with the syringe. He caught his error in just enough time, though. Fifty dollars' worth of smack couldn't be wasted.

Dante reached for the syringe again, and the pounding got louder.

"I said shut the fuck up!" he screamed, before turning to bang his fist against the wall. "Quit making all that goddamn noise!"

But the thudding didn't stop. It seemed to make the walls vibrate and the door rattle.

"Fuck it," he muttered before finally retrieving the syringe from the carpet.

If Kiki insisted on playing loud music and couldn't respect the rules of his house, she would have to live elsewhere, and he would tell her so. But for now, he had other things to worry about.

Less than a minute later, Dante injected that sweet brown sugar into one of the veins in his left arm. When he felt the rush of the high overcome him, he quickly undid the belt wrapped around his bicep and slumped back against the bedroom wall. He smiled dumbly and closed his eyes.

Tee had been right. This was *much* better than the Oxy, and the effect was much faster. He didn't know why he had fought so long not to take heroin. If he had known it was this good, he would've done it sooner!

Dante had finally decided to take the plunge after he had gotten out of jail on the trumped-up assault charge after Charisse had called the cops on him. Kiki had bailed him out the next morning. By the time he stepped out of the precinct doors, he was already enduring withdrawal symptoms. He had the shakes and the sweats that were soaking his dress shirt. He felt sick to his stomach. He immediately reached into his suit pocket and realized the cops had taken his pills. Of course, they had!

Probably dumped them in the toilet or stole them. Assholes, he had thought with contempt.

"Are you okay, Daddy?" Kiki had asked as she gazed at him worriedly in the rearview mirror while she drove. Tee had stared at him from the front passenger seat with amused interest.

By then, Dante was keeled over in the backseat of the Jag, moaning in pain.

"No, I'm not okay," he'd almost wept. "I need my pills! Just give me my damn pills!"

She drove him straight to his condo in Reston and helped him upstairs. He scoured his entire place, searching his medicine cabinet, dumping the contents of drawers on the floor in search of bottles he may have forgotten. Kiki and Tee helped him look, but none of them could find an additional stash.

He was out. Good God, he was out, and there was no way he could get any more from his supplier at that late an hour.

Kiki offered to take him back to his mother's old home to see maybe if some was there. When they arrived, he collapsed onto the lone, stained mattress in the guest bedroom, writhing in agony. Kiki left to go to the nearby drugstore get him some medicine for the chills and fever.

"I'll see if they got some extra-strength Excedrin, too, until we can hook you up with something better. Maybe that'll help you, Daddy," she had called out to him as she walked down the hall.

He would've laughed if he weren't in such agony.

Excedrin . . .

She might as well give him peppermint candy with how helpful an over-the-counter drug would be in getting this nasty monkey off his back!

Meanwhile, Tee had stayed behind. She had sat on the floor beside him, watching as he groaned and moaned.

"You know," she said, "I don't got no Oxy, but I got something else that can help you. All you gotta do is say the word." She then dangled the plastic bag in front of his face and grinned.

He wasn't in a position to say no, and she didn't even charge him for his first hit. In fact, she prepped it for him—warming it up, tying off his arm, and injecting him. The moment was as memorable and blissful as the night he lost his virginity underneath the school bleachers when he was twelve years old. He wished it would've lasted forever.

"Daddy! Daddy!" Kiki called out.

Dante's eyes fluttered open when he felt her roughly shake his shoulder. He squinted up at her and smacked his lips. "What?" he croaked.

His mouth felt heavy and dry. His brain was sluggish. He glanced up and saw that Kiki had two grocery bags in her hands.

"You passed out again, didn't you?" She slowly shook her head and glared at Tee, who stood beside her. "I don't know why you gave him that shit! It was supposed to make him better, not worse. Now all he does is lie around and get high! He's been like this for the past four days. He hasn't even washed, and this damn room smells like piss!" She nudged Dante's shoulder again. "Daddy, did you pee on yourself?"

Four days? Dante squinted. He hadn't really been here four days, had he? He glanced down at himself. He was still wearing the white dress shirt and slacks from the day he had gone to the prosecutor's office. And yes, there was a wet spot on his gray slacks.

Well, look at that, he thought dazedly. He snickered.

"This shit ain't funny!" Kiki shouted. "You can't just sit around in your own piss all day!"

"Oh, leave him alone. He ain't botherin' nobody," Tee said, kneeling down in front of him. She grinned. "You get to use his credit card and his car. He gets to have his fun. Seems like a good deal to me."

"You owe me rent for this month, and stop blasting music," Dante babbled. "I'm tired of hearing that shit. The neighbors might start to complain."

"What?" Kiki snapped, staring at him in confusion.

"Stop blasting music or . . . or I'm kicking your ass out. You're making the walls shake with . . . with all that noise."

Kiki sucked her teeth. "Nobody was blasting music! I haven't been home all day. You're hallucinating! That shit is fucking with your brain!"

Tee started to laugh, and Kiki punched her in the arm, silencing her. The young woman reached into one of her grocery bags and pulled out a bottle of Gatorade and a turkey club sandwich. "Here!" she said, tossing both onto Dante's lap. "Eat something!"

Dante glanced at the cellophane-wrapped sandwich with disinterest.

"Nah, I know what he really wants," Tee said before reaching into the pocket of her saggy, ripped jeans. She pulled out another plastic bag and tossed it to him.

He grabbed for it eagerly.

Kiki shook her head and sucked her teeth again. "I hate fuckin' junkies," she muttered before walking out of the bedroom. Tee followed her, chuckling to herself.

"Don't listen to her. Have fun while you can, ol' man," she said to him, shutting the door behind her and leaving Dante to his spoils.

Dante opened his eyes again to darkness. A hazy blue sky was on the other side of his bedroom window, illuminated by a nearby street lamp. He couldn't tell if it was late at night or early in the morning, but the time really didn't really matter, did it? He just felt the urgent need to get high again.

Dante pushed himself up from the mattress, hearing the rusty bedsprings squeak beneath him.

He'd just had the most wonderful dream. He had dreamed of having a threesome with both Charisse and Leila. In the dream, he had ordered them to go down on each other, which they had done with zeal. He had them go down on him, which they had each performed just as heartily. He had finished the sexcapade by doing them both doggie style until they screamed with orgasmic delight.

As they slumbered, he had crept from the bed, reached into his night table drawer, pulled out a Glock, and shot them both in the head. The rush he had felt in his dream as he killed them was better than the one he'd felt while they were having sex.

As he now sat in the dark, he smiled thoughtfully, looking forward to falling asleep and having that dream all over again. But he was content to put off the fantasy for now. Instead, he focused on the task at hand. It was time to take his medicine.

He reached in the dim light for his drug stash, which sat on the floor beside him. He did the same steps he always did with the same steady reverence of one taking holy communion.

First, tie off the arm.

Second, light the spoon.

Third, fill the syringe.

Fourth, insert the needle into your arm and lower the plunger.

Fifth . . . pure bliss.

His eyes started to feel heavy again just as he heard the bedroom door creak open. His head lolled to the side and he looked up, expecting to find Kiki or Tee standing there. Instead, he saw a dark, looming figure. He saw the glint of the muzzle of a handgun.

He experienced no alarm. The drugs dulled his senses. He only squinted, trying to figure out who was standing in front of him. The shadowy face wasn't recognizable—at first. Then he realized who it was.

"*Renee?*" he said, almost with awe.

But she was dead. Kiki had assured him she'd had her killed. He could even remember seeing the news stories that showed she had gone missing. But here she stood and, strangely enough, she was wearing the same outfit she had worn the night she'd shot him a year ago in the parking garage. The same frilly trench coat and knock-off Louboutin high heels. Was he hallucinating again like Kiki said?

"Renee? What . . . what are you doing here?" he mumbled.

She didn't answer him. He watched as she raised the gun and pointed it at him. Her eyes were flat and lifeless.

He slowly shook his head. "I'm sorry, Renee. I'm sorry I tried to kill you," he slurred. "I should've just taken you to Barbados like you asked. I'm—"

He didn't get to finish. The bullet in his head, at point-blank range, stopped him.

Chapter 29

Paulette

Today is a beautiful day, Paulette thought. *Yes, a beautiful, lovely day!*

She hummed to herself as she sat in front of the mirror at her makeup table, applying blush to her cheeks. She felt buoyant, like she was suspended on a cloud. She hadn't been this happy in months—maybe even *years!*

"You're in a good mood," Antonio said before leaning down to place a quick peck on the nape of her neck.

She smiled at her handsome husband in the mirror's reflection. "Of course I'm in a good mood! Why shouldn't I be?"

"No reason." He adjusted his gold cufflinks then the knot in his tie. "I just didn't know you were this excited to see your brother get married. I thought you didn't want him to tie the knot."

"Oh, keep up, Tony! That's old news! I've made peace with Terry's engagement. He found a woman that he loves and he wants to spend his life with her. I can't begrudge him that. I'm sure the wedding today will be beautiful. It will be . . . it will be *marvelous!*"

"Marvelous, huh?" Antonio raised his brows in amusement. "That's quite an adjective, baby."

"But perfectly appropriate, considering the circumstances!"

She then reached for one of her perfume bottles. She removed the glass stopper and dabbed the tip along her neck and jawline, filling her nose with the scent of vanilla and lilacs.

"If you say so." He shrugged before heading to his walk-in closet to retrieve his suit jacket. "Maybe you know something I don't."

Paulette smirked at his retreating back. In fact, she *did* know something Antonio didn't.

She'd finally gotten the results of the DNA test yesterday. Paulette had almost avoided going to the website to see them, feeling sick to her stomach at the prospect that Marques Whitney was really the father of her son. She told herself that maybe it was better not knowing at all.

"Just erase the email notification and pretend like you never saw it," she had whispered aloud while staring at her computer screen.

But she realized how ridiculous that sounded. She had secretly collected samples from her husband and son for a reason—*two* good reasons, in fact: peace of mind and the chance to learn the truth. She couldn't let this opportunity escape her.

Paulette had taken a deep breath as she clicked open the email, preparing herself for the worst. She was lucky to have been alone when she'd read the results because she'd immediately burst into tears. It was there in black and white. "The alleged father's probability of paternity: 99.7%." So Antonio was indeed Little Nate's father.

"Oh, my God," she had whispered as she sobbed, clapping her hand over her mouth. "Oh, my God!"

It was like a weight the size of a boulder had been lifted

from her. The baby she had always wanted to have with Antonio was really theirs. She couldn't tell her husband, but she wanted immediately to tell Miss Claudia the good news since it was she who had encouraged her to finally get the answer she needed. But unfortunately, her nanny had been on vacation the past few days, and today Paulette had been so busy getting ready for Terrence's wedding that she hadn't had the chance to talk to the older woman.

I'll tell her tomorrow, she now thought as she recapped her perfume and rose from the makeup table. For now, she'd have to keep the precious secret to herself.

Ten minutes later, Paulette and Antonio emerged from their bedroom. They walked down the staircase hand in hand and were greeted with the sight of Miss Claudia sitting on the couch with Little Nate on her lap singing along to a children's cartoon.

"We should be back by midnight at the latest, Miss Claudia!" Paulette called to her. Antonio handed her a shawl that she wrapped around her shoulders. "Thank you again for doing this!"

"Oh, it's not a problem, and don't rush home. You two go and have yourselves a good time! We'll be fine," Miss Claudia called out before returning her attention to Nathan. She clapped his tiny hands together as another song started on the television screen.

Paulette blew her son a kiss before stepping out the door that Antonio held open for her. She looked up at the cloudless sky, closed her eyes, and did a long intake of breath—savoring the world around her. She then exhaled, opened her eyes, linked her arm through Antonio's, and gazed up lovingly at her husband.

"Let's see my brother get married," she whispered.

The moment Paulette and Antonio arrived at the sunset ceremony, she looked around her and breathed in audibly.

She had never seen anything so gorgeous—including her own wedding. While Paulette had chosen a church overflowing with roses, hydrangeas, and freesias in every pastel color imaginable for her own wedding day almost three years ago, Terrence and C. J. had chosen a design that was much more understated but just as awe-inspiring.

They had set up the ceremony at the top of a hill overlooking the Chesterton Country Club's golf course, under a grand old oak tree that was draped with hanging candles, crystal pendants, and white wisteria. A single crystal chandelier hung from the largest branch where the minister and Terrence now stood in between two stone podiums also featuring candles and white roses. A trail of white rose petals served as the runner. A string trio played a soft melody for the hundred or so guests who waited patiently in their Chiavari chairs for the ceremony to begin.

Paulette took her seat in the front row next to Evan and Leila. She squeezed Antonio's hand.

"I did not expect it to be *this* nice," she whispered into his ear, making him roll his eyes and chuckle.

She leaned toward Leila. "Okay, admit it. You helped her with the décor, right?"

Leila turned to Paulette and shook her head. "Nope. C. J. did it all by herself. She didn't even use a wedding coordinator."

"That's impossible! I thought she wasn't the girly type, but it all looks so . . . so feminine! So perfect!"

Leila shrugged and grinned. "People can surprise you." She then turned, leaned toward Evan, and kissed his cheek before wiping at the pink smear of lipstick she left near his goatee.

"Ain't that the truth," Paulette mumbled with a laugh. Just then, the string trio changed its music from a soft melody to the "Canon in D Major," signifying the start of the wedding march. Everyone rose to their feet for the bride's entrance. C. J. appeared, and Paulette's chin almost dropped to her chest.

The young woman stood alone at the end of the aisle. She had pinned her curly hair back from her face with delicate diamond hairclips and wore makeup, taking her from her usual plain-Jane self to a show-stopping beauty. C. J. was a vision in white, wearing an empire waist charmeuse and lace gown with caplet sleeves and a cathedral length veil that trailed behind her.

Paulette did a double take. Was that the same dress C. J. had worn at the bridal shop—the wedding gown that Paulette and Aunt Ida had shamelessly ridiculed? Ida had even said the dress reminded her of the doily her grandmother had kept in her foyer.

It looked like, despite their vocal disapproval, C. J. had worn the dress anyway.

Good for her, Paulette thought as bride drew closer. She reluctantly had to admit that C. J. had made the right choice; she looked amazing in that dress.

Paulette watched as C. J. held her hand out to Terrence, and he took it within his own. Paulette's gaze locked onto her brother's face. She expected him to be smiling ear-to-ear. She was in for a surprise.

Instead, Terrence was biting down hard on his bottom lip, trying to hold back his tears but failing miserably. One trickled down, then another. After a few seconds, the floodgates opened. He released a hiccup, and the tears poured from his eyes and down his cheeks.

In all the years she had known him, Paulette couldn't remember Terrence openly weeping. Not "cool as a cucumber" playboy Terrence Murdoch. Half of the audience stared in shock. A few of his buddies began to laugh openly. C. J. grinned and reached up to wipe the tears from his face.

"I love you too, baby," she mouthed, and the tears came even harder. He was damn near sobbing! He wiped his nose on the back of his hand.

"Oh, damn," Antonio murmured. "Did anyone tell him that they haven't even said their vows yet? Is he gonna make it through the ceremony?"

Paulette elbowed her husband in the ribs and stifled a laugh. It was embarrassing but sweet to see her brother like this. The tears and snot showed the truth: he really did love C. J. He obviously adored this woman! And Paulette could see the same adoration reflected in C. J.'s eyes as she gazed up at Terrence.

Finally, after another awkward minute, Evan rose from his chair and handed Terrence a tissue. He whispered something into Terrence's ear before giving him a congenial slap on the back. He then sat down again next to Leila.

Paulette didn't know what Evan had said to him, but Terrence immediately wiped his eyes and blew his nose before tucking the tissue into his tuxedo pocket. He pushed back his shoulders and nodded.

"I'm . . . I'm ready now," he said, clearing his throat.

The minister then began the ceremony, nodding and letting his eyes sweep across the crowd. "Dearly beloved, we are gathered here today in the presence of these witnesses, to join Courtney Jocelyn Aston and Terrence Xavier Murdoch in holy matrimony . . ."

Paulette and Antonio jostled for space on the crowded dance floor, grooving with the other couples under the twinkling light of the reception tent to the popular R & B hits the DJ played. She and her husband had been dancing for the past two hours, downing several glasses of champagne and working up a sweat while they were at it. Paulette suspected that if she headed to the ladies' room, she'd see herself in the mirror and find oozing makeup and sweated-out edges, but she didn't care. She has having too much fun!

Antonio didn't seem to be turned off by her bedraggled appearance, either. Quite the contrary, her husband couldn't keep his hands off of her. He grinded her from behind and kissed her bare shoulder.

"I hope Nate sleeps the whole night because I've got something planned for you later," he whispered seductively into her ear, making her smile.

Paulette glanced to her left and spotted the bride and groom doing their own bit of grooving and grinding. C. J.'s arms were draped around Terrence's neck. His arms were wrapped around her back, though his hands now drifted to her bottom as a slow song kicked on the stage speakers. C. J. returned his hands to her waist. She started to playfully chide him just as he lowered his mouth to hers. Her words died on her lips, and she tightened her hold around him.

Staring at them knowingly, Paulette suspected that she and Antonio weren't the only couple that had big plans tonight.

I just hope they pace themselves, she thought with a chuckle.

As Antonio continued to grind behind her, she reached into her purse and pulled out her cell phone. Even though she had called to check on Nate and wish him good night three times, all her calls had gone to voice mail. She glanced down at the glass screen to see if Miss Claudia had gotten her messages and finally called or texted her back. She hadn't. Paulette's smile disappeared.

"What's wrong?" Antonio asked as she turned around to face him.

"Still haven't heard back from Miss Claudia!" she said, shouting over the music.

"Are you starting to get worried?"

She hesitated, then shook her head. "No, I'm sure it's no big deal. I bet she got tied up with something or was putting Nate down for bed and didn't want to wake him up to answer the phone. Besides, it's already eleven o'clock! She probably fell asleep on the couch and forgot to call us back."

Antonio eyed her. He linked his arms around her waist and pulled her close. "You say that, but the look on your face says differently. Be honest. Are you worried?"

She sighed. "Okay, maybe a little. We should head home now anyway. It's getting late."

He nodded and stopped dancing. "Let's say good-bye to the newly married couple and call it a night."

"Sounds like a good idea."

"Don't fall asleep yet. We're almost home," Antonio said during the drive back home.

Paulette turned away from the passenger side window to look at her husband. Even in the darkened car compartment, she could see him smiling. "I'm not asleep, honey, but I am tired."

"I'm tired, too." He yawned. "I know I said I was gonna tear that ass up tonight, but I may need a rain check on that one. Guess I can't hang like the old days."

She smiled and lay back against her leather headrest. "I won't hold you to it. We can always try again tomorrow."

She sat forward in her seat as Antonio turned onto the side street leading to their colonial, eager to see their baby boy and get a good night's sleep after such an uplifting day. All she wanted to do was ask Miss Claudia how the evening had gone, go to the nursery, give Nate a kiss on the cheek, and go to sleep.

As they approached their driveway, Antonio suddenly braked, making the car lurch to a stop. Paulette had to brace herself to keep her forehead from colliding with the dashboard.

"Damn, Tony!" she shouted. "Why'd you do that?"

"Where's her car?" he asked.

"Whose car?"

"*Miss Claudia's!* Why the hell are all the lights off?"

Paulette turned away from her husband to stare at their house's exterior.

Antonio was right. Miss Claudia's gray Toyota Corolla wasn't in their driveway, and every light was extinguished, excluding the exterior light that they usually kept on when they knew they would be arriving home late.

Paulette instantly got a sinking feeling in her stomach. She had called Miss Claudia twice tonight and had gotten no answer. Maybe something really had happened. Maybe she had fallen ill and had to be rushed to the hospital with Little Nate in tow. Maybe she had gone on an errand, taken Nathan with her, and gotten into a car accident.

Paulette didn't wait for Antonio to pull into their driveway or turn off their SUV. She threw open the passenger side door and ran up the walkway. She could hear her husband shouting behind her, calling her name, but she ignored him. Her hands shook as she removed her keys from her purse and then opened the lock. She stepped into her pitch-black foyer, then turned on all the lights, filling the space with blazing light.

"Miss Claudia!" she called out frantically. "Miss Claudia, are you here?"

There was no answer. She rushed into the living room, only to find all of Little Nate's toys still strewn on the carpet. A magazine Miss Claudia had been reading still sat open on the coffee table.

It was like a moment frozen in time.

"Miss Claudia, where are you?" she yelled, feeling her

heart pound like a snare drum in her chest. She opened her purse to remove her phone and started to dial the woman's cell number just as she heard Antonio call out to her again.

"Baby! Come in here!" he called from the kitchen.

She ran the distance between the two rooms, dodging around furniture, and listening to the line ring in her ear.

She found Antonio sitting in one of the kitchen chairs, staring at a sheet of paper.

"Oh, thank God!" she cried with relief, hanging up her phone as the line once again went to a voice mail message. "She left a note! Did she say where they are?"

When Paulette saw the look on Antonio's face and the tears in his eyes threatening to spill over, she went numb.

"*What?*" she cried hysterically, reaching for the sheet of paper. "What did she say?" she asked, as she snatched the note from the table.

Then she read it.

"This letter is for Mr. and Mrs. Williams but in particular, you, Paulette, because you are a mother and you will understand my words. There is no greater pain than having your child taken away from you. This I know for sure. I think about my baby every single day, ever since you took him away from me. I don't know for sure how you did it, but I know in my heart that you did, even if the police won't believe me! Now you will feel what it's like. You will feel my pain. Nate will be safer with me than he ever will be with you. I will never get my son back—but being with Nate has been like being with him. He does look so much like his daddy!

"Paulette, if you ever want to see your baby boy again, you know what has to be done. Tell the world the truth. Tell them all what you did."

When Paulette finished reading the note, she started trembling.

"I don't . . . I don't understand," Antonio said feebly. "Why did she take him? What does she mean?"

Paulette now realized why Miss Claudia had seemed so warm, why the older woman had seemed so familiar when she first met her. She remembered her now, though she had only met her once before.

She had been lying on Marques's bed back when they were sixteen, back when he was her first real boyfriend and she had not yet discovered what a low-down user and manipulator he really was. She remembered lying back on his Spider-Man bedsheets while he kissed her collar bone and her neck. Suddenly, his bedroom door creaked open. A dark-skinned woman had stood in the doorway, haloed by the hallway light. Seeing that they were no longer alone, Paulette shoved him off of her and scrambled to cover herself.

"Damn, Mama! Can't you knock?" Marques had asked, sucking his teeth.

The woman had smiled. "I'm sorry, baby. I didn't know you were having company."

"Well, I am," he'd snapped.

"It's . . . it's nice to meet you, Mrs. Whitney," Paulette had whispered as she tried to button her shirt.

"It's Rhodes, honey," his mother had said. "And it's nice to meet you, too."

She'd then shut the door behind her.

"Miss Claudia is . . ." Paulette paused. "She's Marques's mother."

She then set the note back on the kitchen table and crumpled to the floor.

Chapter 30

Paulette

When Paulette opened her eyes, Antonio was huddled over her, gently shaking her shoulder. "Baby, wake up. Wake up!"

For a fleeting moment, she'd convinced herself she had been dreaming. She hadn't come home to an empty house and hadn't discovered Little Nate missing, after all. Antonio hadn't discovered the letter from Miss Claudia explaining that the older woman had taken their son in revenge for murdering her son, Marques. Paulette was waking up in her bed the morning after her brother's wedding to realize it had all been a horrible nightmare induced by too much champagne, a bad hors d' oeuvre, and sleep deprivation.

But she quickly realized she wasn't lying in her bed but on kitchen tile and, from the stricken look on Antonio's face, she knew it hadn't been a dream. She was still living a real-life nightmare.

Paulette slowly pushed herself up from the floor as Antonio eased back. "We . . . we need to call the p-police," she said, rubbing the spot on her head that she'd hit when she'd fainted. Tears pricked her eyes again. Panic seized her in its viselike grip, clearing her malaise. "She took our son, Tony! They have to find her! We—"

"We *will* call the police, but before we do, I need to know what the hell is going on," he said, taking her hand and pulling her to her feet.

She nodded as she slumped back into one of the kitchen chairs. He pulled out the chair facing her and sat down. "What you said before you fainted . . . that Claudia is Marques's mother. Are you sure?"

"Yes! Yes, I'm sure! I didn't remember her before, but I sure remember her now. She looked different back then. She was skinnier . . . younger, and . . . and she didn't have dreads. But when I read the letter and what she said about Marques, it all fell together. It all made sense!"

How could she have been stupid enough to trust her? Why hadn't she put the pieces together before?

"And she knows what happened to him. She knows that I . . ." Antonio hesitated and looked away. "She knows how he died." His eyes flashed back to hers. "Did you tell her?"

"No! No, Tony, I would never do that!" she shouted, furiously shaking her head. "She must have figured it out from the investigation. Maybe someone said something to her . . . one of the detectives must have. But I never did!"

"Okay. Okay," he said calmly, nodding. "At least there's that."

Paulette stared at her husband, unnerved at the fact that Antonio wasn't hysterical like her but very cool, almost reserved. His son had just been kidnapped. Shouldn't he be more emotional? Shouldn't he be more concerned?

"So if she doesn't know for sure that I killed him, she can't go to the cops with that info unless she has some—"

"Tony," Paulette said, reaching across the table and grabbing his hand, "she took our son. Every hour that goes by means more distance between her and us. It'll make it harder to find him! Why are we sitting here talking about this stuff when we should be calling the police or—"

"No, she took *your* son," he said, yanking back his hand, making her fall silent. "Not mine. That's what that whole letter was about, right? She took her grandson because she didn't think you deserved him, and she refused to let him be raised by the man who murdered his father."

"But he *is* your son, Tony!"

Antonio shoved back from the table and walked away from her. He braced his hands on the edge of the farm sink and stared out the kitchen window. "No, he isn't. I . . . I accepted Nate like he was my own. I love him. I would've done anything . . . *anything* for him! But I guess I . . ." He lowered his head. "It just . . . it just wasn't meant to be."

"Just wasn't meant to be?" She stared at him in disbelief. "*What are you saying*, Tony? Are you saying we shouldn't try to find him? We should just . . . just let her kidnap Nate? So I'm supposed to sit by and let her steal our baby!"

"Paulette, I'm a murderer, and you've been lying to cover up a murder! What kind of goddamn parents are we anyway? Life is telling us that I don't deserve to be that boy's father!" he argued, showing his first sign of tears. He ran his hand over his face, choking back sobs through gritted teeth.

"No, it isn't!"

"Then *why* is this happening?"

"Because she lied to us! Because she'd intended to do this shit all along, and I was too stupid to realize who she was and what she had planned. That's why!"

"Maybe I was just fooling myself when I thought I could make things right," he continued, as if he hadn't heard her. "I thought I could keep my family together and put the past behind me. But I can't! I killed a man and thought I could get away with it. I tried to raise someone else's son as my own, and now he's gone! And she refuses to bring him back . . . to let you or me see him again until we tell the truth about what happened, until we tell the world. That's what she said! She's blackmailing us, Paulette!"

"I know. I know," she whispered, now in agony and feeling it twice over seeing him go through so much pain— pain that once again she had helped to inflict. "But we can't just give up! We deserve our baby, Tony! You deserve to raise your son!" He stubbornly shook his head, and she rose from the kitchen chair and walked toward him. "He's your son! Do you hear me? I took the DNA test last week. Marques is *not* Nate's father."

He twitched as if given an electric jolt. "W-what? What did you say?"

"I said I took the DNA test. I got the results. There's a ninety-nine point seven percent chance you're the father. Nate is yours."

She watched as he slumped against the kitchen counter and his face changed, as a myriad of emotions flashed across it. He closed his eyes.

"You said it didn't matter. You said you didn't care. But the question was tearing me apart! I needed to know the truth, and now I do: Nate is yours and mine. He's our baby—not hers—and we have to do *whatever* we need to do to get him back. Please, Tony . . . we need to call the police."

He didn't answer her for several seconds. Finally, he opened his eyes and dully nodded. "Let's . . . let's call them."

She reached for the cordless phone near one of the cabinets and began to dial 9-1-1.

After the police arrived at the house, everything faded into a blur. It felt like a hundred officers had trekked through their house, collecting evidence, scouring every room for any trace of Nate or Claudia. They asked questions—*lots* of questions—about Claudia, about what had transpired that night, and about what had happened earlier that day. She and Antonio answered robotically, as if they had methodically synced their stories and lies prior to the police arriving.

Yes, Claudia was their babysitter.

No, she had given no indication that she might do something like this.

No, they had no idea why she would kidnap their son.

The only time one of them faltered was when one of the detectives asked, "You said you came into the house and realized she had kidnapped your boy. How did you know it as soon as you arrived?"

"Huh?" Antonio had answered numbly.

Ever since Paulette had revealed the truth about Nate's paternity he had been in a daze, almost like a zombie.

"Why did you assume he had been kidnapped?" the detective elaborated. "Why hadn't you just assumed she'd taken him out on an errand or . . . or something? You said she does that on occasion."

Paulette and Antonio had glanced at each other then turned back to the detective. Antonio had cleared his throat. "Well, we . . . uh . . . we found a—"

"We found his room empty with the lights turned off," Paulette rushed out, panicked that Antonio would reveal the letter she now kept tucked safely inside her bra, the letter that would reveal who Claudia really was and Antonio's guilt. "She didn't even leave his nightlight on, which she always does. When we saw that, we knew something was really wrong. We knew something was . . . different."

The detective had looked between them before gradually nodding. "I see."

After a few hours, the cops left with hollow promises to find Nate. The phone rang throughout the night with calls from family and friends—Evan, Leila, and even poor Terrence, who had planned to leave that very morning for his honeymoon in Jamaica with C. J. when he got the news and immediately canceled their travel plans. They all offered to come over and hold vigil with the anxious couple, but Paulette declined. Reina called when she got word of the kidnapping and ignored their request to be left alone. She'd shown up at their door in rollers and a pink bathrobe, screaming and wailing, blaming Paulette for Nate's disappearance and "that bitch who I knew wasn't right the moment I met her!"

Antonio had let his distraught mother sob on his shoulder for a good two hours before the older woman finally collapsed on their living room couch and fell asleep.

But unlike a snoring Reina, Antonio and Paulette couldn't sleep. Instead they lay in bed together, staring at the ceiling, unable to get the rest they sorely needed for the press conference that was scheduled for early the next morning.

"Why didn't you tell the cops about the letter?" Antonio whispered in the dark.

"If I told them about the letter, we would have had to tell them about Marques and his murder. They would've asked questions. They might find out the truth."

The bedroom went quiet.

"Maybe it's about time that they know the truth," he whispered, making her snap her gaze away from the ceiling. She turned her head to face him.

"What?"

"I said maybe it's time they know the truth."

"Tony, if they found out the truth, you could go to jail. You could face the death penalty."

"You don't think I know that?" he hissed. "You don't think I realize what I'd be doing? This isn't a choice I wanted to make, Paulette, but it looks like I'm going to have to make it." She watched as he slowly eased up from the mattress, threw his legs over the side of the bed, and walked across the bedroom to a small desk they used as their writing table. He turned on the table lamp.

"What are you doing?"

"I'm getting our son back," he said, opening a desk drawer and pulling out a sheet of paper. He dug into the drawer again and removed a fountain pen. "You saw what she wrote. 'Tell the world the truth. Tell them all what you did.' So tomorrow at the press conference I'm going to do that. I'm going to say what really happened that night. I'm going to tell the world that I killed him, and then she'll give us our son back."

"Tony, you don't know that!" she shouted as he pulled out a chair at the desk. "You don't know if she was lying or just crazy or if she's—"

"Paulette," he said firmly, turning toward her, "we *have* to end this. You told me to do whatever I have to do to get our son back. That's what I'm doing."

She then watched helplessly as he sat down and began to write. He wrote about the events preceding the murder and what had happened that night when he strangled Marques. He apologized for the pain he caused. He wrote and he wrote—crossing out words, tearing up sheets, and starting over again. He finally stopped when the sun came up and his hands were sore and there were bags under his eyes.

"Please don't do this," she said, realizing that she had already lost her son and may well lose her husband forever.

"I have no other choice, baby."

As they washed and dressed, it felt like they were preparing for a funeral, not a press conference. Paulette broke down into tears several times. When the rest of their family arrived, no one questioned her puffy eyes and solemn expression. She was a worried mother, but they didn't know she was a grieving wife, too.

"Are you ready?" Evan asked as he stood in their living room, dressed in a business suit. So was Terrence. Though she knew it was part of his job now, she didn't think she would ever get used to Terrence wearing a suit.

Paulette nodded up at her brothers. "I'm ready," she whispered, dabbing at her eyes with a tissue.

Antonio nodded, too, patting his breast pocket—the pocket the contained the written confession that he would read in only a matter of minutes. "Ready."

They opened the front door and saw all the mikes set up under their portico along with the swarm of people. Paulette should have known that a Murdoch offspring being kidnapped would make big news in Chesterton. Nearly a dozen reporters, photographers, and cameramen were waiting in their driveway, being held back by two police officers. A few still spilled onto the front lawn, trampling the tulips along the stone border.

Some of the neighbors across the street and next door had come out of their houses to watch the hubbub. They stood under porticos, squinting and craning their necks so they could get a better view of the chaos happening at the Williams residence.

Paulette stepped onto her front porch, feeling very sick, like she would vomit right there on the brick pavers.

"Are you all right?" Leila whispered into her ear, rubbing her shoulder. "Are you going to make it?"

Paulette limply nodded, linking her hand through Antonio's arm, leaning against his strong frame for support. The Marvelous Murdochs and their spouses huddled near the door where a group of officers and a dour-looking man in a dark suit already stood.

At first, Paulette didn't recognize the man but then realized it was the lawyer Evan had hired on their behalf. She watched as he nodded at the throng that gathered at the foot of the stairs, signifying the start of the press conference.

"Thank you for joining us today. I am representing Mr. and Mrs. Williams, the parents of Nathan Williams. As you know from previous news reports, Nathan, or Little Nate as he is known by his family, was last seen on July fifteenth in the company of his babysitter, Claudia Rhodes," he began. "The family has reason to believe that Ms. Rhodes has abducted Nathan and are offering a substantial reward for any information regarding his or Ms. Rhodes's whereabouts. In addition to that, Nathan's parents would like to issue a formal statement."

He then turned to Paulette and Antonio. "Go right ahead," he said, gesturing to the mikes.

They both hesitated for a few seconds, staring back at the eager faces that peered up at them. Finally, Antonio took a step forward and Paulette squeezed his bicep, silently begging him not to do this, to not throw his and their lives away. They could get Nate back without doing this. There had to be another way. But he glanced back at her, and she saw the resolve in his dark eyes. She knew it was pointless to try to stop him, so she stepped forward and stood next to her husband.

If Antonio was going to step before the firing squad, she wouldn't let him do it alone.

She watched as he reached into his breast pocket and pulled out the confession. He unfolded it, loudly cleared his throat, and licked his lips. When he opened his mouth, she sucked in a breath, like she was preparing to be shoved under water. She closed her eyes.

"There are no words to describe the torture you endure when your child is taken away from you," he began, staring down at the pages. "The sorrow that my wife, Paulette, and I feel in having Nate ripped from our home and our lives is equally indescribable. I want my son back. I *need* my son back. I want him safe in his mother's arms, and I am willing to do whatever I have to do to achieve that." He looked up and grimaced, then returned his attention to the words on the page. "For that reason, I . . . I want to confess that I—"

"They found him!" one of the reporters suddenly shouted in the crowd. "They found him! I just heard it over the radio. One of the cops picked her up during the traffic stop. Nate was in the car with her."

"What?" someone yelled back.

"Wait, they found him *already?*"

Everyone began shouting—the reporters, the cops, and the Murdochs. Antonio's face went blank. Paulette's eyes began to water. Reina fell to her knees and started screaming hysterically, thanking God up above.

Paulette turned to her husband, ripped the confession out of his hands, and hugged him for dear life.

Epilogue

There had to be flowers—lots of flowers, Leila had insisted on it. There also had to be candles—tea lights, tapered candles, and candelabra. She wanted them on every table and in every corner.

"Whatever you want, baby," Evan had assured Leila as they made plans with a wedding coordinator to renew their vows. He assured her that she could have the wedding she had wanted all along—not some rushed ceremony in a judge's chambers like they had had two years ago.

The ceremony had turned out to be everything Leila had hoped for and more, as was the reception. He knew Leila would look beautiful in her wedding dress, but she had exceeded his expectations. Throughout the day, Leila seemed to glow from the inside out.

"Thank you," she whispered into his ear as they sat at their wedding table. Angelica was in his lap, licking the icing from their wedding cake off her plump little fingers as she wiggled to the band music.

"For what?" he asked, turning to Leila.

She caressed his cheek. "For doing this. For trying your best. For loving us."

"You don't have to thank me, Lee."

"Yes, I do! You stuck it out when you didn't have to."

"Neither did you," he said, leaning over and kissing her. "Thanks for staying."

He watched as she blinked back tears. "Don't make me mess up my mascara again," she blubbered.

They weren't the only couple that had "stuck it out" so that they could find something close to a happy ending. There were several others around the reception room who had traversed seemingly insurmountable obstacles, but managed to make it through, over, and under them.

Evan's gaze shifted to his brother, Terrence, who was currently on the dance floor doing the electric slide with Isabel, Diane, and a few of the other reception attendees. No one would guess this was the same man who had fractured his leg, lost his eye, and battled depression a few years ago. A very pregnant C. J. stood off to the side of the throng with Terrence's son, Duncan, in her arms, smiling and laughing at her husband.

Though Duncan's arrival had been quite the surprise for the young couple, the two seemed to be making it work even with the occasional "baby mama drama," Terrence had conceded a few times to Evan. Despite the hiccups, C. J. adored her stepson and had taken to being a stepmother like a fish to water. For that reason, Evan had no doubt she'd make a wonderful mom when their baby arrived in two months.

Paulette and Antonio were also surviving and thriving despite the chaos in their past. Little Nate was a well-adjusted toddler, showing no signs of the trauma he may have endured during his kidnapping. Even now he laughed and squirmed in his mother's arms at their reception table while his father tried to shovel food into his mouth.

Paulette and Antonio could have fallen apart during the kidnapping and Claudia Rhodes's trial afterward, but they actually seemed to have gotten stronger. During her sentencing, they had each talked about learning the art of remorse and mercy and shocked the judge and prosecutors by asking for Rhodes to receive a reduced sentence for her crime. Because of their request, Rhodes would only serve fifteen years for the kidnapping instead of the thirty years to life she had faced.

"She was in pain and she made a bad decision," Paulette had confessed to Evan when he asked her why she and Antonio had requested leniency during the sentencing. "Tony and I know how that feels."

Of course, not everyone had reached their happy ending. Their half-brother Dante never got one, which was lucky for them, since his cherished dream was to destroy their family and everything that had been important to them.

It had been more than a year since Dante's murder. Their half-brother had been found dead in his late mother's house. The cops had also found two other dead bodies—two young women who were naked in bed in one of the upstairs rooms. All of the victims had been shot in the head, at point-blank range.

The cops didn't know what to make of the young women or the squalor they had found in the home, but judging from the several pounds of weed and heroin in the house, they figured someone living there had run afoul of local drug dealers. Maybe it was a hit put out by the competition, some of the cops speculated in the news stories that had circulated for weeks after.

Evan considered it ironic that Dante had been killed merely because he was in the wrong place at the wrong time, considering how many people out there had *wanted* to kill him—Evan included. But thanks to the many people he had crossed, death had been following Dante around for years. It was bound to find him eventually.

Evan hadn't spoken to Charisse in more than a year after he sent her one final email saying he could no longer have contact with her for the sake of his marriage and out of respect for Leila. Despite that, she had persisted. Charisse had tried several times to speak with him again, even going so far as showing up at Murdoch headquarters unannounced, but he stoically kept his distance. Finally, she gave up. The last he had heard she had moved back to the Caribbean with her mother—to a beach community— and she hadn't attempted to contact him since. The only exception was the week before his wedding, when he received a bouquet of two dozen white roses at his office with a mysterious note attached.

"I hope you're finally getting what you wanted, Ev," the note read. "I truly hope you're happy."

It wasn't signed, but he caught a whiff of a familiar perfume emanating from the parchment to let him know who had written it. He gave the flowers to the upstairs receptionist and ripped up the note. He would never respond, but he also hoped Charisse was finally happy, because he certainly was.

"Everyone is dancing now," Evan said now, turning to Leila, who was smiling at the crowd. "Wanna take another spin on the floor before the night is over? After that we can head home, set up Isabel with some popcorn and a movie, and put this one to sleep. Then we can get started on our second honeymoon," he whispered, wiggling his brows seductively.

She chuckled. "Sure! Why not?"

They both rose to their feet, each holding Angelica's hand as they walked to the dance floor.

TO LOVE & BETRAY

Shelly Ellis

ABOUT THIS GUIDE

The suggested questions are included to enhance your group's reading of Shelly Ellis's *To Love & Betray*.

DISCUSSION QUESTIONS

1. Leila initially agrees to sleep with Dante in order to get him to withdraw his testimony accusing Evan of attempted murder. Do you agree with her reasoning for doing this?

2. Paulette hasn't taken a liking to C. J. She doesn't like that C. J. lied in the beginning in order to get close to Terrence. Do you think Paulette is just being protective of her big brother or are there other factors at play?

3. C. J. has decided not to reveal to her colleagues that she's engaged to a Murdoch because she doesn't want people to treat her differently. Do you think that is the only reason why she doesn't openly discuss her engagement to Terrence?

4. Paulette becomes angry at Antonio when she finds out that he revealed to his mother that he may not be Nathan's father. She feels like it's another example of his ongoing lack of trust in their relationship. Do you agree with her assessment, or do you agree with Antonio, who believes she's overreacting?

5. Terrence doesn't want to take over the public affairs division at Murdoch Conglomerated but agrees to do so after both Evan and C. J. talk him into it. Is taking on such a big job a smart move when he's still battling clinical depression? Why or why not?

6. Aunt Ida's fiancée, Michael, keeps making romantic

advances at Leila, but she doesn't tell Evan. Do you think that was a smart decision on her part?

7. Charisse reconnects with Dante, and they develop a sexual relationship again. He suspects she has an ulterior motive for reconnecting with him but pursues her anyway. Besides sexual attraction, why does Dante toss aside his caution?

8. Aunt Ida gives advice to Evan on how to handle Dante. Do you think he should have taken her suggestion or let things play out as it did?

9. Evan and Leila make up after their blow-up over Dante and Charisse. Would you have made the same decision?

10. Paulette and Antonio requested the judge issue Miss Claudia a reduced sentence for her kidnapping charge. Do you agree with their reasoning?

11. Dante is finally dead and police suspect it is drug related. Do you think that's the reason he was killed?